PRAISE FOR KATY EVANS

"Katy Evans's books are like a roller coaster; the excitement, anticipation, and absolute thrill of the ride keep me coming back to her awesome romances time and again."

—Kylie Scott, *New York Times* bestselling author

"Katy Evans, your men are soo delicious and soo irresistible that life stands still and I can't get anything done until I get to the end of the book!! :)"

—Tricia, *iScream Books Blog*

MILLION DOLLAR
DEVIL

OTHER TITLES BY KATY EVANS

MILLION DOLLAR
DEVIL

katy evans

Montlake
Romance

Published by Montlake Romance, Seattle
www.apub.com

Amazon, the Amazon logo, and Montlake Romance are trademarks of Amazon.com, Inc., or its affiliates.

ISBN-13: 9781542043809
ISBN-10: 1542043808

Cover design by Letitia Hasser

Cover photography by Wander Aguiar

Printed in the United States of America

To it all

She'd make the devil into the perfect man.

THE ONLY MAN IN THE ROOM

PROLOGUE

Lizzy

The room is packed—everyone who is anyone in the city is here. All the movers and shakers. The most influential reporters, bloggers, you name it. I grip his arm tighter as he leads me into the ballroom of the five-star hotel we rented out for the launch. I suppose I'm more nervous than he is. I glance up to my left and see his masculine profile, and my stomach clutches. He has a face that—until now—only existed in my dreams. Hard jaw, chiseled to perfection. Firm, plush, kissable lips. Sharp, pristine blue eyes that feel like lasers zeroing in on me. He catches my gaze, and the devil's smile suddenly playing on his lips is worth a million bucks.

That's exactly how much it cost me. What *this* guy cost me. I would've paid so much more.

It's like he's the only man in the room. Like he belongs here. Confidence oozes out of his every pore. Masculinity envelops him as perfectly as his custom black suit. He walks like he owns the place. My heart beats harder and harder for him.

I can't believe I got him to agree to this.

Women are vying for his attention. His moves are smooth. Sophisticated. Elegant.

"An autograph?" a young woman asks shyly.

He takes the notepad and pen she extends and scribbles his name, his voice low and rough. "There you go." Beneath all that polish is his raw masculine energy. The determination that brought him here.

"James . . ." I halt him before we go any farther. "Whatever happens . . ."

He looks at me. A thousand words lingering in his look. "I know."

But does he? I've fallen in love with my own creation. I polished a diamond, and now it's flawless. Perfect. But it's not mine to keep.

He is not mine to keep.

This elite world he's about to join isn't one he was born into. These fans only know him because of me. His place at the top? That's not where I found him.

THE PERFECT MAN

Three months before . . .

My father has been staring in nerve-racking expectation at me for the past three minutes, and I can barely hear myself think. As I sit across from him at his massive oak desk, I'm nervous. I'm more nervous than I ever remember being. I prepared for this meeting all last week, when he gave me permission to bring him my proposal for the much-anticipated launch of our new line of men's designer suits. But it's one thing to talk to my reflection and quite another to have *the* Harold Banks staring back at me. My father isn't always easy to please—hell, try *never*—and his office always intimidates me. It serves as a reminder of one little bitty thing I can't ever seem to forget: I'm not what he wanted.

You see, his office is a shrine of collectibles. All around me, there are pre-Columbian artifacts, old tapestries, framed stamps. My father collects everything, the *best* of everything, except the one thing he wanted to collect the most. Sons. On their first try, my parents had me. And before they could keep trying for long, she left him. Leaving my dad with only me.

I'm twenty-five, dark haired, and green eyed; slim, thanks to healthy eating habits and exercise; and well groomed, thanks to the habits instilled in me by my nannies. A good girl who has never gotten into trouble. I'm a perfect daughter by anyone's standards. But still a *daughter*—one who's trying her best to thrive in a company that caters mostly to men.

I've been waiting for an opportunity to finally prove to my father that I'm a woman who can be an asset to his company—to *our* company.

But a man like my father never takes anyone's word. He expects results, and he expects them fast.

Hence my nervousness. I don't want to bite off more than I can chew. And our new line of suits has been a huge investment for the company. I know my father wanted someone more experienced to handle this launch.

I, however, have other plans and hopes.

"Have you started up that nonprofit yet to help the sick children of Uganda?" he finally asks. He always seems confused about why I want to work in his business rather than do things "women should be doing."

"And what happened to decorating your new place? Don't you have something to buy?"

I pretend nothing he just said bugs the hell out of me.

"I started that nonprofit last year, and it's been doing incredibly well. My apartment is perfect; it doesn't need anything else." There's a pause. I hesitate, then plunge in. "I can work in your business, Dad. Just because a bunch of old-fashioned stuffed shirts run this place doesn't mean I can't run it too. My Stanford degree is just as good as theirs. And besides, I think nobody knows what a perfect man should be like better than a woman."

His eyebrows pull together, and another uncomfortable silence ensues.

Say yes, I try to mentally channel.

"You won't disappoint me, will you, Elizabeth?" he finally asks.

My heart skips a beat, and I suddenly realize, *I've got him!*

With a quick nod, I keep my voice stern and businesslike, the tone my father usually uses with me and that I have been taught to use in return. "I won't disappoint you, Dad. I know I've disappointed you before, but I'm more careful now—"

"Are you? That prick you were dating was hardly a diamond. Rich, yes, but not very well mannered. Standing up my daughter on the day he was supposed to meet his possible future father-in-law . . ."

"And that's why we're not dating anymore. I won't settle for anything but the best, just like you've always told me, Dad."

He nods complacently and straightens his tie. I think I get my OCD from him. I can't ever survive a meeting without him straightening his tie several times. "You're perfect. You deserve the perfect man," he assures me.

My dad has always told me that I'm perfect—and every part of me, down to the pristine designer pumps I'm wearing, is a testament to how much effort I put into looking the part.

I smile at his compliment, wishing he'd spoken it with a little more warmth and that the words *perfect . . . for a daughter . . .* didn't ring in my head.

I want my father to give me one of those proud looks I rarely receive from him. I want him to say, "My daughter is the fucking best, best daughter, best at everything." I want to give him a reason to smile. I know that he's looking for his replacement for when he decides to step down—and I don't want him to hire a CEO who didn't grow up with our company like I did, who doesn't breathe and live Banks LTD like *I* do. I'm a Banks, and if someone inherits my father's legacy, it should be me.

"If you want to prove to me that you can be a competent CEO, then this should be the greatest launch of any line we've ever launched, Lizzy. I won't go for a half-assed job."

"Got it. There would be *no* better CEO for the company when you decide to retire than me, Dad."

"Good. I'm willing to give you this opportunity to show me you've got what it takes, but if you fail me, I'll be up front with you: I'll start prepping LB for the job." Letting this last unwelcome tidbit sink in, he claps his hands together as if that's that. "So, who is the face of our new line?"

Springing into action, I reach into my briefcase and pull out a set of folders. "I've got a list here of attractive, successful bachelor entrepreneurs who embody what our line represents—vitality, masculinity, power, money, class."

"Ferdinand Johnson. I like him," he says as he inspects the first photograph, turning it over to read the details I've put on the back.

A winning smile appears on my face as pride starts to swell in my chest. "I've got an appointment with him at three."

"Gregory Hutchinson. He could do." He nods in approval again, and more pride swells.

"I'm meeting him at one thirty."

He lifts a brow, clearly impressed, but saves any compliments. I never did receive coddling from my dad. My mom left us when I was only four, and I grew up in a world full of men. I've done my best to thrive in it. Butting heads with the best of the best.

"Leave it to me," I tell him as he reviews the rest of the photographs without any comment.

"I will. But be warned, Lizzy: I won't cut you any slack because you're my daughter. Work is work, as—"

"As you've told me before, yes, Father," I quietly concede, pulling the photographs into my neatly labeled folder and easing it into my briefcase.

I step out of the room, my heels clicking steadily on the floor as I stride down the hall. I'm summoning confidence with every ounce of my being as I pass his two secretaries and give them a grateful smile. It was difficult enough to get my dad to give me a meeting, and it was equally difficult to schedule a meeting with each of these eight millionaires. But somehow, I'm going to pick the very best and convince him to be my model. *Our* model. This launch is my baby, and it's my personal challenge to make our men's designer suits synonymous with class and elegance—a staple for the best males of our species.

My dad wants the perfect man. I plan to deliver.

♥ ♥ ♥

"I'm sorry, Lizzy, but no amount of money will get me to agree to this," Ferdinand Johnson said as he finished his coffee, set his napkin aside, and left me staring blankly at the bill.

"The only way I'd agree to this is if you tripled the offer," Gregory Hutchinson said. "And maybe not even then. It simply isn't worth my time."

Keith Halls hardly let me finish. He spent the entire time talking to my cleavage, even though it was discreetly buttoned away behind my silk blouse to show I meant business. I fended off the urge to say *Eyes up here* about a thousand times.

And the others?

The others weren't any better . . .

"'Thanks, but I don't have any time to play Ken to the Barbies out there'? That's what he said?" My best friend, Jeanine, is on the other end of the line as I walk out of my last meeting at 8:30 p.m.

"YES! And that was only *one* of them. Jeanine, it was a massacre. I . . . I'm truly shocked by how rude, arrogant, and plain uninterested they were! What the hell am I going to do now? It's the first shot—the only shot—my father has given me, and I'm completely stumped here!"

Eight appointments. Eight. Nobody cares to be the face of our new Banks LTD men's suiting line. Nobody could give a shit about it. One asked for five million. Another kept glancing at his watch. Another listened to me, nodded, and simply asked, "Are we done yet? I'm playing tennis in half an hour."

These millionaires are spoiled rotten, and I'm reeling from how badly these interviews went.

I tend to beat myself up for any mistake I make because I've been taught that failure is not an option. My father—*the* Harold Banks—believes that famed quote about failure being the road to growth is bullshit. He believes that aggrandizing failure is something only fools who can't get it right the first time do.

He's a tough act to follow, but follow him I do.

As I walk down the street after my lackluster interviews, I can't bear the idea of going back to my father empty handed.

What did I expect? It's not like I haven't been around men like that all my life; they're the same men that my father *might* consider worthy of me. Men like the eight I just met with are the reason I'm destined to be single the rest of my life. They're so self-important that I could've offered them the world and it wouldn't have been enough. Combine them with my dad, and I'd probably get more action as a nun.

"Are there no decent men left in the world, interested in hard work and good money?" I ask her, glaring down as I watch my feet move. "Sheesh, I offered a cool million for their troubles, and all they had to do was launch the product with me, be the face of our new menswear suits, wear them to a couple of events—and that's that."

"You know what . . . the ones who've already made a name for themselves are probably too big for your purposes." She waits a beat. "A million dollars is chump change to Ferdinand Johnson. Maybe you should go smaller."

She's right about that. "Smaller. Hmm. Like . . . where do I find such a beast?"

"I don't know. Take a walk around Midtown? Scour the wine bars? You'll land on your feet. You always do."

She seems to forget I *live* in Atlanta's Midtown, and I've never seen anyone that even comes close to ticking off the boxes on my list. "Besides, I worry anyone smaller might be like Daniel."

"Ugh," she moans at the mention of my horrible ex, who was too afraid of my father to even show up to meet him. "Not every man will be as spineless as him. There are real men out there, I promise. So, what are you going to do?"

"Right now? I want to get hammered, like Ernest Hemingway hammered. Hemingway's best works supposedly materialized when he had a bottle in hand. I'm giving it a try."

"Well, I'd drink to that if I could. Right now, I can't. One of the interns screwed up, so all hands are on deck tonight."

I continue walking down the block with no idea of where I'm going, only certain that I can't go home like this, and I certainly can't go back to my father empty handed tomorrow. "God. Maybe I'm just not cut out for this job. Maybe I'd be better off working for someone else, someone easier to please."

"You're a Banks, lovely. Your father's daughter through and through. You'll think of something and make it happen, Liz." Jeanine is trying to give me a pep talk, but it's hard to let her words sink in.

"I *have* thought of something. I'm getting drunk and not going to work tomorrow," I say.

She laughs, then says, "Okay. Have one drink. It's on me. Then go home and put your mind to work—you'll figure something out."

"I see a bar. A seedy bar, which is good because I don't want to bump into anyone I know in my hour of abject desperation. I'll call you tomorrow—"

"Lizzy, are you sure—"

I hang up before she can protest and stare at the sign. TIM'S BAR.

Wow. I must have switched streets without noticing, and now I'm in a not-so-nice part of town, with my Hermès purse and my Louboutin shoes. I furtively scan up and down the dark streets. Something moves in the shadows of the narrow alley beside me, probably a sinister figure, like all these neighborhoods have. Oh god. Suddenly I feel naked. I might as well have *MUG ME* written on my forehead.

I've never gotten seriously drunk at a bar, for fear of embarrassing my father. At this place, however, good ole Tim's Bar, I'll bet there's no one who's even heard of him or our products. That's just what I need.

But I can't go inside, can I? Who knows what kind of rough, scary people are in there. Growing up, the most badass person I ever met was Sensei Tim, my Tuesday-Thursday judo instructor, and he lived in the suburbs and had a side business selling scented candles.

As I'm debating, Sinister Man steps out of the shadows. He has no teeth and slits for eyes, and impossibly, he's even more sinister in the streetlight. "Hey, sweetie," he hisses.

Oh, hell no.

Exhaling, I push open the door and throw myself inside, skidding to a stop and scanning my surroundings.

About fifty heads swing in my direction, like I'm the entertainment for the evening. It's like the record playing on the old jukebox in the corner suddenly screeches off its track too.

I tuck a lock of hair behind my ear. There's a long, almost-empty bar and a couple of customers having nachos and chips and salsa at the tables.

But as I walk across the tilting cement floor, every single one of those eyes is on me.

What am I doing here, again?

Oh, right. Probably trying to get myself mugged.

No, this is a regular commercial establishment, like any other. I'm sure they'll be happy to have my business.

Summoning my courage, I take a middle stool at the bar and tell the bartender, who's busy watching something on his phone, "Tequila, the finest you have—straight up," in a gruff voice that I hope makes me sound like I can hold my own, in case someone is eyeing up my purse.

He doesn't look up, merely smiles down at whatever he's watching as he pours me something from a bottle called Montezuma and serves with his free hand. What the hell is Montezuma?

Great service. "Um. I said the *best* you have."

He looks up at me, finally seeing me for the first time. A frown of annoyance on his lips. "This is the best, princess. Also the only."

I probably don't want to upset him, seeing how he has arms the size of tree trunks, covered in tattoos.

I take my shot and guzzle it down. It's awful, like paint thinner, squeezing tears from my eyes. Whatever. I tap the bar for another. When my curiosity gets the best of me, I ask, "What are you watching?"

"Jimmy."

"Jimmy what?"

"Jimmy Rowan. The stunt guy on YouTube? He's going to get killed one day."

"Hopefully not today." I frown and peer at the screen. "What kind of stunts does he do anyway? That's so *dangerous.*"

He tilts his phone completely toward me. A guy in a helmet and nylon jumpsuit is throwing himself off an airplane. He's speaking into the camera, saying, "So I was dared to pull the strings fifteen seconds after any sane, normal human being would. So, let's count down from right about . . . *now.*"

My eyes widen, and my insides clutch in concern for the idiot behind the camera.

Fourteen . . .

The static from the wind makes his voice sound shattered, strained.

"Thirteen." The bartender is counting.

I watch the idiot continue his free fall as land grows closer beneath him.

"What an idiot," I mumble, but I'm still unable to take my eyes off the video.

"Five!" the bartender says.

I look away. "Just tell me he lived."

"Oh, he lives." He shows me the camera when the guy finally pulls the cord on his chute, and a few seconds later, crashes into the ground.

The guy growls, "Ouch," then starts laughing, a low, rumbly laugh. I can't help but smile and shake my head.

"And he did this all because . . ."

"They dared him to. Five hundred bucks."

"He did all of that? For *five* hundred bucks?"

"He gets more from the video views. A man's got to put food on the table." He eyes me up and down. "Specially when he doesn't have a trust fund coming to him."

Hell, and all I want is a man to wear my suits and look pretty for a few events. "Why can't I find such a man?" I ask out loud, shaking my head as I push my empty glass forward. "Bartender. Another drink. Please."

I'm on my third.

He pours it for me. "Classy guy, that Jimmy."

"In what dictionary?"

He frowns as he sets his phone back into his pocket and polishes a glass. "Huh?"

"What dictionary would define him as classy?"

His eyes widen as if I've just murmured something blasphemous. "Well, maybe not *your* class. He doesn't own a Rolls. But around here, he's royalty. Jimmy hangs out here all the time." He nods at a dark corner booth situated to the right of the bar. "His office is right over there."

I see the cluttered tabletop and wonder what kind of man leaves a tripod, camera, and old laptop set up in a bar. He must trust the people who patronize this place. Either that or the patrons fear him.

"Jimmy Rowan will do anything for a dare—he's a man of honor."

"If he'd do that for five hundred, what would he do for half a million or more?" I grumble, smiling and shaking my head at the thought. At least I can still smile.

"Hell, shit, ma'am, he'd do anything. What? You offering?" He eyes me with new interest, in kind of a smarmy way, as if he thinks I'm asking to buy Jimmy's services. Who the heck does he think I am? "Ladies go for him."

Oh god, he *does* think that.

"*No*, thank you very much," I mutter. "Ladies or women? I don't think a lot of ladies would go for someone that foolish."

He raises his gaze past my shoulders. Silence falls over the room, and then the bartender murmurs, "Speak of the devil . . ."

There's a loud crash, followed by a ruckus.

"What's that?" I glance around at the commotion.

The bartender smiles. "Jimmy Rowan."

I turn my gaze to the door, and my heart skips a beat. The tall, raw-looking sex machine the bartender refers to doesn't look anything like a *Jimmy*. The guy is too tall and eye catching and too . . . well, *hot*.

I don't recognize him from his video. He was wearing a helmet during the stunt I just watched on YouTube. But right now, he's wearing a head of dark mussed-up hair. Worn jeans that sit perfectly on his narrow waist. And a black T-shirt that looks old and tattered, hugging muscles that only a truly athletic man could ever develop.

Realizing I'm staring as if I've never seen a real live man before, I purse my lips in distaste at myself, blame it on the cheap tequilas, and turn back to my drink.

There's a loud whistle. "Luke!"

"Jimmy!" the bartender greets him back.

I glance past my shoulder again, unable to stop the quiver in my stomach. My eyes fall on him—and rebelliously stay there. His hair is a little too long, reaching his collar and curling at the tips. Dark as midnight. He's smiling as he greets the guys who come over, and the women seem to be sitting up taller or standing and thrusting out their tits or hips. Some are even sultrily walking over to him. He oozes confidence and strength while, at the same time, there's a playful tug at the corner of his mouth that makes him look young and devilish.

He looks . . . dirty. Unkempt.

And wow. Nobody seems to care about that.

He's like some sort of celebrity around here.

I run my eyes over his chest and can't help but notice the way his shirt clings to broad shoulders. His biceps are clearly hard, as the shirt presses to his skin as he moves. His worn jeans embrace his slim hips, and the guy's got long legs, his thighs hugged by the denim material. An uncomfortable little frisson shoots down my spine as he looks up, as if sensing my stare.

"Jimmy!" some girl walking over from the corner calls out.

I snort and shake my head, frowning over how foolishly these girls are behaving. At my snort, Jimmy swings his head to look at me, a dimple under his scruffy beard appearing a little bit as our eyes meet.

Bearded jaw. Roguish smile. Golden tan. White teeth. Eyes so bright and blue it's sort of a shock when they land on me.

Why is it all turning me on? He might be hot, but he is *not my type at all*. I'm me, and he's . . . so raw; he's the most primitive man I've ever seen.

I shift in my stool and turn back to take a quick sip of my drink, bracing myself for another look.

I steal it. My stomach clutches because, oh god, he's blatantly staring at me.

He raises an eyebrow, and I stiffen in my seat and turn back to my drink, listening to a soft male laugh behind me.

"Jimmy . . . you fucking asshole!" I hear someone call.

I turn, and Jimmy is now looking at another guy, who's kicking his chair back.

Jimmy raises one eyebrow. For some reason, the deep bass of his voice causes the hairs on my arms to rise to attention. "I told you I'd find you." Jimmy speaks threateningly to the other man.

"Here I am, fucker," the other says.

They start to face off, winding around the tables to the vacant space between.

"You make it so damn easy," Jimmy murmurs with a scoff. He flexes his arms at his sides, his biceps bunching in a way I fear might make his T-shirt pop.

Why the hell am I here? In the middle of a freaking bar fight? Jeanine would tell me to get the fuck out, but she also would've told me never to come in here in the first place. But I'm strangely rooted to my stool. Before I can take another breath, Jimmy lunges at the guy.

His opponent falls onto the table behind him, and the table legs break with a loud crack, sending him flat on his back with Jimmy Rowan on top.

"Ahh, fuck, Jimmy!" the bartender groans as he swings up over the counter and slides down to the other side, charging over. "Dude, take this outside. OUTSIDE! FUCK IT, TAKE IT OUTSIDE, JAMES!"

Wait. His name is James?

Kind of like . . . Bond. James Bond?

The bartender and another man pull James back, and James shakes his head with a scowl and glares down at the man on the ground. "Fine. I'm fine."

They release him, and James drags a hand restlessly along the back of his neck before he raises his head and looks at me again. My heart skips a crazy little beat as he stares at me; then he seems to recover his anger and dives for the guy one more time.

The crowd watches as both guys punch each other, rolling on the ground, and as the fight continues, I sit here, paralyzed. I'm shocked but can't look away. It's like watching a train wreck.

"JIMMY!" half of the bar cries, while the other half is just watching, like me. Though I have to say a lot of the people here look amused. I'm not.

Again, two men pull James back, and he lets out an angry curse as he's held back, his eyes whipping to mine again.

He stares at me with flaring nostrils, no apology or remorse in his stare. He's not looking away, his stare sexual and blatant, as if he wants me to know it.

I lick my lips, my hands trembling as I reach into my purse and pull out some money. I leave it on the bar. He's breathing hard, his chest heaving and stretching his T-shirt as I quickly sling my purse around my shoulder, grab my jacket, and start walking toward the door.

His eyes crawl over me with every step I take, and I vaguely remember I'm wearing a business suit. My jacket is in my fist, the shirt I'm wearing too white, my nipples pushing against the material. My skirt feels shorter than I'm sure it is, a little tighter than I remember.

I can't fucking wait to get out of here.

What is this man doing to me?

"You cool, man?" the bartender keeps asking this James Rowan guy. The YouTube star. The daredevil.

James gives him a sharp nod, frowning, his gaze focused on me.

The bartender smiles as he follows James's gaze, as if he knows something that I don't.

I'm not so sure I want to know.

It's as if everyone is shocked that James's attention keeps coming back to me.

I'm just as shocked that I can't take my eyes off *him*.

My knees feel wobbly. Every step closer to the door makes my thighs feel weaker and weaker.

Suddenly the other man murmurs, "You lusting after that kitten? Girl can't seem to get away from you fast enough. Fifty bucks—dare you to try to fuck—"

Suddenly James lunges for him again, pushing the two men who try to restrain him away. I squeak and hurry to open the door, ready to leave, but something holds me back. Something—a nagging little whisper—stops me from opening the door. I glance back and watch him move.

This is a guy who will do anything for money.

Anything.

The thought makes me reconsider leaving. *God, Elizabeth, you're not really thinking what you're thinking . . . ? It's impossible. It would never work. This is tequila-thinking, not sane, rational thinking.*

But yes, yes I am. Inhaling a breath for courage, I end up walking back into the bar, closer and closer to the chaos.

"Gentlemen!" I stop them with a loud call, stepping in between them, still not a hundred percent sure I won't get a fist in the face in return for this act of sheer stupidity. "I'm sure we can all settle this like gentlemen, and talk."

The men pause and eye me as if I'm crazy, and it's only then that I realize how dumb it sounds. Men like this don't talk. They just grunt like cavemen and then settle things with their fists. The end.

"Hey," he breathes to me, his eyes catching on my pearl necklace before trailing lower. "Hillary Clinton. Nice suit. Get out of my way."

I look down at my suit. It's not like it's a pantsuit. I look nothing like Hillary Clinton. I know I'm fabulously overdressed for this place, but . . .

James whips a lethal gaze back to the other burly guy. "I'm done talking to you. Your no-good brat goes near Charlie again . . . ," James spits out, flexing his fingers into fists.

"Fuck you, Rowan."

James steps around me, pushes me back behind him so fast that he knocks the wind out of me, then swings out and knocks the guy back with a punch on the jaw. More fighting ensues. I'm woozy on my feet, my heart pumping with adrenaline.

It takes three men to restrain James and two to restrain the other one, and finally, the other guy is pulled back enough to give me space to talk to James.

Something about the eerie silence in the bar makes me more nervous as I manage to capture his gaze again.

He's released, and he instantly jerks his attention to me. He runs his gaze down my body again. His lips curve upward as he drags his eyes back up to mine. But suddenly he's frowning.

"What the fuck do you think you're doing?" His growl is low and deep, causing a little shiver of fear and excitement to shoot down my legs. He takes a menacing step forward, his frown deepening. "Do you want to get yourself killed, lady?"

"Killed, no, noticed, yes." Nervous because he's too near, I stick out my hand. "James, I'm—"

"Jimmy, to his friends," the bartender interrupts.

I pause. Think about it a little. Do I want to be his friend? No. Do I want to be his business associate? Maybe. "James will be just fine," I say.

The daredevil just stares with narrowing eyes.

"I'll take care of you once I'm done," James suddenly croons down at me with a wicked little smile. He nods as if to placate me, and I gape as he turns back toward the other man.

I'm not used to being ignored. Especially by some hot-as-hell idiot who'd risk his life for five hundred measly dollars.

I stomp my feet and cross my arms.

"No! I'm leaving if you don't come and talk to me now." Straightening my shoulders, I add, "I have a lucrative offer for you."

I'm not sure if the last part is for me or *James*, but since I have the floor, I want to give a reason for needing this man's attention.

Oh my god. I'm really going to do this. Am I crazy?

I am completely batshit.

Part of me wants him to say no and laugh in my face. Then I can go home and lick my wounds. Then I'll wake up tomorrow and laugh about how I was so desperate I actually tried to bribe some pretty-faced nobody who probably doesn't even know what a cuff link is to be the face of Banks LTD. And then I'll get to business and try to find a realistic solution to my problem.

But that doesn't happen.

James spins around, frowning as he looks at me. He laughs. He licks the blood off the corner of his mouth, and the move makes my eyes fall there. Unbidden fantasies of getting it on with him trickle through my mind. My lips on his, beneath his, my whole body feeling the strength of his . . .

Gulping, I shove the thoughts aside, shocked that I'm even having them. This isn't the Elizabeth I know. I can't even believe how this guy stares down at me, past really dark slanted eyebrows, through a fringe of superdark lashes, with bright-blue topaz eyes that just laser in on me like there is no one else in the bar.

Does he feel this pull like I do?

I'm scared to find out.

He looks a little reckless as he starts to smile. Like he's planning to do some crazy shit to me, right here, in front of everybody. My nipples harden even more, as if reminding me I wouldn't object one bit.

I clear my throat and smooth my trembling hands down the front of my shirt. I'm just making sure that it's in place.

"I'm Elizabeth." I keep my last name to myself.

James scans my features in a way that makes me blush. "I've got pending business, as you can see, Elizabeth . . ."

"I . . . have another business proposition for you," I repeat before I lose his attention. "One I think you will find much more interesting."

"Yeah? This I gotta hear."

Vaguely, I wonder if I'm too drunk to be thinking clearly. I motion him to the bar, acutely aware of his big body following me. I notice the bartender watching us in amusement. He pours another drink for me. I toss back the tequila shot, gasp as the burn reaches my stomach, and turn to face the YouTube daredevil.

James "Jimmy" Rowan is looking at me cockily. His gaze was on my ass when I spun around—and I can't believe how low I've fallen. How my body keeps jumping from the nearness of this guy. I purse my lips in a fight for control, not believing I'm fishing for the face of our new top-of-the-line product in some seedy bar, with some douchey bearded daredevil they call Jimmy.

But I'm desperate, and I don't like feeling desperate.

I inspect the span of his shoulders. His dark unruly hair. He lifts his head as if sensing my scrutiny, and I catch his gaze. There's intelligence there—maybe he's not a Harvard grad, but with a little, okay, a *lot* of grooming . . . it could work. I suddenly get another uncomfortable squeeze in my tummy.

Yeah, he'll do.

I'm taking this guy home.

I tip the bartender a hundred. "Thanks."

"Whoa. You're welcome. Anytime."

"Let's go, James," I say primly, and he scowls at me, shoots a confused glance at Luke, but follows me out.

Jimmy

First of all. I didn't plan for this. I was coming over to the office when I bumped into Denny and company. Decided I was hankering to tear his limbs off, one by one. Turns out I can do neither because Hillary Clinton here has some business. With *me*.

Right.

Still puzzling over that one. Oh yeah . . . I have some ideas of what business she's thinking 'bout. It's not the first time some classy, high-end chick comes to Tim's Bar and thinks either me or my buddy Luke is some sort of personal Magic Mike.

I like fucking like any other man, but one's got some pride, and I always turn those chicks down. Except why didn't I send this one and her suit out the door?

I scan her profile as she fiddles with her phone, and I assume she's summoning a car service. Her hand trembles. She's a small thing, at least a head and a half shorter than me. Shoulder-length dark hair. Skin like porcelain. She looks like one of those pretty dolls people keep behind glass doors. Never to touch, only to admire from afar.

So why the fuck are my hands itching to reach out and trace her, head to toe?

It's as if her tremors increase as I study her, like she senses my stare. I smile to myself. Hell, I like that I make her nervous.

A part of me wants to make her more nervous, while another just wants to get to the part where we both take our clothes off.

That's what she wants, I bet. And I never take my bets lightly.

"Did you get lost on your way home from . . ." I narrow my eyes as I silently debate. "A tea party?"

"Tea party? Really?" She shoots me a shocked look. "For all you know, I live down the street!" She sounds annoyed that I called her out on how much she sticks out here.

I laugh. "I don't think so. I'd definitely know if that were the case."

"Because you know everyone who lives around here?" She sizes me up, her gaze a little too caressing, if you ask me.

"All the pretty women."

"I'm sure you know them by first, middle, and last name."

"Pet names," I say, lips twitching as I wink at her. "And those are subject to change as we advance from foreplay, the throes of it, and pillow talk."

She bristles a bit, and I wonder if she's spoiled as well as obviously rich. I look at her, wondering if she fucks all nice and clean or all raw and dirty. She tilts her chin up a little higher. "The car's on its way," she says, smoothing her hands primly down her suit.

"I have all night," I drawl easily, crossing my arms.

"Yeah, me too," she says offhandedly.

"Just the kind of thing I like to hear." I give her a lopsided grin. "I like patient women. Means they won't rush me once I get busy."

She laughs sarcastically. "Oh . . . *why* would I be in a rush when I'm standing out on the corner of—where are we again?—with a man I've never seen before at a bar I've never heard of?"

I laugh, then reach out and tweak that little pearl necklace on her throat. Watch her go breathless before I release it. "No one forced ya. If they did, tell me where to find them, and I'll take care of it, but I'm guessing you walked in the bar on your own accord tonight. I'm assuming you weren't dragged here. As for the man you don't know? That's me, and I'm going home with you." I drag my thumb along her lower lip and study her. "Because you forced me. For what reason, I'm still waiting for you to tell me, baby."

She swallows, then rolls her eyes away from my biceps and gnaws on her lips.

"While we're waiting, I have a few questions."

"Like?"

"Like why do you jump out of planes for a few bucks?"

"A *few* bucks? Lady, five hundred ain't a few. I can see where those dollar signs could be a little blurred for someone like you, but for most of us, five hundred is quite a bit." I jerk my chin in the direction of her shoe. "I bet five hundred wouldn't even buy one of these."

She seems to silently plead the Fifth.

Bites that bottom lip.

And damn, why do I wanna be the one who bites it so hard?

I drag a hand along the back of my neck, sharing something I don't usually share with strangers. But can't blame me trying to impress the girl. Hello? She's fucking smoking. And I want her in bed beneath me as hard as I wanted to tear those two men apart just now.

"See . . . I've got some advertisers starting to come up on my channel, but I'm having a hard time getting them to up the amount. So . . . I need to keep attracting attention. Views and followers. Their offers will go up once my numbers climb."

She eyes me as if in great interest, as if she never once considered I might have a brain under all my brawn.

"So, you going to give me more?" I ask her. Not certain whether she wants me for a fuck or not. I wouldn't charge her a dime for that. But I'm curious as to what it is she could possibly want from me, and whether it's a fuck or real business, the kind people do behind closed doors where there are contracts involved and lots of money too.

I wonder if she's seen my channel often. If she came looking for me because she knows nobody can get shit done the way Jimmy Rowan can.

Elizabeth nods and, as if her thoughts are running as dirty as mine, blushes a pretty red color. "Most assuredly. If you agree to my terms."

A car pulls over before us, and the driver steps out. "Miss Banks?"

"That's me. This is us," she tells me as she motions me to the black Lexus, trying to hide that blush, and my dick gets even harder at the mere prospect of having her all to myself in the back of that car.

It hits me right then and there that I know exactly who this walking wet dream of a woman is. But does that hold me back? Hell no.

WOMAN ON A MISSION

Elizabeth

You've lost your shit, Elizabeth.

Your therapist has warned you time and again about how easy stress can get to you, and look at you. Look at what you did!

Instead of continuing with my internal war, I turn to the guy who stands beside me. He looks half-amused, half-still-annoyed that I coaxed him out of the bar. There's also a dash of curiosity there.

Good. I can work with that.

But. What if this guy isn't as great as Luke the bartender implied? What if Luke is a really horrible judge of character?

As I overthink this, James finally takes a step and opens the back door of the car . . .

Hops in first and slides across the seat.

Hmph.

I shoot him a snooty look of superiority as I slide in next to him and reach for the door. After the door is closed, I say, "You're no gentleman. Are you?"

A wicked grin settles on his face as he gives me a sultry look that suggests he has all sorts of ideas for our twenty-minute ride. "And you figured that out after the first or second punch was thrown? If you were shopping for gentlemen, baby, you went to the wrong place."

Stiffening when I find his relentless gaze lingering inappropriately long on my face, I dig into my purse and spritz my palms with a dab of Purell, rubbing them together.

"Want some?" I cordially offer.

"Not of that. No."

I jump a little in my seat when I hear his deep voice in the closed confines of the car.

The driver apparently believes he's been cued to watch. He fiddles with the rearview mirror, and it's trained on us until I glare at him. He readjusts the mirror.

What a perv.

Fighting to relax and exhaling, I give him my address and really focus on my idea. My crazy, out-of-this-world idea: if I can't find the perfect man, I'll create him.

And as the guy with the beard and blue eyes stares back at me, I can't help but give him a smile.

"You should've said what you were up to from the start." The daredevil's voice sounds oddly husky as he stretches his arm behind the seat, his gaze falling to my mouth as he cups my nape in his big fingers.

He pulls me a little closer. I panic and put on the brakes. "Oh, no . . . wait. Not *that*. I have a business proposition for you. *Business.* But let's get you cleaned up first."

He looks at me in confusion, then glances back at my lips with ill-concealed hunger. I lick them. Once. Twice.

"You don't want this? You seem pretty into me." He glances pointedly at my nipples, pushing against my shirt.

"I . . . ah . . ." I try to cover my chest, and when I hear a slow chuckle, I glance back up. "Could you stop staring at my chest?"

I narrow my eyes as the guy watches me. He's grinning as he pulls his eyes up to mine. He smells good. Masculine. Warm and exciting and . . . dangerous.

"You dig my touch. Don't you?" he asks, trailing a finger down my jaw, watching as my lips part on a soft gasp.

I ease back, putting some distance between us. "You're no gentleman." I try to right myself as he gives me a look that says he doesn't care.

"You said that once already."

"Maybe because it's true."

"Or *maybe* because you react to my touch in a way that excites the fuck out of you?" he asks, not smiling, his gaze intent. "And me."

Oh god.

And *oh god*, my dad would kill me if he knew what I was up to.

I shrug away the tequila buzz that has me longing to jump into this man's lap.

Elizabeth, get a hold of yourself. Remember that you picked this guy up in a sewer. Remember what he is here for, and get this done.

I struggle to regain my composure.

"If I'm going anywhere with you, it's because we both know where this is heading." His deep, rough voice is actually a turn-on too. Too bad his words only piss me off.

I stick my chin out and look past the window, hoping we can get to my penthouse soon. "No, actually. I assure you. You have no idea where this is heading."

He looks at me with that lopsided smile. Oh lordy, that's cute. Avoid, avoid, avoid. "So, wait . . . you would actually do *that*, for money?"

He narrows his eyes at me.

"Like . . . prostitute yourself?"

He laughs as if I'm so amusing. "You're hot. I'd let you have the first one for free."

I gape at him. "Let's get one thing straight, James," I continue.

He's nodding as if he's listening, all while he reels me by the arm toward the flat planes of his body, and his lips descend. Shocked, I just sit here, panting as he brushes his lips across mine.

I gasp on contact.

He growls softly. And he tries it again.

Brush. Graze.

OPENING ME . . .

Suddenly I'm tasting him—he tastes of coffee with alcohol, a little metallic from the blood on his mouth, his tongue wet and slick as he flicks my own. He tastes forbidden. Dark. *Sexy.* He shifts me closer to him. Our mouths parting wider now, tongues licking at each other, over and over, both of us going at it like we need it.

I can feel his hardness pressing into my hip bone as we both taste one another, him groaning, me moaning, acting desperate as if this is the only chance we'll get.

I try to remind myself this is insane. I don't know this guy, but I'm kissing him like he's the only one in the world, grabbing his shoulders, letting him devour my mouth—and do I *feel* devoured!

His tongue caresses mine, creating an intense wave of pleasure through me. No man has ever made a kiss make me want in this way, make me crave with desperation and mindlessness. My sex aches and clutches. The void has never felt this empty, this painful.

When we pull away, I'm gasping, and the guy growls and pulls me back to him. "Mmm, maybe even the second one, too, heiress. I want more of you, and you want it too."

His lips descend again, and this second kiss is just as intense, his hands gripping my ass and driving me so insane that I'm suddenly straddling him, my fingers rubbing his muscular forearms and biceps and shoulders.

I've never kissed a guy with a beard before. It's a little prickly, but it's naughty and wicked. As my hard nipples brush against his strong chest, the pleasure is excruciatingly sweet. Too sweet. Too exciting.

Moaning as I tear free, I look at him, gasping for breath.

We size each other up.

Stare at each other's mouth.

Amusement sparkles in his eyes, mixed with heat and something dark.

I shake my head. He shoots me a lopsided grin, the grin of a demon, for sure.

His bold gaze traps mine as he frowns. "What got you so riled?"

"You. You really sleep with women for money?"

He shakes his head and reaches for me again. "But I'll make an exception, since you're the one offering, and I like the looks of you."

I straighten. What have I gotten myself into? "No. We're not supposed . . . I didn't invite you to my house to . . . you know what . . . call me Lizzy. It's less . . ." Serious. Intense. Intimate. *Ugh.*

I stop talking when we pause at a Midtown traffic light. My breath catches, and I look around as if I'm seeing the city for the first time. If we're already in Midtown, then that means we've been romping across the back seat for the last fifteen minutes.

Our driver adjusts his mirror again. He's getting his jollies, but I ignore him.

Groaning, I gradually return my attention to James. He's thoughtful too. I wonder what he's thinking of when he gives me a hint.

He responds by bracketing his arm around my hips, drawing me closer to his hard male form. "You know how to use those lips—don't you, Lizzy?"

What? What's he asking? Does he think I'll blow him?

Lizzy . . .

Good lord. It's not much better when he calls me Lizzy either.

I groan and slide onto my side of the back seat. James smirks and watches me.

I clear my throat. "If you could control yourself, Mr. Rowan, I want to discuss some business," I say, finally back to my senses.

"Fine. I'm curious. I'll give you that. I'm all for business . . . Miss Banks." He winks on that last.

I blink at his use of my last name.

He knows my name. He called me Miss Banks.

I cringe at the thought of this guy knowing me—or worse, maybe, my dad.

"Have we met or . . ." No. We haven't met, and I don't have time for games. "How do you know me, exactly?"

He watches me in complete silence, which is probably a struggle for someone like Jimmy Rowan, but for James, the man I plan to create, this is good.

I can work with quiet consideration.

He crosses his toned arms. "Read the papers, don't I?"

I shrug. "I don't know. *Can* you?" I shoot back, partly having fun, partly annoyed.

He ignores the dig. "The driver mentioned your name. I put it along with your first name, and voilà, recognized why I felt like I'd seen you before. Everybody knows you. You're the poor little rich girl, heiress to a fortune. Harold Banks's only daughter. He's the man who easily pleases millions of customers but couldn't satisfy the little woman at home."

"That little woman was my mother."

"I'm just repeating the story."

"It's one I'd like to forget."

Even though Mom left a very long time ago, what he said is true. Locals can't recall what kind of winter we had a few months ago or even tomorrow's forecast, but when it comes to lifestyle gossip? Atlanta doesn't forget.

My dad was one of the first men who took his company global with online shopping and a worldwide promise: *If you're not completely satisfied with your product, return it for a new one.*

Sometimes I wonder if that's why Mom left. Maybe she'd traded Dad in for a newer version. At the time, that was the running joke.

"Back to business," I say, refocusing. "If you'll trust me, you'll be the surprised one in the end. I'm the answer to all your prayers."

He runs his fingertip down my jaw. "I don't pray."

"After this, you may."

"Honey, if I go down on my hands and knees, want to guess whose legs will be propped up on my shoulders?"

My breath catches. I can't pretend that his raw look of masculinity doesn't spin my libido-meter. Steeped in wild danger, the synergy between us is electrifying.

I try to recover, but why is it so hard to stay aloof with the tequila buzzing through my system and this unapologetic tower of testosterone buzzing so near?

He just raises his brows.

The driver pulls in front of my building. James looks up and snickers. "Exactly what I expected." He takes out an old-looking cell phone with a cracked screen and punches in some numbers. "Charlie, listen . . . something's come up. No, not that, not yet. Anyway, I'll be home late. Call me later." He hangs up, looks at me.

I don't know what to say. The whole car smells of him.

I wiggle a little bit farther away so I don't have to sniff his scent. But oddly, I still feel his hands on me. I fight to shake the feeling off. Wondering how a guy who's a complete stranger and nothing like the guys I usually date can make me feel so restless.

Focus, Elizabeth. This is about business and business only.

Right . . .

THE MAN ON MY COUCH

We pull into the circular drive of my condominium complex. The doorman opens the door to the cab, and we step out.

James whistles.

I know my place is nice. Not as nice as my dad's, but I can't complain, because Daddy's paying for all of it. All. Of. It. I know that makes me a spoiled princess. But I couldn't tell him no, that I wanted to make my own way in the world, because in his world, he's supposed to keep me. That's a fact of his life, like that the sky is blue. He pays for everything for me—my house, my car, my credit card bills; hell, he even has a housekeeper come in every day to fill my refrigerator with food.

He knows all these strings tying me to him just make it harder for me to leave, like my mom did.

It's frustrating to feel so "managed" all the time, especially when I want to prove to him that I'm a capable girl and can do fine on my own.

One of the doormen studies the hunk of dirty man flesh next to me, then pulls me aside as James struts toward the entrance. "Are you in trouble, Miss Banks?"

Probably. I give him a reassuring smile. "No, no trouble."

We head up the elevators, and then I lead him into my sprawling apartment. James Rowan seems larger and larger as he enters my space. I suppose it should alarm me, but I'm too drunk and too excited to rethink this whole thing. Yes, my hormones maybe got more of a workout than I wanted them to, but I'm trying to get them under control now.

Oh my fucking god. Did I really kiss him?

If my father had been a fly on the wall during that, he'd be lying on the floor mat of that cab right now, a dead fly.

James glances around my pristine place and whistles. "Damn. Nearly as nice as the owner." He winks at me, his voice deep and flirty, and I feel a blush creep up my cheeks.

Scowling at my reactions to him, I sigh. "Just . . . clean up, okay? Towels and everything you need are right through there." I point to the restroom, sighing as the guy heads down the hall. He pauses at the door to the guest bathroom, eyeing me as I sway a little on my feet. I'm suddenly ready for bed, too exhausted and intoxicated to think clearly.

"Tough day, huh?"

"Says the guy with the bloody fists."

"I won't mention the other guy." He shrugs as if it's no biggie.

"You mean *boast* about the other one."

Another roguish smile, making me wonder what that dimple on his cheek will look like without his beard. "Appreciate you letting me clean up here." He turns to head into the shower, and I stop him.

"Wait. James. Wait. Stand there. Don't. MOVE. Let me look at you again."

Facing me, he narrows his eyes, standing still for me to walk up to him and slide my eyes up and down his frame.

Trying to ignore the odd little boil running through my veins, I assess him as clinically as possible. Taking in his pros, his cons, everything about him. Needs a little shave. Nicely built. Mmm. *Very* nicely built. And I bet he'd be a bargain too. I could probably save some money by offering him less. I mean, he nearly killed himself for $500. Men like him have no shame.

"Do you have a screw loose or something?" he growls softly.

I jerk my eyes up. Okay. I'll start the bidding at one hundred. He'll probably lap that up.

We will have our work cut out for us, though. It'll take time. I'll need to *buy* time—but it will be worth it. Because underneath the daredevil there's something terribly mesmerizing, and I can't wait to discover it.

I will take on the near-impossible task of turning this guy into the most perfect man the world has ever seen—I just need to control my attraction to him in the process.

Jimmy

When I woke up this morning, I didn't think I'd be finishing up the day in a place as swanky as this one.

But wouldn't you know it? My life's full of adventure.

Fuck, everything is white here. The walls, the carpets, the sofas, the towels. I hope she pays her housekeeper a mint.

I'm the only smudge in the place. Knew that much when I saw the way the doormen were looking at me. Like I ain't even human.

I check the mirror to find the markings of a fresh bruise on my cheek. Denny's lucky. I should've knocked his teeth out tonight. I probably would've if it hadn't been for Elizabeth.

Hell, I should've knocked him out anyway.

That guy? What a bastard.

I yank a bath towel from the linen closet and place it on the vanity before entering the walk-in shower. The light-colored walls and ivory marble tiles are something I've only seen in movies.

This gigantic bathroom is larger than my bedroom. Shit, my whole house would probably fit in here.

As I work the shampoo into a lather, I think about Charlie again. Best kid in the world. He's thirteen years old but looks about nine, and because of it, he gets his ass handed to him on a regular basis. Fucking Denny and his family of assholes. How could a grown man encourage his younger brothers to bully a kid?

Damn, it makes my blood boil!

Yeah, so I may have to pay Tim for the bar damage. The person I became tonight is the person Denny knew he could pull out of hiding. It was too easy, and I guess it concerns me.

It only took him a minute to drag my rage to the forefront. Was that the goal all along? I didn't want a fight.

Hell, Charlie didn't want this fight. Charlie ain't into that. He's such a calm, sweet kid that he's paid very little attention to my tips on defending himself—and that concerns me too. He begged me to stay out of it, and maybe I would've, if Charlie could hold his own, but he can't.

And he won't need to.

He has me for that.

My mind turns back to Elizabeth. Hell, my mind isn't the only thing weighing in right now.

Elizabeth Banks. The Elizabeth Banks. From the fucking newspapers.

Who knew that in person, she'd make my cock stiff as fuck? Who knew that I got off on the country-club set? What I'd give to run my fingers through that silken black hair, stare into those emerald-color eyes, and just screw around until morning light.

I stroke my dick, thinking of her sweet little body, the way her nipples spiked with just a bit of friction. If she gets cranked up over a little foreplay, I wonder what happens when she's into an outright grind.

My hand tightens as I leisurely pump up and down. I close my eyes and think of her smile. Those perky fucking tits.

Damn.

What I'd do to earn my place in her bed. What I'd do to spread those soft thighs, clasp her slender hands, and find that easy late-night rhythm.

Hell. I'd probably fuck like a maniac and scare her to death.

I wonder then if she likes a lot of foreplay or if she gets right to it. Does she like wild sex in numerous positions, missionary, or climbing aboard and riding?

She seems so prim and proper. She dresses like a woman who's in control, but she needs to let her hair down.

I'll gladly help her with that.

On the drive over, she acted all timid and shit, but as soon as our lips met, she felt that chemistry. *I felt the connection.*

I should be hightailing it back to the house. Instead, I'm here in her museum-size shower, stroking myself while thinking of one hot piece of strange tail.

I stop.

She's more than a piece of ass. I grit my teeth and revisit her earlier words.

Does she really have an offer for me, or is that some sort of pickup line?

If the deal is as good as she thinks, and I hope it is, maybe I'll be able to provide Charlie a better life, a safer place to call home, and maybe even some new clothes. That shit doesn't come cheap.

Rap. Rap. Rap.

I freeze. Dammit.

"Everything all right in there?"

I press my head against the wet tiles and stare down at my erection. "Yep! I'll be out in a minute."

"Take your time!"

Not a chance.

That'll come later.

When I'm taking my time and working on a woman. On a damn classy woman.

Elizabeth

Everything's foggy when James emerges from the bathroom. I smell him first. He smells like my hand soap and shampoo, both of which have a vanilla base.

And then I make the mistake of looking at him.

Holy lord. He has a towel slung over his hips, and . . . it's not even one of my big bath towels.

It's like a hand towel.

I didn't even know I had towels that small. Or maybe he's just that big.

He has leg muscles to kill for. His back is like a ski slope over a perfect ass. I gawk at his chest, at the dark wet hair on his pectorals, glistening on the planes of his sexy-as-hell body as he sits next to me on the sofa.

Wha?

I can't even think a full word.

Wha?

"So, is this a normal routine for you?" he's saying, as alarm bells go off in my head. Too close! Too naked! Too close!

"No." I jump off the couch and point to the kitchen. "Want a drink?"

"Not yet." He shoots me that devil's lopsided smile again. "Why would I need a drink when I could sip on you?"

From this vantage point, I have a perfect view right up the towel, between his legs. I fight to avert my eyes. "I brought you home because—"

"Look. We don't need to talk. We can pick up where we left off."

Oh god. He is almost naked. And he's hairy and hard and . . . naked on my couch. And I'm still drunk and thinking tequila thoughts, and when was the last time I had sex? I can't even remember. "That's not . . ."

"Say nothing." He reaches for me and drags me to him. "Nothing at all." His lips skim mine. "Let your body do the talkin', honey." He's crooning now. Sexy, sultry.

The "honey" part snaps me out of the trance. "I need a minute."

"Hurry," he says, patting my bottom when I pass him.

I jump. Men do not swat my ass. Especially hot naked men who are nowhere near my type. My type is the Ivy League guy who has his own dynasty to manage. Not him. Not . . .

What the fuck am I doing?

As soon as I'm behind closed doors, I kind of wobble over to the bed and sit. Really. What. The. Fuck. Am. I. Doing? I acted on impulse, and now?

I'm here. He's out there. We're alone. Behind. Closed. Doors.

Whatever possessed me? When did I cook up the idea that it would be fine to create a man since I couldn't find one? Sure, in the broad scheme of things it's possible, but I don't have time for a long shot. I need a solid finish.

I need to impress the unimpressionable. I want my dad's approval.

And this is a fucking stupid-ass way to go about obtaining it. Even bleary from too much tequila, I know that Mr. Doesn't-Even-Know-How-to-Shave isn't going to get me the Daughter of the Year Award.

I had too much to drink and need to nod off for a minute.

Just a minute . . .

As I close my eyes, I think of the last few hours. I'm sitting at the bar. James is the focal point. Everyone loves him. There's a fight and an endless conversation with the bartender. I see a beast of a man, a man who seems interested in me.

I'm interested in him.

There's a fight, and I break it up. My shirt is torn, stripped away from my body. Suddenly, I'm hot. Aching. Desperate.

My eyes fly open, but James isn't there, so I return to my fantasy because this is getting good. I latch on to the dreams and let them have me. Maybe these visions are a sign of what's to come. Or maybe they're just a warning.

I am NOT interested in him. In any way, shape, or form. He is my little project. That is all.

But I'll indulge the fantasy. Just for tonight. As long as I don't let it get out of hand.

And you won't, Lizzy. He's just a dirty, sweet-talking guy from the street. Keep your head about you.

♥ ♥ ♥

I sleep restlessly, having dreams of my launch failing miserably, people laughing at me, at us, at Banks LTD. I dream of bloody lips on mine, and feeling bloodied hands touching me, and feeling restless and reckless and waking up horny.

I shift in bed, exhaling, glaring at my ceiling over my dilemma.

I hear snoring. I groan, my head pulsing. Stirring, I peer around the room and realize the snoring is coming from my living room. I wrap a silk robe around myself, slide into my fur slippers, and start padding out but freeze when I see a pile of flesh and blankets on the sofa.

Ducking behind my massive entertainment center, I gasp and draw the sash on my robe tighter around me. My eyes widen, and I start when I see the muscles on that body. A pillow covering his face.

There's a guy sleeping on my couch.

A breathing, living, RANDOM guy!

I bolt to my room, fully prepared to slam the door and lock it, if necessary, and call 911. Instead, I stand there addled and narrow my eyes as I peer out my bedroom door.

What have I done?

Shit.

I can't believe what I did.

I take a quick shower and change—with the door locked—and then I pace nervously in my room. He could be a rapist. Some felon. A thief. And I let him into my place.

But the guy is also a businessman in his own way. Honestly, I was impressed with the size of his YouTube business, and I'm pretty sure I could even help him grow that more after we're done with my project. I'm certain he and I could find some common ground and a win-win situation for the both of us.

I pace and pace, shocked that I—Elizabeth Banks—brought him into my gorgeous Midtown apartment.

I'm surprised the doormen even let me bring him upstairs!

A worrisome thought hits me: Did they think I bought myself a male escort last night?

The image of dirty, bearded, bar-brawling, testosterone-laden James Rowan making love to me slams into my brain, and I'm envisioning that this man likes it hard and rough and raw, makes hard and rough and raw noises, and moves his hips in the same way.

The thought unexpectedly makes me so hot that I squirm and shake my head as I try to push it away. The worst part is that the guy is nowhere even *near* the kind of guy I always go for.

I always go for guys who are educated, polished, elegant. *Classy. Boring.* Not that boring and classy are interchangeable, but sometimes they can be. *Rowan* is neither.

Another shiver speeds down my back as I remember the way he brawled at the bar.

I'd never seen a real bar fight before. The men I date would never do that. I suppose because they hate getting their hands dirty. Think themselves above it. It isn't the way classy, educated people are supposed to behave.

But to be honest, I can't say some of my "friends" proved to be as educated and classy as some might expect.

No.

Dropping off the face of the earth after I assumed we were dating isn't really a classy thing to do. It's the kind of thing only a loser would do.

A thing that only my most recent ex, Daniel Winfrey, would do.

Daniel was a normal guy. He was wealthy, but not Banks wealthy. Dartmouth educated, interesting, and cute. But he was apparently too intimidated by my father to endure a dinner with him. He stood me up the night of our introductory dinner at my dad's place, and from that moment forward, I've feared that being my father's only daughter will prevent me from meeting a lot of men who would be great catches in other families.

In fact, I don't think there is another man out there who will ever meet my father's standards.

No.

My father wants perfection in every sense, and the thought of failing him, or of the only two men in my life having an awkward relationship, makes me want to retch.

So no.

That's why I've avoided dating for a while. Why should I go through the motions if they'll either get too scared to face my father or prove to be completely different from what I hoped for?

Those few failed relationships have plagued me with self-doubt, and for the past few months, I've had to replay our breakups a million times to figure out what I did wrong. I can never seem to find out—so I've decided the best course of action is to focus on Banks LTD and let the other parts of my life just adjust.

I'm not going to let this opportunity go to waste. Sure. This guy could use a good hand, but if anyone can create the perfect man out of a classless, crass, bearded bar brawler, it's *me*.

I'm a detail person.

I won't miss anything that needs to be done.

This guy is an up-and-coming YouTube star.

Which reminds me . . . I flip open my laptop and check out his channel once more. He has over two hundred thousand followers. Wow. That many people either find him entertaining or want to see him die?

Impressive.

I could totally work with a guy who seems to connect with the public in the way this one does.

I watch another video as he sleeps. It's an older clip with foggy images, but I'd know that body anywhere:

"Dared for a hundred bucks to jump my bike over that car over there. Watch this." He hands the phone to a little boy that can't be over eight or nine. "Charlie, get over here—now Charlie's holding the phone . . ." He grins into the camera.

"Careful," Charlie peeps out happily as he trains the phone on James.

"Me? Careful? Never." James winks, laughing that deep laugh as he heads over to do his stunt.

My stomach is in absolute knots as he crafts a makeshift ramp and takes position on his bike. A bike that's almost too small for James's big frame.

Obviously the guy survived the stunt because he's currently sleeping in my living room. But still, I am breathless as I watch him pedal the bike, push up into the air, fly across the top of the car, and land with a flourish.

A childish "woot!" comes from behind the camera, and James hops off the bike, approaches with a slow, cocky male swagger, and peers into the video lens as he says, "See that? Yeah, fuck you, too, and give me my money." He winks and turns off the camera.

Who's Charlie?

I realize that maybe it wasn't a mistake. Maybe this is the sort of guy who will value the money I can offer, and I desperately need someone who's willing to work hard to make my launch happen.

Bracing myself with a breath, I march outside, half expecting to find all of my artwork and silverware gone. But no, he's still asleep. I stand before him, surveying him. Nice chest. A little hairy but we'll take care of it. Muscles all over. Bodywise, I have nothing to complain about.

Too much facial hair, though. Hair too long as well.

Oblivious to me, he shifts on the couch. He's perfectly relaxed lying there, shifting around, displaying a peek of his ass.

Oh my god, he's naked on my couch?

My eyes widen. I alternate between being curious and angry and thoroughly, disturbingly . . . a little bit aroused.

I take a picture of him sleeping and shoot it to Jeanine.

Me: Fuck, marry, or kill?

Jeanine: Fuck. No regrets.

Me: I need a man that women will want to both fuck and marry. He needs to look like Prince Charming.

Jeanine: Dude I'd fuck him even with that godawful haircut and without a shave. And Prince Charming is way overrated.

Me: Right. But not marry this one? YET?

Jeanine: You marry that thing, and your dad will disinherit you. Where did you find him?

Me: It's a secret.

Jeanine: Wait just a damn minute. Is that dude in your apartment NOW? Did you sleep with him?

Me: No . . . but he is fuckable, isn't he?

Jeanine: Yes, but . . . that's about it. Please tell me you're not thinking of anything else.

I pause just long enough for her to get exactly the idea that I'm thinking.

Jeanine: Holy fuck! No. Back away. Bad idea. Your dad will kill you if he finds out! When I said you should go smaller, I didn't mean cockroach small.

And I wonder who I've been texting this whole time.

Jeanine: Your dad has high expectations and Lizzy? That guy on your couch? Will not meet your dad's expectations. EVER. Even with a shave and a cute suit. Wake him up and GET HIM OUT OF THERE.

Before I can respond, Jeanine pops back with: Do me a quick favor before you send him on his way. Lift the blanket, flip him over, and take a CLOSER snapshot.

I think about it, smirking.

Me: Jeanine, I still need the perfect man.

Jeanine: Perfect? There's no such thing, Lizzy. You might as well go to a lab and create him. Like in Weird Science.

Exactly, I think; then I survey him again. He's tall, and I like tall men. He's very masculine, and I like those too. A shiver runs through me as I inspect him. Because though he's not clean or polished, I'm viscerally attracted to him.

And that means other people will be too.

Jeanine: What gutter did you pick this one out of?

I wince. Is it obvious?

Me: I know he looks a little rough now, but . . .

Jeanine: I'd REALLY do him. Even without a shower or a shave. BUT THEN I WOULD THROW HIM BACK IN THE GUTTER.

Me: You're not the only one.

I don't tell her about the intense romp in the cab. She probably wouldn't believe me anyway.

Jeanine: Yum yum.

Me: Tell me about it.

I inspect the breadth of his shoulders. His dark, rather longish hair.

Hmm. Okay, so, we have slightly under two months until the fashion season begins with the West Coast Fashion Week in LA. There will be a few other dinners with major buyers in between. Then, a month later, the season culminates at the biggest event of them all, Men's Fashion Week in New York City.

This is doable.

I think.

Exhaling, I march to the kitchen, bring out my trusty notepad and pen, and start making a list.

Haircut.
Shave.
Wax.
Eyebrows.
Skin care.
Wardrobe.
UNDERWEAR!!
MANNERS!!!!!!

I walk the length of the sofa, tapping my pen against the notepad as I try to imagine what he'll look like when I'm finished with his transformation. The full makeover will take a lot of work. We'll definitely need to work on his manners too. If he's going to own the Banks look, he needs to be the total package. No slipups. We have to make every single person in every room he walks into think that he's the real deal, born into high society, a regular English freaking lord.

I wonder for a minute how hard it would be to get him to speak in a British accent.

No, scratch that—I have enough work on my hands as it is.

I circle him again, thinking about all the things he'll need to learn. It would've been much easier if I'd hired someone with the right skill set.

Maybe if I'd done my man shopping at the local country club, I'd have a chance. But I shouldn't even count on this guy knowing how to tie a simple bow tie. Maybe even a regular tie.

Ugh. I've got a lot of work ahead of me.

He shifts, open his eyes. He looks at me, and I start.

"Well, well, well." He sits up onto his elbows, a slow smile curving his mouth as he stares at me.

I jump a little, pricking angrily. "I'd appreciate if you wore something when you sleep on my couch. It kind of grosses me out to sit there now."

He raises one sardonic eyebrow. "Are you always this prissy, baby?"

I grab his dirty clothes and send them flying at his chest. "Get dressed. We need to talk."

He just piles the clothes in his lap and stares at me, and he smiles, then lifts a picture from the side table. It's the one of me taken three years ago, from my Stanford graduation. Puts it down.

As I walk away to let him change, I hear him say, "Tell me something, sweetheart."

The thick way in which he says *sweetheart* makes me halt in the middle of a stride. "Yes?" I'm afraid to look back, scared if I do that I'll never be able to turn away.

"Look at me."

His voice is husky, his demeanor stern.

I turn, unable to refuse. Gasping at the sight of those abs and pecs, I can't help but focus on his clothes, the torn shirt that he holds in front of what must be a very erect, very hard, and maybe even BEAUTIFUL cock.

Maybe isn't even a possibility here.

Every inch of this man is perfect. Raw and unrefined, but *perfect*.

At least from what I can see.

But I'm pretty sure his confidence is a testament to past compliments that he's probably earned in many beds—or maybe in the back seat of a cab.

A wicked shiver runs down my spine as I remember him groping me, and my own body reacts as I run my eyes along his muscles.

"What?" I'm uncomfortable, and it's not right, dammit. This is my home, my fortress, and this man makes my world tilt.

His roguish smile proves he knows what his presence here does to me, what his naked body makes me think about.

He curses under his breath. "Great. Just what I need. A prim and proper princess when the lights are on. You always wear a suit?"

He drops his clothes to the coffee table, and I struggle to keep my composure, not that keeping one's composure includes gaping at a man's bare cock and imagining what it might feel like to . . .

Dammit to hell.

Stop. Just stop it.

And I don't know if I'm trying to mentally convey the message to James or if I'm ridiculing myself here, but either way? I can't seem to avert my eyes no matter how much I want to.

Do I even want to?

Fuck no.

I mean, I'm a grown woman. I've seen a man's dick before, but this . . . man . . . and HIS dick?

Whoa.

He watches me until he deliberately pulls on his T-shirt and drags it across his tight stomach. The tip of his cock brushes against the hem of his shirt, but I still don't look away, and I'm not sure why.

I don't behave like this, not under most circumstances anyway, but I didn't ask him to lower his clothes. I didn't tell him to show me what he's made of—delectable inches and inches of perfect male.

He smirks as he holds out his arms. "Seen enough?" His voice is thick and sultry. My stomach constricts in response to his tone.

I turn away, but hiding now is a moot point. "I see you're not shy."

"Nope. So if you're a princess by day, what are you by night?" he gruffs out.

I hear the rumple of his jeans as he drags them on, and I face him again. "What do you mean?" My own voice sounds odd. Sort of . . . crackly.

He left the fly open.

He.

Left.

His.

Fly.

Open.

My eyes hurt from the pain caused by wanting to look down again but forcing myself not to.

My eyes fall for a second. I stare at the thick, hard . . .

I pull them back up, glaring at him in some sort of automatic self-preservation mechanism.

There's that smirk dancing on his wicked lips again.

"So snippy in the morning," he croons devilishly. "Can't blame a guy for asking. Last night, I felt the heat from your gaze all the way across the room. This morning? Those pretty eyes are ice, heiress."

He inches closer, and I steel myself against his approach, swallowing back the nervousness that I refuse to let him see.

He bites his lip and quickly grabs me by the back of my neck, and I yelp in surprise.

His body heat envelops me. Excites me. Worries me.

"So, Elizabeth Banks. Do ya always turn into a man-eater after happy hour?" He grins as he lowers his head and keeps his lips a breath away from mine. "Because if so, after the way ya ran your eyes all over me? I wanna know where to find ya between say, seven and nine tonight?"

"I—" *Desperately need some sex therapy now, but I'm not sure if that requires a professional, or a bad boy like James Rowan.*

"I'll be right here. Working. And you won't be . . . the last thing I plan to do is eat a man like you. You're not my flavor. And I don't want to get indigestion." I brace myself and say, "Listen to me. That's not what this is about."

I huff and free myself from James's grip as he releases a low, deep chuckle.

Taking charge of the situation by shooting him a "down, boy" glare, I head to my office, located to the right of the living room. I take a seat in my office chair, prop up my glasses, and start adding more things to my list.

Occasionally, I lift my gaze and study him. He tugs on his shoes and finishes gathering his limited belongings. As he threads his belt through the loops, I hold my breath. He takes his time with the buckle, and it's a lame effort to tease me.

Only, it's not really that lame, because it's working.

He's a stone's throw away. RIGHT THERE. In my living room!

I crane my neck, but it's no use. I've already witnessed the best part of this show, the way he slowly pulled on his T-shirt and covered a rather impressive chest, the way he teased me with his cock, looked on in silent anticipation as if he expected me to . . . *to what, Elizabeth? Surely the guy wouldn't ask you to fuck.*

Oh yes. This guy definitely would.

That's part of what scares me, part of what makes him so hot.

He lifts his head as if he senses my stare, and I catch a sultry look in his eyes only to get another uncomfortable squeeze in my tummy. I look away.

He starts walking over. I stare at my nails, exhaling. I can't continue ignoring him because suddenly he's standing right in front of me. I also need him. I asked him to come home with me and still haven't told him why. My gaze fastens on his worn sneakers, before sliding up his denim-clad thighs, up a body that any woman would die to feel above her.

Am I *seriously* thinking these things?

Okay, Elizabeth, you need an orgasm, or you'll attack the first hot guy you meet.

But this guy isn't hot; he's more like . . . raw and primal. The sexiest guy I've ever met.

I blow out a hard breath and realize he hears me, all while this undeniable need wells up inside of me. It's there not because I'm basically looking for "any" man, but because I'm looking for the "perfect" man.

I have high expectations.

"Take off your glasses." His voice is low and deep, and this close, it makes a little flutter of nervousness race through my system.

"Excuse me?" I lift my head.

"Take off your glasses, and look at me."

Wow. The nerve of him! I bristle, but I pull my glasses off all the same. His eyes are so blue it's like I'm swimming in a Tahitian sea.

"You're giving me a hard-on of the kind I never ignore. I want to fuck you well and deep—and I think by the look in your eyes, you wouldn't object. So why don't you show me your bed, and we get right down to it?"

I know I'm attractive. Sometimes men approach me with some lines like *Do you have the time? Can I have your phone number? I think I've seen you before.* But wow, this one? Way too blunt. We'll definitely need to work on his subtlety. He managed to both get my attention and piss me off in just a couple of seconds.

My palm itches at my side. He smiles slowly. I'm sure women fall at his feet willingly when he says such things.

I try to remind myself that I am not just any woman. I am Elizabeth Banks, and he's . . . someone I picked up in a trashy bar.

He thinks he's getting laid.

I should lay him out.

Instead, I paint on a look of real interest, stand, and tell him, "Sit."

He chuckles, seems a little wary, but eventually sits and watches me with more brewing interest than before.

"So, you do anything for a bet?"

I butt my hips against my desk and wait with my arms crossed. It's deliberate. I want to look unapproachable, professional. More importantly, I want him to see me as a woman in control.

"Don't worry about the money. I was kidding last night. I don't fuck for money. This one's for me."

I eye him, my heart pounding as I shoot him a look of disgust. "I have no intention of hitting the sack with you."

"Don't you." It isn't a question because he doesn't believe me. "Okay then." Amusement curves his wicked lips again.

"In case you haven't noticed . . . these are designer heels. This is a Frida, a totally authentic designer. I'm the sort of woman who selects only the best," I go on.

"You'll never find the best—nobody will ever reach that standard. Which explains why you're so starved."

"Excuse me . . ."

He cocks his head, surveying me as he slowly stands.

"What . . . ?" I press.

"You're parched, and I can sate this thirst."

I don't believe him because I saw the women at Tim's Bar. They weren't there for the drinks and good service. Those crooning broads were there for him.

One taste of pleasure from this guy, and I'd probably grovel for more.

Leaving insatiable women in his wake? That's this guy's game.

He walks forward. I put my arms out to stop his catlike approach, and I quickly slide away from him, sure that I can't take his touch, not here and now, not when I'm dressed for the corporate world and planning to tackle the day with the confidence and luck of a pariah. "Don't do that. I can't think when you do that."

"Then don't think." He reaches out for me, and I spin away.

"Whoa. Stay right there. Halt!"

He narrows his eyes, and I whisper, "Let's discuss this business proposition that I have for you. An offer."

"I have a sweet proposition, too, a sweet suggestion of my own. Want to hear it?"

God damn him and that sexy smirk!

"No." But I do. I so fucking do. Instead of giving him the opportunity, I say, "It's going to take some effort, but if you can do all those stunts you do, then you can do this as well."

"Want to know what else I can do well?"

Frustrated, I say, "That's understood."

"What is?"

"Look. I get that you're *good*. I'm sure you're very skilled in all the ways that matter." Jeanine always says to feed a man's ego. "Now can we move on?"

"If we can move to your bedroom."

"We can't." Not yet. Refusing to acknowledge the flush creeping up my cheeks, I continue, "But you need to act the opposite of your usual self."

He looks offended. "What do you know about my usual self?"

"Plenty. I'm a good judge of character."

"Then you shouldn't be so quick to judge. We could be having a blast right now. Alone. In your bedroom. In that *great big*, massive four-poster bed."

I swallow. How does he know that I have a *great big, massive four-poster* bed? I want to let the comment slide, but curiosity wins. "How do—"

"You have nightmares."

"Me? No."

"If you say so." He folds his arms over his broad chest. "Go on. I'm listening." He's scowling now, looking impatient.

Something about this man screams that he's not the kind to be trifled with. Never mind that his chums call him Jimmy. He's intimidating as hell, but I won't let him intimidate me. I'm a Banks, after all.

I quickly rummage through my head, trying to remember if I had any significant dream the night before. Coming up empty, I shoot him a scolding little look and say, "Stepping uninvited into a lady's bedroom? I could teach you a thing or two about how a real gentleman should act."

"Sweetheart, I need no lessons—"

"Which brings me to my business proposal. I need you to become the perfect gentleman, *be* the perfect man. I'll shave you, give you a new look, show you how to act around women—men—everyone. You can keep the clothes—just give me three months to be the face and help me launch my new menswear line. If you can do that, I'll pay you a hundred thousand dollars. Any questions?"

"Yeah. What's in it for me?"

"Didn't you hear a word I just said?"

"Every last one of them." He gives me that rogue look again, the one that lets me know that he wants a perk or two to sweeten the deal.

"Cash," I snap. "Isn't that the language you speak?"

He narrows his eyes. "I speak English. But I can speak Dollar, too, if that's all you know."

I thrust my arms out. "Come on. Don't lay this on me. You do stunts for five hundred dollars—" I stop. Is it an insult to call a poor person poor? "You're on a limited budget, aren't you?"

He laughs, moistens his lips, and shakes his head. "I might be poor, lady, but my pride's rich as Midas, and I don't beg."

"Beg? For what?"

"Sex, money, you name it."

"I never said you did."

"You're saying cash is my language when clearly it's more yours than mine. And I can talk Dollar just fine, like I said, but I have other interests too. Right now. For example. You."

"Excuse me?"

"What if I decide I want you?"

My eyes widen and my lips part, and for a second, I feel a little vulnerable because I don't know how to respond to that. I've never been come on to by a guy who tells it like it is in the way *this* devil does. It's infuriatingly sexy, and it makes me want to negotiate with my body. Great. Like *I'm* the prostitute now? "Not an option," I finally force out.

"Then I'm not interested." He stands.

Wait. He can't be turning me down. I offered him more than he probably makes in . . . I don't know. A lifetime? I mean, he nearly killed himself for five hundred bucks, and he won't help me for three months for two hundred times that?

He takes a step toward the door. Then another.

I'm losing him.

My heart races as I follow him. Is he serious? He's leaving?

"Wait! James, wait!" I rush around to stop him and realize I'm out of breath when he stares at my rapidly rising chest. "Five hundred," I blurt. "I'll pay you five hundred thousand. But for that much, you're going to have to agree to a few things."

He raises an eyebrow.

"First, I'm not part of this deal. If you accept this offer, I'm your boss. You have to stop acting like you want to get in my pants 24-7, because frankly, it's infuriating." And I might have a moment of weakness and give in. "That's not how a Banks man would behave. You have to have a little bit of decorum. Tact. Got it?"

He lets out a low laugh. "So a Banks man . . . doesn't fuck?"

I ignore him. "Second, I know you've got your own business, and you're building something for yourself. You have a lot of followers and people connect with you, and I respect that. What you learn with me can help you take it over the edge and make you into an even bigger success—but you've got to help me first. Your business is *not* priority now. For the time that you work with me, you're exclusively on my project—which includes you NOT being Jimmy the YouTube guy and instead being James Rowan, the perfect man that I will teach you to be," I say. "So. From now on, you have to be James, suave, sophisticated, and debonair. But I can't have you dressed like a prince and getting in bar fights and doing crazy stunts while you're working for me, or whatever it is that you do or *are*."

"Daredevil." He studies me for a long moment before scanning the corners of the ceiling, suspicion creasing his forehead for a long moment until he seems to be struck by a realization. He's suddenly groaning, "Fuck this. Who put you up to this? Is this like a candid camera thing?"

He whirls. Takes another step toward the door. Definitely looking frustrated and annoyed by the thought of being played.

"A million!" I shout at his broad back. "Okay? One million dollars. But I won't go any higher."

He freezes. He doesn't turn around. "One *million*?" he murmurs.

"Yes."

It's another full ten seconds that he just stands there, frozen, before turning back to me.

"So, let me get this straight. You want to make *me* into an exclusive, hoity-toity dildo for a new clothing line? Is this some sort of joke?" His eyes darken, but I can't tell if he's pissed because he thinks I upped the price to avoid being in his bed or if he's intrigued because $1 million in three months is a sweet deal.

"Look around. Does it look like I'm joking?"

"Yeah."

I arch a brow. His smile fades when he realizes I'm serious.

"So as I asked before . . . do you have any questions?"

"One." His gaze is intent, determined, lethal. "Why me?"

"Nobody else would do it. Any other questions?"

He eyes me. "Your boyfriend wouldn't do it?"

"I don't have a boyfriend. I'm waiting for the perfect man. The real version of what you're going to play. Any other concerns?"

"One more."

"Which is . . . ?"

"Where do I sign?"

MAKINGS OF A GENTLEMAN

An hour later, I'm on the phone with Jeanine, whose law firm has helped Banks LTD on numerous occasions. "Can you draw up a contract for me, please?"

"Oh, no. No, no, no, no, no, no, *no*," she says, so many times I'm afraid she's stuck on repeat. "Do not tell me."

"Come on," I beg. "You'll see. He'll be good. He may be a diamond in the rough now, but when I get done with him, every socialite in the city will want to be on his arm."

"Doubtful. But fine," she huffs. "I warned you. What do you need?"

I set the phone down and call James into the room. "I'm sitting here with James Rowan, the man I told you about. You're on speaker."

"Technically, you didn't tell me much about him. You just sent me a piece of his ass."

"What's she talking about?" James asks, a stern edge to his voice.

My face heats.

"James, meet Jeanine, my attorney, who failed to keep client privileges when she blabbed all about the picture—a snapshot of your ass, no less—that was sent to her earlier via *confidential* text messaging."

He raises an eyebrow. "You took a pic of my ass?"

I give him an apologetic shrug.

"Right," she says in a slow, sarcastic drawl. "Lizzy knows I like to see the people I'm working with. But not just their asses. Let's go face to face?"

I snort. She only insists upon that when the guy is as hot as James.

"Hang on," I say, pressing the button and propping up the phone in front of James while waiting to connect. "Okay, there."

"Nice." She focuses on James. "Can you turn around so I can get a better look at the merchandise?"

Exhibitionist that he is, he stands up, but I push him down. "Jeanine," I warn.

"Relax. I want to see if he's worth the mill."

"I'm worth it, baby," he says, leaning back in his chair. "I want half the money up front."

"Not a chance," she says.

"It's fine, Jeanine."

"I'm in charge here, Lizzy," Jeanine says, looking out for my interests. "What experience do you have, James?"

"What kind do you need?" The brash, hard-driving alpha cocks his sexy head, and his eyes darken.

"Um . . . being photogenic? Acting?"

"I have it all, lady."

"References?"

"Plenty." He shoots me a crooked smile. "Check my YouTube comments."

"YouTube? Oh boy," she mutters. "Lizzy, give us a few minutes to work out the details."

"Perfect."

They discuss our contract while I pace the living room. When they're finished, I hear him say, "Deal."

I blink. Holy shit. Did I just get myself the face for our Banks LTD new menswear line? This bearded, crass, dirty-talking daredevil? Where the hell am I going to even start with the guy?

"We have a little under three months total, including one month to teach you the basics before we start touring and paying visits to the biggest store buyers in the country. The two biggest shows are West

Coast, in five weeks, and New York, a few weeks after that. There's also an ad photo shoot. After that, you're off the hook."

"I'm not doing shit until I get the money that lawyer just promised me," he dares me as he flings open my fridge and takes out a quart of milk.

I swallow and take out my checkbook. "Do you . . ." My mouth runs dry. I'm nervous. "Do you take checks?"

"Checks, cash, sex. As long as it's smoldering-hot grunge sex." He's undressing me with his molten eyes, and I squirm in my seat.

What exactly is grunge sex? It sounds positively divine. I cut my gaze up at him. With this man, any kind of sex would be earth shattering. "What did I tell you about that?"

"I'm kidding, Lizzy."

He called me Lizzy. My heart sort of flutters. It sounds as sweet as the aforementioned sex, the sex that he claims to joke about.

The sex that I need.

The sex that I can't stop thinking about.

SEX WITH HIM.

"Of course, if you're interested, say the word, and I'll make it happen." He guzzles down the milk directly from the carton, then wipes his mouth with his sleeve as I give him a warning look. "And yes to the check."

"Great." I'm glad he clarified. He keeps this straight face as if he wants me to wonder how far he'd go, how far he could take me.

"You won't hear from me again until it's cashed."

"Wait, what does that mean? Where are you going? Remember, you have to keep this under—"

"Relax. I don't want people to find out I'm your paid monkey-suited Banks puppet any more than *you* want people to find out."

"How do I know you won't back out on me? I need some insurance. And don't drink directly from my milk quart! You're so much work already!" I groan, already feeling my stress level rise. I mean, I told him, stop it with the coming on to me 24-7, and he's clearly not following that part of the deal. Will it be as hard to get him to follow any of my directions?

James takes another long guzzle, then covers it and shoves the carton back in the fridge, walking back to me as he digs into his back pocket and takes an envelope out of a torn wallet.

"Inside that envelope is one of my most prized possessions. I'll be back for it when my half a million dollar check is cashed."

I pick up my phone and read Jeanine's text:

Pay him half but send him on his way with some firm instructions. If he owes back rent, utilities, anyone or anything, have him pay his bills. This guy is the face of your new line. He should look the part. Talk later.

"Top cabinet, to the right. That's where the glasses are. For your milk."

He ignores me, still holding out the wrinkled envelope. There's a new somberness in his eyes. I take the envelope, staring down at it, tempted to open it but somehow feeling like I have no right to. I set it carefully aside, and we stare.

"Deal?" he asks, his gaze intent.

"Deal." I slip my fingers into his large, long tanned ones, palms connecting as we shake.

It's like I've got a hold of temptation's hand, and that comparison drives me to release him and say, "I look forward to working with you, Mr. Rowan."

"Jimmy."

"James."

THE FIRST DAY OF THE REST OF JAMES'S LIFE

We exchanged phone numbers before he left, and now I'm heading to work, angsty as I reach the Banks corporate building. A part of me is hopeful about the deal I just made, while another part is still blown away by my ballsy move.

My whole life I've tried my best to be as perfect as possible, but I'm never really sure that I buy my own act. I'm not sure my dad buys it either. Hence, my desperate need to prove myself to him.

Though our menswear suits line was my idea, that's not enough to satisfy my dad's need to know that I can handle this business—in every aspect. And I don't want to disappoint.

I'm fretting over how to introduce James to my dad. He will ask about progress. And I'm not ready to introduce them yet. I need time. I step into the elevators of the Banks corporate office, chewing on my inner cheek as I try to think of what to do, when LB steps into the car with me.

Ugh.

Nearly a head shorter than me, balding, and always simpering with his beady little snake eyes, LB Lee, my dad's right-hand man, always goes out of his way to derail my perfect plans. As thirsty to be CEO as me, his success rides on *my* failure. Right now, he's the last person I want to see.

"Going up to the executive floor?" he asks, obviously noticing the lit button.

I nod.

"Appointment with your dad?" he presses.

"Nine a.m. sharp. You?" I feel special because I'm his first.

"Nine fifteen. I'm early." He shoots me a boastful smirk as if this makes him better than me, his eyes glinting in glee.

Early . . . or snooping? I want to ask.

I don't think anyone aside from HR really knows what LB stands for, but all I know is he's worked here since I was in elementary school. I like to think his initials stand for "Little Bitch" because, well, the reference fits. LB is a yes-man and kisses Dad's ass for sport. To make matters worse, Dad relies on LB for just about everything, which must only fuel LB's belief that one day he'll hold the corporate reins and close to a billion dollars in assets.

Sometimes I dread that if Dad doesn't take me seriously . . . LB will succeed.

When we arrive at the top floor, I step out and notice my dad's office doors are wide open. Which means he isn't in.

I take a seat in one of the chairs outside in his waiting room, greeting one of his two secretaries with a smile.

LB goes up to kiss her ass and pulls out a candy from his briefcase for her. Like one of those pervert strangers that offer poisoned treats to kids or something.

I resist the urge to roll my eyes, when suddenly the elevator opens, and my dad steps off, zooming straight toward his office doors.

"Good morning, Mr. B." The secretary hurries around her desk to greet him.

"Elizabeth," is all my dad says, ignoring LB as he disappears inside.

I leap to my feet and follow him inside.

"Good news, Dad. I have secured the perfect man for our campaign."

Dad shrugs out of his crisp black suit jacket and hangs it on the back of his chair before taking a seat. "Is it Johnson? Where is he?"

He's looking around as if I have him stuffed in my briefcase.

"Well . . . no . . ." I glance around the collectibles in the office as if I lost my explanation somewhere there. "He's going to cash the check, so it'll take a few days to get the contract squared away."

I exhale after that. That will at least buy me a few days.

"Right, then. I expect to meet him. Next week?" He flips on his phone to check his calendar, as if ready to schedule me. "Anyone I know?"

"No. Which is even better. He'll be fresh to the market and blow any of the options I previously showed you out of the water."

He lifts his head, his bushy eyebrows flying up in wonder. "Really? I'm intrigued."

I nod happily, nerves curving like pretzels in my stomach. "Yep. Prepare to be wowed." I use my hands to make an exploding motion.

Okay, Elizabeth, this is overkill, and he'll know something fishy is up. Stop overselling!

I'm rescued by the phone ringing on his desk, and I exhale a ragged breath as Dad picks up with a brusque "Yes? Aha. Put him through." He listens to the other end, his expression darkening. "That's correct. If it's ready for me to view, I'll take a flight out today. Don't make me waste my time," he warns before he disconnects the call.

"That was Steven Marx on the phone. We're well underway on the final expansion of our Minnesota warehouses. I'm flying to Minneapolis. I'll be home in a few days—if I don't decide to tour some of our other storage facilities afterward." He stands and summons his secretary, who appears at the door with LB.

Dad waves LB into his office, and I cringe when LB says, "Mr. B., Elizabeth. Always a pleasure to see you both so early in the morning."

"What a fraud," I whisper under my breath, but Dad's scowl proves I was louder than necessary.

"LB, I want you to be Lizzy's second on this menswear-line launch. It's our biggest launch in years, and it has to be perfect." I feel LB's superior smile as my father looks at me. "I want you to keep him up to date on the preparations. *All* preparations. West Coast Fashion Week is not very far away. Do you understand me?"

I nod like a toddler who was just told to stop throwing her Cheerios on the floor.

He motions to his secretary about needing to book a flight to Minneapolis, ASAP.

After Dad collects his laptop and some files, he plants a kiss on my cheek. "If you need anything, you know how to reach me."

"She'll be fine," LB says.

I want to deck him until Dad beams. "Of course she will. She has you."

On second thought, decking is for sissies. I want to kick him. In the balls. But I smile politely and give my dad a beaming smile.

"Please. I'm a Banks. I don't need anyone to be fine. I've got everything under control. Don't worry, Dad. Leave everything to me."

"And LB," he reminds me, as if everything I just said went in one ear and out the other.

"Right," I mutter. UGH.

LB smiles at me. "Elizabeth, we should set up a meeting later to go over everything you're working on."

Grrrr.

I step out and leave them to their business, heading to a lower floor, to a temporary office I'm using for now.

I'm thinking hard as I head to my desk.

Dad's business trip couldn't have come at a better time. It's just what I need to get James on the straight and narrow gentlemen's path. But how am I going to get LB off my case?

Suddenly, it comes to me. There are two main things I'm tasked with for the new menswear launch. First is getting our new face photographed and ready for the events. Second is scheduling all the meetings with various buyers to introduce him around. If I handle the first one and give LB my list of buyers so he can schedule our meetings, then he won't be able to tell my dad I'm keeping him totally in the dark. And if he asks to see the model, I can fudge a little.

I can do this.

I spend all day working on the plans for the big launch as well as reviewing our designs, then head home at five p.m. Pulling out my phone, I text Jeanine as I ride in the back of a company car home.

Any news on my guy?

Jeanine: You mean sexy Thor with dark hair and perfect ass?

Me: I checked my bank statement online. He hasn't cashed the check. I need that to happen asap so I can get started.

Jeanine: Don't worry on that. He's signed the contract, so you're good to go. You're going to need all the time you can get to transform that beast into a beauty.

"Thanks, Roger," I tell the driver as he drops me off.

I'm marching briskly, phone in hand, toward my building when I spot a tall man leaning against the building's mirrored walls.

Dressed in light denim jeans and a white old T-shirt, something about him makes me take a second look. He's very . . . very . . . hot, but he does not belong in this neighborhood in the least. I'm surprised the doormen didn't shoo him away for loitering.

He's looking down at his phone, and I pretend I'm not that into him when I suddenly recognize the phone. The beat-up old cell phone with the cracked screen.

I jerk back to look at his face as he lifts his head.

What the . . .

It's HIM. Oh god. In daylight he looks more . . . dangerous.

Edible.

Scrumptious.

He smiles a dimpled, bearded smile as he pushes off the wall.

As though he knows his effect on me.

"Hey," I blurt out. "I didn't . . . know you'd be here."

I stumble on the sidewalk edge, and he quickens his steps, but thankfully, I recover before he has to come save me. Trying to save face, I breeze toward the elevator and push my floor number. "You haven't cashed the check?"

I shoot him a sidelong glance.

My tummy is tumbling.

Nervous because . . . um, the back-seat-of-the-cab thing?

The delicious-hands-on-me thing?

All that. Six-feet-plus thing.

Yeah.

"I'll get to it. Don't worry. Have a good day?" he asks as he runs his gaze over my business suit.

"Yes. You? Beat anyone up?"

"No." His lips curve.

"So it's . . ." I'm unsure. "*Not* a good day?"

"Oh, it's a good day."

I fight the overwhelming urge to grab his face and plant a happy kiss on his jaw. He smiles down at me.

My angel's working overtime to give me time to introduce my dad to my guy.

And he is here now, so we can get started . . .

Definitely a good day. "Do you want dinner? I was going to order in."

He nods. We go upstairs to my apartment. As hungry as I am, the OCD part of me can't stop looking at that forest of hair on his face and picturing what's underneath. After all the selling I did to my dad, I hope it's not hiding a massive birthmark or a double chin.

"You know what? We have time to shave you before dinner."

"Excuse me?"

"You heard me." I set my bag down and extend my hand. "Come on. And I can get to know the real James Rowan while I shave you."

"This wasn't what I was planning when I stopped by here. Ya know?"

"Oh, I know what you were planning. But that's not good for business, and we're in business," I say, taking his hand and pulling him into my bathroom.

I pull up the seat of my vanity and pat it. "Sit here."

He's reluctant before he drops down on the seat, his body engulfing it. "I like my beard," he says, rubbing his chin in the mirror. "You'd like it, too, if you just got me between your legs."

I give him a look.

He gives me an innocent shrug. "I don't get complaints. That's all I'm saying."

"Thank you for that bit of info," I say stiffly. "But we're going less Paul Bunyan with our launch and more Michael Bublé."

"Who?"

"Forget it. Lean your head back."

I open a drawer and pull out a brand-new razor from my "new stash"—where I keep a set of new toothbrushes, a new toothpaste, a box of Q-tips, and fresh sets of razors. When I pull out the razor and look down at him, my breath hitches.

He's sitting there with his head tilted a bit back, his blue eyes trained on me. Swallowing, I try to recover by fanning a towel around his shoulders, hoping that he doesn't notice my trembling fingers.

I've never shaved a man before, and now here I am, hoping I don't cut him.

"Are you good with razors?" He cocks one brow.

"I'm terrible with them. Any final words before we do this?" I grin down at him before grabbing the shaving cream and lathering it on his face.

"Guess that was my way of asking if you've ever shaved another man? Elizabeth?"

I pause before looking down at him.

He's looking straight into my eyes, and for a second there, I feel as if he can see right through me.

Clearing my throat, I'm suddenly carefully raking the razor over his tight jaw. "Why do you ask?"

He laughs. "Why not. Answer me." His timbre drops.

Wow. This guy. I'm the one with the razor. But he acts like he's the one with all the control.

I frown for a second, then relax and concentrate as I drag the blade across his chin. "Well, I . . . I don't have a boyfriend. And I've never shaved anyone for the hell of it. Never worked in a barbershop."

"I'm a lot of work." He grins up at me. "So why me, baby?"

"I'm . . ." I scowl down at him. "I'm not your baby. And maybe I think you're worth it."

"Maybe I am." His lips are thick, full, and completely beautiful.

Eyes up, Elizabeth.

But god, those baby blues aren't much easier to look at.

"So, what do you want to talk about?" he asks, crossing his arms and exhaling as he relaxes in the chair.

I try to focus on the task, not wanting to nick him. He needs to be perfect. God, and he smells so good. I try not to notice. "Why don't you tell me about yourself?"

"Where do you want to start?"

I think a minute before deciding. "Let's play a game. I'll ask a question. You answer it."

"That's not a game. That's called prying, baby."

"It's for a good cause. Stop calling me baby!" I laugh, wondering if he's doing it to distract me.

He smirks.

"What do you want to know?" He tilts his chin higher, and I almost nick him. He flinches and grunts. "Watch yourself. *Baby.*"

"Don't move. *Devil.*" I check the blade to be sure there isn't blood on the end. "Favorite color?"

"Black."

"These questions pertain to fashion."

"Still black."

"Pinstripe?"

"What the fuck is that?"

I bite my lip. "What ties do you like?"

"Cartoons."

"Really?"

"Nah. Just checking if you were paying attention. I don't wear ties. Don't wear suits either."

He doesn't? Oh god. This is going to be even tougher than I thought. "Never? Okay, well, if you were going to wear one?"

"I like red. Sometimes black and white. I'm not one for flash."

I smile. "So . . . why did you agree?"

"Easy. Because I want you writhing in bed beneath me."

I fumble the razor, try to play it off, but catch a glimpse of myself in the mirror. I'm red, completely flushed.

I lift my gaze, and a half-shaven James Rowan with a foamy jaw is staring at my mouth.

"What did I tell you about that?" I ask calmly.

"What?" he asks. "I forget."

"My eyes are up here, Rowan. And you'll kindly refrain from the come-ons."

He lifts his gaze, and they gleam mischievously and intelligently. Predator-like. "Can't help it. Love to see you blush."

"I'm not blushing."

"Sure you are."

Of course I am.

"Anyway . . . so why did you agree? For real." If my hand stopped trembling, maybe I could finish this whole thing?

"I don't know. Charlie, I guess."

"And Charlie is your brother?" I can't help but be curious.

"He's my everything."

I blink at that. Shocked by the honesty of his words and gaze.

"He's all I have," he adds, gruff and somber.

I ease back, taking a moment to switch sides. "You were punching the guy at the bar because someone hurt Charlie?"

"Yeah. Charlie's . . . he's too damn wiry. He don't like to fight."

I quietly finish shaving him and drag a damp towel across his jaw. I'm touched by his words and protectiveness over his brother.

"There," I say, stepping back so James can lift his head and meet my gaze. He slowly comes to a stand. I turn him to the mirror. Our eyes meet in the reflection.

And holy mother of god.

I can barely breathe.

JAMES ROWAN IS . . . *IT*.

I marvel how I didn't get cut shaving that jaw. All hard angles, square and mean and masculine. And that perfect little dimple, right in the center of his chin. Yum.

"Smoothly shaven. Now when you want to kiss someone"—I pat his square jaw—"your jaw won't feel bristly."

I start to exit my bathroom when he steps forward in a flash, seizing my elbow in his grip as he turns me.

"Want to give it a try?" He smiles amusedly.

"Right!" I roll my eyes, and he laughs at my immediate flush.

He takes a step closer, boxing me in. I swallow, but not because I'm afraid.

Because he nerve-racks the hell out of me.

His voice turns thick, and suddenly his arm is around my waist, and my hand is on his chest. His flat, muscular, warm chest—the definition palpable under the cotton of his T-shirt.

He lifts my chin with his thumb. "You've been thinking about me. Haven't you?"

His gaze blazes so intently that my lungs can't seem to get enough air. I nod, breathless.

I lift my hand and run my fingers over his smooth jaw.

"In a business sense, yes. Professionalism is very important to me."

"And your *pleasure* is important to me."

"James. Don't break the contract on your first day." I laugh, and he chuckles and buries his face in my neck, his breath tickling me.

"You smell good."

"Mmm. So do you," I say, then curse myself the second it's out. *Stop encouraging him.*

Even though, yum. He *really* smells good.

We remain like that for a second, until he uncurls his arms from around me and lets me go.

We're smiling as we make eye contact.

But the air leaps between us, like electricity.

I need to call Jeanine and get her to talk some sense into me before I do something I'll regret.

"We need to get your hair cut too. But I leave that to a professional." My voice is a little thick as I pull out my phone and dial. I hope to get my favorite stylist, Sherry, to pull an emergency makeover. I need to keep him as quiet and under wraps as possible during this transformation period, and I know she will be discreet.

"Sherry, I need a huge favor. I need a total makeover, and I need it stat." I laugh. "Of course, I don't need a makeover—you just gave me the perfect shoulder-length haircut." I eye my Perfect-Man-in-the-Raw. "It's for a guy. Uh-huh. My company is using him for the face of our new line. It's top secret. But I need it all—haircut, waxing all that bear chest. Pedicure, manicure. Eyebrows. The works."

She gives me a slot for tomorrow at noon, during her lunchtime. And I quickly head to the living room and write down the address for James and hand it over after I hang up.

"We have a lot of work ahead. Tomorrow, meet me there at noon. Get your life squared away. You'll be mine for three months."

James Rowan then surprises me by pocketing the address and asking, "So for three months, does that mean you're mine too?"

"I . . ."

I hold my breath, wondering if anyone in their right mind has ever said no to the guy.

"Oh, and . . ." He grabs me by the chin and scrubs his thumb along my lower lip. "You're not waxing me."

I try to suppress a shiver from his touch. "Um . . . not me. But someone is waxing you."

"*No one* is waxing me."

I sigh, getting the feeling this guy will be the death of me.

SPA DAY

I'm flipping through the magazines outside the spa when I get a call from Jeanine.

"How goes it with Thor?" she asks me.

"He's not exactly Thor anymore," I whisper into the receiver. "I have him at the spa now, and he's getting more sexified with every passing minute."

"Seriously? I want pics."

"He'll definitely look the part. Whether he can act it . . . I don't know. He's stubborn and has absolutely no manners whatsoever."

"Not to mention the whole caveman thing and that godawful accent."

I pause. "He's not dumb," I say, but she is right about his slow, easy, fuck-proper-speaking accent. "I just . . ."

"Maybe you can get him to keep his mouth shut."

I frown. "He does not keep his mouth shut, that's for sure. Especially about . . ."

"About what?"

"He's always coming on to me. He doesn't possess a lick of subtlety. Even if it is in the contract, he's constantly trying to . . . you know."

She laughs. "Ah. You live a hard, hard life, Lizzy my dear, with a gorgeous man wanting to fuck you. So, are you having trouble keeping it in your pants? Is that what you're saying?"

I let out a huge breath of air. "Yeah."

"Well, the contract doesn't officially prohibit sexual contact. It simply says that *he* must treat you in a professional manner. But if you were to treat him in a not-so-professional manner, there's nothing he can do about it."

"You mean he's the one in breach of contract? Not me? So I could sleep with him and treat him like crap and demand the million dollars back, and he'd have no recourse?"

"Yep. The contract definitely favors you, sweetie. I told him to run it past his lawyer, but he didn't have one."

I rub my eyes. It feels wrong taking advantage of him like that. Dirty. "I don't even know why I'm having this conversation with you. It's stupid. It's against everything my father wants for me. I need to focus on business."

"You're contemplating it because he's hot as fuck," she says. "If I had that opportunity, girl, I'd be all in too."

Great. Just another reason for me to want him. Like I need any more.

I end the call and am checking the time when my phone pings.

James: Real men don't get manis and pedis.

An hour later: They damn sure don't get facials.

Massages? Really? Infrared?

Where you at, Liz?

Where you at? No. *Liz?* Hell no.

No response? 'S okay. Can't talk now anyway. Freezing my balls off in a machine that uses subzero temps. What the fuck are you doing to me? I thought you wanted a man! I'm being treated like a prissy teenage girl.

73

An hour later: Where are you, Ms. Banks?

Better. He doesn't sound like a rapper.

I type out a quick response and hit send.

Me: I'm right outside. Where you left me.

James: I'll never complain about a massage again. Nothing but fond memories here.

I frown at the implication but assume he's just trying to get a response, something to hint at interest.

Never going to happen, James. I grin, then think of his exposed cock. A tingle settles in my hips and a little lower, which is a little too pleasurable for my liking.

James: She's great. REAL attentive if you know what I mean.

Me: Sherry is a happily married WOMAN with three kids, a dog, and a white picket fence.

James: Sherry? Psht. She had to go out. I got Wanda. And THANK YOU for putting Wanda ON me.

Wanda? What the . . . ? No. No. HELL no. I booked Sherry for a reason.

Broad has great . . . hands . . .

The dot-dot-dot bit is intentional. She has great boobs, and she's shown them to everyone. In fact, she's a breast-implants influencer.

Can you imagine? What does a breast-implants influencer do in her spare time? Flash random guys?

You should see what she does with her little finger when she drags it across . . .

You know what? Fuck him. AND his dots and her little fingers. I'm pacing outside when the doors open, and Sherry steps out. Behind her is James. Partly blocked from view.

74

I glare at whatever pieces are visible, realizing he WAS trying to get a reaction.

"All done. Everything except . . . well. He'll tell you." Sherry beams at me, then glances past her shoulder and lets him step out. "Well, Mr. Rowan. You're free to go."

I'm standing here.

Speechless.

Drooling in my mouth.

As he fills my complete line of vision.

All six foot plus of him.

"Well?"

He's speaking. He's asking me something. Hands in his pockets, glare on his face.

He approaches, and I almost lose my balance. This guy, this hot-as-hell man, is like WHOA . . . I can't even describe him.

Only I can, but it'll take a minute.

I run my eyes all over him, taking it all in. His hair cut shorter to enhance his incredible features. He even smells amazing. I can tell he pulled out his best jeans, loafers, and T-shirt for today, and though he rocked them when we went in, right now he's totally rocking the world. My stomach ropes in with excitement and dread over his black, stony look.

I realize I'm ogling him a little too much before I finally smile up at him and, to hide my blush, turn my attention to the cashier.

I flip out my card. "Checking him out."

They charge me for everything and swipe my card, and we climb into the back of a cab as I give the driver the address of our next stop. I suppose I should've driven my car over here so that I could tuck our purchases in the trunk later, but I'm so used to riding in company cars provided by my dad, used to having my hands free to work from my phone and keep in touch with the office while we head from one place to the next, that it didn't occur to me to take my car out for the day until now.

It would certainly give me something to do other than sit here with a very hot James Rowan far too close to me. It's not like I'm able to get any work done here with the guy staring at me the way he is.

He's still squaring his jaw, obviously pissed at me.

"I know you maybe didn't enjoy that so much. So we'll go shopping. I'm treating you to some fabulous casual clothes," I tell him.

I'm checking the receipt as we drive and realize they didn't charge the waxing.

"They forgot to charge the waxing."

"Baby . . . they didn't charge it because I told you. No one would wax me." He reaches out and tips my head back, seizing my gaze.

"What do you mean?" I shift, uncomfortable when struck with his new, neatly shaven face.

He raises one brow. "She tried." Nostrils flaring, he grabs a fistful of his T-shirt and simply yanks it over his head, tousling his hair. Now that he's bare chested, I see a sliver of waxed skin on a massive chest, nestled amid a dusting of hair.

I bite down on my smile as I struggle not to laugh. "She only waxed one strip?"

"Hurt like hell."

"Aw, poor baby." I can't help but laugh and shake my head, then turn back again to look at that one strip of waxed skin amid a mass of hair.

God. And his chest. His pecs.

I'm drooling in my mouth.

"Well? Heiress? I expect an apology."

I twist my mouth thoughtfully to the side. I tell myself not to ogle. *Do not ogle and definitely do not think of touch—*

Impulsively I reach out to stroke my fingers down his smooth, tan skin. "It'll grow back."

Realizing what I just did, I retrieve my hand.

My eyes fly up to his.

The look in his eyes simmers with intent.

He smiles.

Oh.

My.

He speaks on a softer note. "How about we go back, and I wax my dick?"

"James!"

Laughing, I slam a fist to his chest, and he laughs and grabs my arm by the wrist and pulls me closer. Leaning down. "I'm serious."

"No. I can work with a hairy chest. Nobody is going to see it." *But me*, I think. Where did that thought come from? He's not mine. This is business; I need to remember that.

I grab his T-shirt from his lap and toss it back at him. "Put that on, please."

He grabs it and pulls it on with one swift motion. "Say it." He rolls the fabric down those impeccable abs with one hand.

"What?"

"What you were thinking." When I only stare, he adds, "Who's the only one who's going to see my half-waxed chest?" One black eyebrow is up in challenge.

I swallow. "Fine. ME! But only for business purposes," I quickly add.

And when that damn flush creeps over my neck again, all I hear is James's low devil laugh in the closed confines of the cab.

TIM'S BAR

Jimmy

"Nice look, man!"

Luke looks surprised as he pours two shots. I pull out a stool with my foot and drop down on the bar. "Yeah. Well. Thought I'd get a shave," I lie.

We lift our glasses. "Salut."

"Shit, man, I'd never seen you without a beard. You look . . . fuck, I don't know. Like those guys on billboards." Luke cackles like it's some sort of joke.

I growl. "Yeah, well. If you only knew the half of it."

"What do you mean?" Luke frowns.

I shake my head, tossing back another shot without answering.

I'm going insane.

Fucking insane.

Elizabeth . . .

Woman's driving me fucking insane.

"Not very talkative today, huh, Jimmy?" Luke prods.

"Nope. Just want to sit here and simmer for a damn minute, if that's all right with you."

"Simmer from what? You sound frustrated."

That's the unanswerable question. I can't even say. Due to the fucking contract, there ain't a whole lot I can talk about.

"'Cause I *am*," I growl, giving him a look that demands he cut it off.

Luke raises his hand. "Okay, man, I'm backing off. But I'm here, you know. Me and all the tequila you need."

"How about one more, to start." I raise my empty glass, which Luke promptly refills. I shuffle through some notes, scan a couple of emails, and call home.

"What's up, kiddo?"

Charlie says, "Do you know what time it is?"

"Late. Sorry. Did you do your homework?"

"Always."

Charlie is such a good kid. "I'm proud of you." I tell him often since our parents aren't here to do it.

"Can you be proud of me at six in the morning? I've gotta get some z's."

"Yeah. See ya tomorrow. I'll be there to make you some breakfast."

"'Kay . . ." His voice drifts off, and the line goes dead.

After Luke calls some drunk an Uber, he locks up and saunters over. "Look, Jimmy, I'd never met your woman before the other night."

"She's not mine." The bite in my response is because I'm frustrated to the point of blue balls here.

Fuck this.

Can't pretend my pride doesn't hurt and that she's not a whole shit ton better than me. Completely unavailable. And there I am, letting her shave me, like a dog playing tricks in the hopes she'll throw me a bone or two. No bones, just boners.

When I signed her contract, I had nothing to lose. That was my first thought. *Why not? I've got nothing to lose.* And I needed the cash. I'm constantly two months behind on rent, always teetering Charlie and me on the edge of eviction. A million dollars can buy me a hell of a lot of wiggle room. Maybe get Charlie into a private school, away from assholes like Denny's brothers.

But maybe I should've thought about more than just the money, for once.

Lizzy pitches a helluva deal, but what if I want more? I might. I mean, we're adults. We could have sex without the strings. Right. Thanks to Lizzy's BFF adding a written clause to the contract about my not attempting to form a relationship with Ms. Banks herself, those strings are pulled pretty damn tight.

And thanks to her stubborn need to keep me at bay, well . . .

I'm pretty fucked.

Not a good thing, as I'm a man who likes to do the fucking.

Luke shoots me a look that proves he already knows the thoughts that are stirring up my brain. "She stumbled in here looking for a drink, and that's all there was to it. She didn't have a motive. She may have been down on her luck. She was pretty negative until she met up with the likes of you, and it's like you were the angel come down from heaven to rescue her from her problems."

I'm not sure what I'm allowed to tell him about our arrangement. If anything. I'm not sure about anything about this whole deal anymore.

"More like the devil of temptation who will take her nowhere good." I drag my hand down my face and wonder what the hell she really saw in me to do this whole ordeal.

"Was she the inspiration for you doing something different with your hair?"

"Fuck you, Luke."

He laughs. "Looks good on ya."

I hold up my hands. "Do these look any different to ya?"

"No. Why?"

"I had a fucking manicure. Can you believe that?"

"Damn."

"Yep." I'm not sure what his one-word response means. If his expression is any indication, he's impressed. "I'm stumped."

"I can see why," Luke says, nursing his beer. "She's keeping you up, and you haven't even fucked her. Have you?"

"I'm working on it. Believe me."

"Don't get hung up on her, Jimmy. Women like that come out of the womb with their men practically chosen for them. They know exactly who'll get that ass for life. Their families arrange it. I know we'd never think of this 'cause your parents were simple people who loved each other and worked hard for what they had."

"My folks worked nonstop to provide the best that they could. Hell, my parents weren't rich. They were comfortable, but ordinary. Dad was the best man I've ever known, and Mom . . ."

She would've approved of Lizzy. I scoff at the thought.

I wonder if that's why Elizabeth Banks is so appealing to me? Is it because I know Mom would approve, just like I know she would've disapproved of the long string of women I had before? Couldn't see introducing a single one of them to Charlie.

Luke and I talk about the night, mine and his, and when we wrap things up, I can't help but think of Elizabeth. Everything about her intrigues me. The way she tries to do the "right" thing but is so tempted to do the wrong one.

Next to every other word out of her mouth says that she's disgusted by me. But her body? Her body is anything but turned off by me. That fact alone makes me hungry for more. More real, ungoverned responses, not the shit she's been taught to say and do by Daddy Warbucks.

Oh, yeah, for sure the man wouldn't approve of me. But I don't really care what he thinks. It's his daughter I want beneath me—*fuck* the rules of propriety. Lizzy may follow them to a T, but I've never had any problems breaking a few in my own self-interest, and for sweet little Elizabeth to lose her cool beneath me, I'm capable of breaking them all. Every last one of them. If she wants me enough—and I get the feeling she does—she'll keep me around even if I break a few of those contract clauses.

A short time later, I'm on my way home when my phone rings. I don't recognize the number, but it's local, and I answer without considering the time.

"This Jimmy?"

"Who's this?"

"A friend."

"Yeah? My friends usually tell me who they are as soon as I pick up."

"Not this one." Static fills the line. "Shit. I don't have a good connection. I'm calling about your kid brother. Text you the address. Meet me in twenty."

The line goes dead. Seconds later, an address is sent, and I know the place. Every thug in Atlanta knows the neighborhood.

It's where boys become men and men become criminals. Correction. They become thugs doing twenty years or more in the state pen.

Fuck my life.

I don't have time for this shit. This is why I accepted Elizabeth's offer in the first place. I don't want to earn my honor or Charlie's freedom in a street fight.

Right now, it doesn't matter what I want. I flip through my contacts and find Luke's number and get him on the line. "Hate to ask, but I may need some backup tonight."

"What do you need?"

I tell him. He says he'll be there. "This is about Charlie, Jimmy."

"Yeah, I know."

"Street rule is if you take 'em all down, they'll leave him alone."

"Then let's end this."

"On my way."

The fight ends about as quickly as it begins. Luke's a brute, and while he was late, the gang never expected me to have backup. Having another guy show up for Charlie was a surprise, and it worked out to our advantage. After Denny's brothers and their crew flee, Luke and I stand around and shoot the shit, half expecting to see another round with different guys.

When no one shows, Luke gets all sentimental. "Charlie has a tough time. If you ever need me again, I'll be here. Tell Charlie the same."

I have nothing but mad respect for this guy. I wish Charlie could find a friend who has his back.

Then again, siding with Charlie could get a good kid knocked up pretty bad.

It's almost dawn when I creep inside our cottage-style house. The floorboards creak as I make my way to the bathroom. My cheek is swollen. My back is sore as shit, and my eye is turning a different color by the second.

I splash some water on my face and head to the kitchen.

"What the hell happened to you?" Charlie is already at the small table. "Let me guess. Somebody wanted to give you a haircut and shave, so they beat the hell out of ya until you agreed?"

"Very funny." If only it were that simple. "Want bacon and eggs?"

"Toast is fine."

"Coming right up." I nod at his open book. "Thought you did your homework last night?"

"Mine, sure. Didn't do Hank's."

I grimace. "Why would you do Hank's?"

"So you don't get your ass kicked again tonight." He glances up at me. "I'll do the kid's homework from now on, and there won't be a problem."

I toss some bread in the toaster. "First, I didn't have my ass handed to me. Thanks for the vote of confidence. Secondly, you're not doing Hank's homework. From now on, if a kid threatens you, come to me. I'll handle it."

"This time, a haircut. Next time they'll shave your head. That's the way these people roll."

"They didn't bring out the clippers, Charlie. I had the cut and shave yesterday."

"Okay, well, in that case . . . who is she?" Charlie pours himself some juice.

"Just a woman."

He shrugs. "Does 'just a woman' have a name?"

"Elizabeth. And it's just business."

"Don't believe you. Since when do you hold frozen peas to your face?"

"Since you asked, we might as well do this now." I tap my fingers against the table. "But you gotta keep it under wraps, okay? I'm the new model for an exclusive fashion line. Banks Limited. Have you heard of it?"

"A model? No fuckin' way."

"Language, kid. I'm guessing that's good?"

"Hell yeah! I bet you're making a busload of cash. Are you?"

"I will be. Yes."

He does a dance with an arm pump. "That means I'm asking for the new Xbox for Christmas."

I laugh. "Yeah, maybe. Let's take one day at a time."

"Don't fuck this up, Jimmy."

"Hey, no. Watch your mouth."

"Seriously, bro. This is an awesome chance for you. Sure, I'd like an Xbox, but if you do this, maybe we can afford to get real equipment for your channel. Go real places." Another arm pump. "Maybe now you can choose your stunts a little more carefully too. Now I won't have to worry about you getting yourself killed for a couple of bucks."

I start to tell him that his perception of a couple of bucks and a few hundred is about as screwed up as my boss lady's, but he's already talking circles around me.

Charlie's never looked happier, and for the first time in years, I see the light at the end of the tunnel. Charlie and I may make it out of the slums after all.

PROMISING

Elizabeth

I hardly slept. I was too excited, my creative juices flowing as ideas on the big launch in two and a half months flitted across my mind. Not to mention the memory of James Rowan sans beard, with that adorable dimple on full display and that mean, square jaw out in the open. Damn.

Add in what Jeanine and I talked about. I could use him and that body of his for a quick roll in the hay, and no one would have to know about it.

It was almost too much temptation to bear. It kept me writhing in bed, sleepless, all night.

Bursting with adrenaline early the next morning, I call my dad to see if he got into Minneapolis okay.

"Of course I got in okay. Why wouldn't I?"

He sounds annoyed that I'm calling, and I stupidly realize I'm interrupting something. "Well, sometimes flights—"

"I fly private." A meaningful silence. "I'll see you when I get back."

"Dad, take your blood pressure medicine!" I yell out as quickly as possible so that he hears the reminder.

There's a long silence. "What?"

My stomach sinks as I realize.

"You forgot them. Didn't you?"

His silence definitely confirms that he did.

"Dad, how can you be such a hotshot in business and at the same time not take care of the most important thing—your health? How long are you staying?"

"Couple more days," he grumbles.

"I'll send them over."

He lets out an annoyed sigh. "Have you been in touch with LB? He told me you haven't given him any of the plans for the West Coast Fashion Week, which is concerning him."

"Oh. I was just planning to do that today," I lie. Shit.

I hang up with my dad and call his secretary to get the hotel address as I head to his place.

I hate it when he doesn't take his medicine. He starts getting headaches and doesn't sleep well, and worst of all is . . . he puts himself in danger. Which isn't like James Rowan, who does it on purpose. I know my dad simply forgets, but *still*.

My dad lives in THE apartment building of Atlanta, in THE penthouse of the city. Anyone would kill for this spot, but my dad would do the same to anyone who tried to take this away from him. He's become who he is by hustling hard and often. And although he wasn't born exactly into old money, he's climbed society's ladder carefully and methodically until people believe that he is the be-all and *end*-all of the city.

I head straight for the medicine cabinet in the master bathroom.

Pulling them out, checking each of the labels, and sticking them into ziplock bags. Aside from the labels on the bottles, I add Post-its with "a.m." and "p.m."—he needs two pills, twice a day, for both his systolic and diastolic numbers—and then I add one more Post-it that reads, "Take these daily!"

Once I've got it all perfect, I zip up the bags, stick them inside a padded envelope, and label it with the hotel address. And as I'm ready to leave, I pause as I cross his bedroom.

On the shelves lining the sides of the flat-screen TV, among books and collectibles, sort of hidden, is a framed photo of him and me. I can't even remember who took it, but it is one of the few photographs that we have together.

Taking it in hand, I cross the room and set it on his nightstand, then step back to see how it looks. Surveying, I turn it just so, until it's perfect. Then I organize the rest of the stuff on his nightstand—a Tiffany clock, a notepad and pen, and a tall reading lamp. Smiling when it looks good, I flip off the lights and head to the mail room.

I pull out my phone and open up an email to LB: An update for you on the menswear launch. I'm in the process of shoring up all the details for the West Coast Fashion Week launch, which I'll send to you later today. Getting our model ready and I'll have photos and a bio for you shortly.

I inspect the email and hit send. Good. That ought to shut my warden up.

Except he messages me right back.

Do you really even have a model or are you just buying time?

I'm fuming as I read it and decide not to reply. Images of walking into Banks LTD with a gorgeous, perfectly groomed, and to-die-for handsome James Rowan fill my head as I head home just in time to meet with James—except, forty minutes later, James still hasn't showed.

It's 9:48 a.m., and I'm still waiting for His Majesty, King James Rowan, at my place when I grab the phone and try his number for the tenth time. It goes straight to voice mail.

Whoa. *Wait a minute.* Is he backing out on me?

Did he cash the check?

After checking my bank statement and seeing he hasn't, I grab the keys to my Audi and drive downtown, hoping I can remember how to get to Tim's Bar.

As soon as I enter, Luke points to the far corner, where I immediately spot a long set of denim-clad legs hanging off the end of a booth.

I pause with a sigh of relief.

"He had a late night. Just got into the office 'bout two hours ago after sending Charlie off to school. I'll wake him in a few minutes, huh?"

I check my phone, worried we don't have minutes to spare. "We needed to be somewhere at ten."

"Like I said . . ."

"I heard you," I say, not meaning to be short and snappy, but we have an appointment with Michael, and I can't allow tardiness from anyone. Especially me. "Fine. *I'll* wake him," I say, marching over.

"I bet you will," Luke mumbles.

The clickety-clack of my heels tapping against the concrete floor is the only noise in the vacant bar. I'm guessing the drunks on this side of town are probably like James, sleeping off the aftermath of the previous night's party.

Bending down to shake him, I pause when I spot a photo on the table. It's a picture of James and a boy who looks like him. *Must be Charlie*, I think, staring back at James again. My breath catches in my chest as I'm struck by his clean-shaven face once more.

I study him for a moment.

Why do I love watching him when he's out cold?

Leaning a little closer, I narrow my eyes, and that's when I see IT.

A very dark circle shadowing his left eye.

No. No, no, no. He didn't do this. He knows how important his face is to me. It's in his contract.

Of course, there are a lot of things in the contract that James seems keen on forgetting.

I want to punch him again. I frown as I look at the bruise a little closer. "What happened?"

His eyes fly open. Bluer than blue. He grabs my wrist and hauls me forward. "No fighting," he says, voice thick with sleep.

"Then how did you get this?"

"I mean . . . no fighting with *you*."

I scowl at him, then lean over and mumble, "Are you sure you can read? Because I did put a clause in the contract that you were not to mess up your pretty face, Devil."

He pulls me over him as if I don't weigh a thing.

Shit. This is not how I planned to start my morning.

You're not just making out in cars, Elizabeth—apparently in bars anything goes?

I fall still on top of him.

I try to breathe, and that proves difficult. Especially because against my stomach, I can totally feel James's . . .

JAMES.

"Uh-huh," he says, staring into my eyes, as if reading my thoughts.

He starts smirking very, very slowly.

The smirk even reaches those mischievous blue eyes, the eyes that were almost perfect when we last met.

One still is.

"Let me go." I push off him. "James, what happened?"

"This?" He pats the swollen flesh. "It's nothing."

"You got in a fight," I say. "I told you to get your life sorted out. I told you that you needed to—"

"And I did. I am. But maybe . . ." He drags my hand to his mouth and kisses the tips of my fingers. "Maybe you need to keep closer tabs on me."

Trying to right myself and pull my dress down at the same time is nearly impossible. Obviously, James doesn't miss it.

"One kiss and I might let you up." His voice is gruff but mischievous.

I hurriedly peck his lips to appease him, but instead of releasing me, he licks his bottom lip and looks at my mouth even more intently. I groan. "I thought you were an honorable man, Devil."

"Baby . . . I said *might* for a reason."

"Which is . . . ?"

"Totally dependent on the kiss." He tips my face back with his thumb and forefinger, eyes drinking me in. Eyes that shine too intently on my face for a guy who's probably hungover. "Want to try again?"

My heart skips.

"I need . . . thank you . . . up, please."

"Oh, I'm up."

I resist a laugh. "That's not what I meant."

"But it's what I meant." He laughs, slowly getting up to his feet. He cups the back of my head. "Kiss me again."

"*I* didn't kiss *you* to begin with."

"The hell you didn't," he says, eyeing me with such lust that it makes me nervous. "We'll be damn good together. You'll see."

"No. I won't. Because we aren't doing this. I told you."

"Why not? You're into this. Into me. Do you deny it?"

"James, I'm your bo—"

"I'm no one but Jimmy here. Come here." He bites down on his lip, watching me under thick dark lashes with eyes that shimmer like pools. "I want to tell you something." That grin is carnal, dangerous. "It's a secret."

I can't help but steal a glance at the bulge in his jeans. "You're just full of surprises, aren't you?" I try to pull away when he loosens his grip, but I quickly realize that this is a trap. Can the guy tell I'm curious by nature?

"Come closer," he says, motioning for me.

"I don't have time for your . . ."

He locks his hand around my neck and drags my ear to his mouth, where he whispers, "If we weren't at Tim's Bar, I would've taken you from whimpers to moans in less than a minute. Next time you wake me up, think about that."

"I will indeed." I want to sound and act professional, but his hot breath on my neck sends a cascade of goose bumps straight down my back.

He smiles. "Good. Now how about I take you somewhere for a change?" he asks.

"Where?"

"To eat. I'm hungry."

Oh, I'd love to see just what he considers to be food. Probably something as unpalatable as that tequila behind the bar. "Sorry. We need to meet Michael. I'll pick you up a bagel on the way."

"And Michael is . . ."

"A genius. You will meet him soon. Come on, Devil. He will love you."

I lure him out of the bar and his ridiculous *office* with a sway of my hips, his long footsteps quickly catching up with me.

"And you," he croons as he swings open the bar door and lets me pass, "will love me too. *Baby.*"

His eyes glimmer.

I jerk my own eyes away as quickly as I can, because I'm not sure whether the wicked shine in his baby blues excites or scares me.

OUT WITH THE DEVIL

I sip my Starbucks latte and sit on the large chaise in the main fitting area of Banks LTD. I keep looking down the hallway, hoping no one else from the company will come in and see my work in progress.

"Where's LB?" I ask Michael, our head tailor, as I pull the plans for the West Coast Fashion Week from my files and email them to my nemesis, as promised.

"Probably slinking along the sewer, where he belongs," he mumbles, his lips closed upon straight pins.

Ah, one of the millions of reasons why I love Michael.

When it comes to LB or me being the top dog eventually, I know for a fact Michael is rooting for me.

For the past hour, Michael has been all over James like a bee on honey, covering him up in the suits I selected for this fitting. I can see James is a bit irritated. He seems completely moody, and I sense that a guy like him doesn't like other men to be sliding their hands up and around them while they ooh and aah.

Now Michael smooths his palms over James's back, then steps aside to contemplate the fit. "Puuurfect, love. This jacket embraces that toned body. Oh yesssss, darling, it does."

James is just looking at me with a glare that could shoot bullets.

I wish James would act a little less like the brooding tough guy from the streets and more like the person I want him to be. But Michael is clearly in love, nonetheless. Plus, I know I can trust Michael, even if I can't trust many other people in my life.

Dragging my eyes down the perfect pitch-black suit draped around James's frame, I brush some imaginary dust off his rounded collar. "Is it hot in here, or is it just me?"

"Oh, darling, it's not just you." Michael jabs his finger at James.

James doesn't miss it, and if his expression is any indication, he's had enough of fittings. He's still caught up on the pair of cuff links we've given him. All the Banks shirts require cuff links. When I handed them to him, he said, "I don't fucking wear earrings."

I showed him how to use them, and he watched me, his gaze dark. "What the fuck is the purpose of this shit? Buttons aren't good enough?"

Michael strokes James's collar before he eyes me. "Fitted look is elegant, don't you think?"

"Definitely. It's—he's—perfect." I thumb through a few styles and locate a notch collar on one of the dinner jackets. "Let's try this one."

Michael immediately removes the current jacket from James's shoulders and snaps his fingers at one of his assistants, who hurries to set it aside.

"Your father must be so ecstatic about our new face. I can see it across every billboard in the country already," Michael tells me.

I glance back toward the doorway. It's empty. I'm going to have a heart attack if I have to keep skulking around with James like this to get my work done. "Yes. My dad is, uh . . . thrilled."

Michael raises his head. "Or has he even met our delightful model yet? LB got in touch with me this morning. You know him, snooping around. He mentioned your father had asked him to keep an eye on it."

My flush is suddenly rising up my neck and cheeks. Anger mingled with frustration over my dad not trusting me. Hardly taking my phone calls but still having plenty of time to discuss me with LB. And also mortification, because when I lift my gaze, I can see James's blue, blue eyes fixed on me.

He sees me.

Before him, I'm naked and bare.

I look through a rack of ties and select a simple red one, since he said that was his favorite. I avoid his hot gaze as I drape it around his neck. "Know how to tie one of these?"

He shakes his head. "Like I said. Didn't even wear a tie to my parents' funeral."

Hmmm. "I'm supposing a bow tie is a big no, then, huh?"

Michael doesn't bat an eyelash. He nudges me out of the way and shows him how to tie the thing, effortlessly.

"Michael, would you be able to give James here a thorough lesson on how and when to wear each piece?" I ask.

James gives me a look. "You don't think I know how to put on a jacket? Just 'cause I never tied a tie before don't mean I'm an idiot."

I roll my eyes. "There are certain occasions befitting of different pieces, and you need to understand that."

He salutes me.

"Oh, and that snake LB," Michael continues with a nod. "He put a call in to some of us, asking if we wanted in on a little bet he has going on. Can you believe? He's betting on you failing at this, Lizzy. The balls on that little parasite!"

"I think we're done for today; thank you, Michael," I say, flushing even more because James is listening.

"Thank fuck." James exhales, his nostrils flaring as he rips the tie from his neck and jerks the jacket off of him with an angry yank. "Fucking straitjacket."

When he finally steps off the platform, I almost can't look back into his eyes for fear of what I'll see there.

"Now will you let me take you someplace?"

Surprised, I jerk my face up. He's wearing a white button shirt, a perfectly smooth area of his tan chest exposed.

"Only if we can call it a business dinner. It'll be a chance to practice your manners," I say, needing to get out of here.

He laughs and starts to button the shirt back up. "Call it whatever the hell you want, if it'll make you feel better." He motions to his gorgeous body, clad in the shirt and slacks. He can almost pass for a man from my side of the world. "Do I meet with your approval?"

Oh, hell yes. But I can only nod dumbly.

"We can take my car." I fish out my keys as we head to the parking lot.

I decide this is just as good a time as any to start teaching him how to treat a lady. So I stop in front of the driver's door of my car.

"Open the car door for me, please?"

James is already heading to the passenger side like he can't wait to get out of here.

He pauses, confused. "Why? You've got two hands."

"They're to embrace the flowers you give me, not open my own doors when a man is around," I say.

He exhales in frustration, nostrils flaring as he stalks around the front of my car, grabs the remote, unlocks it with a beep—and swings the door open.

Our shoulders brush as I step in.

"Want me to fasten your seat belt too?" he asks, his voice gruffer than it was a few seconds ago.

I hesitate, the look in James's eyes unreadable. "If you want . . . ," I answer, my voice thick.

He does.

The brush of his fingers against my body as he straps my seat belt makes me stiffen, wild, white-hot shivers crackling through my system.

I exhale when he eases back, the cologne I spritzed on the guy only yesterday teasing me. I bought him my favorite by Tom Ford. I wonder if that's why I can't get enough?

I'm a little worried about what kind of low-class dive he's going to take me to. I'm not a fan of fast-food places; they smell like fake food and a lot of grease, if my teenage memories are accurate, with several documentaries claiming the food is barely fit for human consumption. But he gives me directions, and we end up having burgers in Shake Shack. A first for me.

And definitely not my last.

"Gosh, this is really the best hamburger *ever*," I declare a half hour later as we sit side by side in a small booth at a corner of the restaurant. I can't really teach him table manners here, but . . . I'll let that slide.

"Good, right?"

I nod, licking my fingers from the last bite and happy I've still got a lot of fries to go through. "How did I spend my whole life missing this?"

"What? You never ate Shake Shack before?"

I cringe before admitting, "I've rarely eaten fast food at all."

And as expected, he gives me a look like I just crash-landed to earth in a UFO.

"Geez. So what? Do you want to talk about it? What's the deal with Dad?" He leans back a bit and studies me.

I'm so surprised by his question I don't know what to say for a long moment, opting to lift my drink and take a cool, quick sip from my Diet Coke.

I set it down, opening my mouth as I try to come up with some lame lie. Instead I say, "I just had a moment. My father is a rather strict man, and it's difficult for me to gain his trust. I wish he would call me instead of LB—his right-hand man. I called him this morning just to say hello, and . . ." I shake my head. "Needless to say, I could tell he'd rather I not call."

He leans back in his chair, eyeing me for a moment. "I can't say I remember what that feels like. Having a difficult father. But if he's asking someone to keep an eye on you, it means he cares in his own way."

I'm literally not breathing. "No," I say, frowning. "My father wants an eye on the business—specifically on the part of the business I'm managing. He's afraid I'll screw something up."

"Gotcha."

"I mean, I know he loves me. But when my mom ran out on us . . . I guess he feels like he needs to keep eyes on me so I don't go and do the same."

"You're a grown woman."

I roll my eyes. "Try telling that to my father."

"We lost our family some time ago," he adds, shifting closer. His eyebrows are drawn, as if it causes him pain simply to talk about it. "For the longest time, Charlie wouldn't talk or eat. I wasn't much help then. Our parents and sister were in an accident, and instead of being grateful to have survived, I resented being left behind. It took a few months for me to process everything, and while I was processing, Charlie became the kid everyone bullied. Now, he needs a boost of confidence. That's not fucking coming if he keeps getting beat up every time he heads off to school." He sighs and clenches his jaw, playing with a fry for a second before tossing it back into the basket. "Anyway. I've got plans for him. Big plans."

"Like what?"

"Send him to a solid, good private school. Giving him the best chances I can to make something of himself."

I nod in agreement, this revelation inspiring me and my thoughts about him. It hurt me, to lose my mother. But as far as I know, she still breathes. But to lose your whole family?

"So you raised him on your own? Didn't you have relatives who could help?"

"None who were in any better shape to help. My cousin Maria stayed with us during the school year. Her parents were drug addicts, and she cared for them more than they cared for her. The only stability she had was my parents, and I wasn't about to take that away from her when we lost them."

"So you supported her too?" I can't wrap my head around it. "How old were you?"

"I'd just turned eighteen."

"James."

He shakes his head and sticks his hand up. "Don't feel sorry for me. I did what I had to do. I did what I wanted to do."

"And Maria?"

He smiles slowly. "She graduated with honors. Fell in love with radiology and became a tech. Married her first patient. Can you believe that?"

"I'm so happy for her, for them!"

His laugh is easy and hypnotic. "So am I. If you're ever around them for a minute, you'll know that they're exactly where they need to be. They can't keep their hands off each other."

"If only the rest of us could be so lucky." My eyes meet his, and I become increasingly twitchy and look away.

So that's why he's a daredevil. That's why he does what he does. He was all alone. And that's why maybe . . . in some subconscious part of him . . . his troublesome relationship with death keeps him coming back to taunt it over and over again. Or maybe it's not all that complicated. Maybe he just likes the adrenaline rush.

As I think these things, I realize James is stealing fries from my basket.

I glare at him and pull my basket a little closer. "Hey. Don't put your fingers in my basket unless you want to lose them, *okay*?"

He lifts his hands, palm up, as if he's innocent. *Yeah, right.*

"What?" he demands as he lowers his hand suspiciously close to my basket again. "You're a pinchpenny with your fries?" He steals one from my basket again, popping it into his mouth and munching, savoring it.

When he grabs yet another one, he sticks half into his mouth and leans forward. As if expecting that I—*me*—will lean over and bite the other end straight out of his mouth.

"Ew. I'm not. Here. Have them all."

I push my basket toward him, flustered when he smirks and grabs the end of the fry, pushing the rest into his wickedly sexy, *smirking* mouth.

James tsks and pushes back my basket. "I've got some, thanks. Just want to eat a few of yours. Taste better, for some reason. Yep." He nods when I can only gape with an open jaw. "What? Did they give you special ones?"

Noting the twinkle in his eye, I shove at his hard shoulder and shoot him a glare. "Of course they do. I'm special *everywhere*. And if you paid attention, I'm trying to make you special too," I joke.

"Your money is the same as everyone else's here, Elizabeth," he says with exaggerated somberness; then he lifts his lidded drink, sipping from the straw.

I smile, suddenly not being able to remember an evening like this one. Where I didn't have to worry about anything and simply enjoyed. "Thank you for the burgers. I was thinking that maybe it's too stressful for you to be trying on all our suits with Michael and the Banks team milling around. So maybe we can continue with you trying on our suits at my place tomorrow—gives us more privacy until you're ready?"

"You mean you don't want me to be out in public yet," he says, setting down his drink and looking around. "At least, *your* public. Got it."

"What? No . . ."

His glance falls momentarily to my lips. "It's okay. I do what the boss tells me. And believe me. I'd dig the alone time."

Trying to distract him and get rid of the awful knots in my stomach, I reach out to toss a fry to his chest. "I need a good night's rest. Take me home, kind sir." I raise my hand exaggeratedly.

He stares at the back of my hand. "Now what?" He lifts those thick-lashed eyes of his to mine.

I realize I'm making a fool of myself and lower my hand. "You gently help me to my feet, offer me your elbow, and escort me home," I say, rolling my eyes and laughing as I stand.

He shoots me a curious glance as if wondering where the hell I left my uptight persona. "Just checking how drunk you are."

"You can't get drunk on Diet Coke."

"Ah, but what do *I* know of what they give the special people in their drinks here?"

He sets his hand on the small of my back and leads me out to the parking lot.

I'm keenly aware of that hand and the fact that his thumb is moving very slightly on my back as we approach my car when voices halt us.

"Hey, JIMMY. Jimmy *Rowan*? Shit, I hardly recognized you! Remember me?" One of the blond twentysomethings peels away from his group and walks over to shake his hand. "Man, it *is* you. You did a dare to help get a wheelchair for my sister. Remember how we emailed you?"

"Damn, Bert! Of course I remember you and your sis." James whistles as if amazed they're face to face again. Then his eyes shift to me, and they widen as he realizes his blunder.

"Man, you remember my name! You're so cool!" Bert gushes as he shakes his hand. "Hey, when's the next video?"

James's voice is suddenly stiff. "I'm sorry. I need to go."

The guy leans closer, staring at him. "Are you kidding me?"

He shakes his head. "No. Sorry. Have a good night."

Then he jogs in front of me, away from the guy, who's staring after him. A wheelchair?

I glance at him as we board the car, surprised that he swings the door open for me.

Guilt creeps in when I think of *me* being the reason he had to shut down his fan's enthusiasm.

"Fan of your channel?" I ask as I climb in.

"For a long time." There's a bite in his voice. I can tell he hates having to turn a fan away.

He shuts the door and walks around the front of the car toward the passenger side.

He's learning.

He's doing everything I've asked for.

But for the first time, I wonder if I'm teaching him the right things.

I try to reassure myself that I'm not doing this to be mean. My future position as CEO rides on the success of this project. I found James in a filthy bar, brawling like some uncivilized beast come from the Middle Ages! For the people of my crowd, someone like James is not worth their time—it's true that they would look down on him. How can I get them to purchase what he's selling if they believe he's beneath them? Nobody can know where I found him.

For his efforts, he's getting a million dollars out of this deal, a new wardrobe, a new life for his kid brother, and a lesson in how to act like a civil human being. He's going to be thanking me one of these days, just like Bert just thanked him.

I repeat that to myself over and over, trying to feel good about my project once again as he gives me directions to his house.

His place is a small crumbling little piece of crap in a bad neighborhood, with an overgrown postage-stamp lawn and a few garbage cans strewn all over the driveway. People sit out on their stoops, watching with interest as I pull up in my Audi. Besides Tim's Bar, I don't think I've ever been in such a bad neighborhood, ever.

I can't help thinking, though, about that fan he had to turn away. The knot in my stomach that appeared when James turned him away doesn't ease. "James, I—"

"I'd invite you in. But my brother's there."

I nod.

He looks at me briefly, then gives me a grin and says, "See you tomorrow, boss."

And then he slams the door.

As I watch him jog up the steps to his front door, I realize it's the first time he didn't try anything.

And it may have been the first time that I would have let him.

Strange that even though I told myself I didn't want to go anywhere with him, when I pull into his driveway to turn around, I sort of don't want to leave.

Jimmy

As I climb the steps to my house, I'm thinking of that guy I met in the parking lot of Shake Shack.

If there's one thing I hate about this arrangement, it's dismissing my fans. Denying where I come from. Pretending like I'm above it all. Because these people? They're the reason I still exist. This neighborhood might not be flashy, but I like it. People look out for one another. I like Tim's; I like doing stunts. Just because I'm playing her damn fantasy man for a few months, I don't want to turn my back on the things that make me who I really am.

But Lizzy doesn't go for any of that shit. And something tells me her ideal guy wouldn't either.

Inside, I hear Charlie run up to the door to see if it's me. "You're home!"

"Hey, tiger."

"Where were you? You hungry?" he asks.

I slam my palm to my forehead. "Goddammit. I was out for burgers. I should've brought you some." I eye him. "What'll you have?"

"I've had dinner already. Maria made me."

"She still here?"

He shakes his head. "Just left. Told me to tell you to text her when you got in."

I shoot her a text saying, I'm home. Thx. I owe u.

Maria: Anytime. And no. You don't!

I toss my phone aside as Charlie buzzes around me like a little bee. "Hell, what'd she give you? A bucket of sugar?" I ask.

"No. Pizza. Want to play *Call of Duty*?"

I slump down on the couch and automatically grab a remote, exhaling as I resist the urge to rub my chest and get rid of this odd pressure I felt during dinner with Lizzy.

Lizzy.

I saw her working today. I was impressed, to say the least. She rolls her sleeves up and gets right down to it. Smart, organized, with a touch of sweet that makes me want to take a bite out of her.

Within seconds she'd taken control of the situation with getting me dressed. Measuring me head to toe. Trying out slacks. Shirts. Jackets. Tuxes. Showing me how and when to put them on and wear them. I was floored by how good I looked, and even more floored that I didn't hate it half as much as I thought I would.

And what the hell was it with me telling her about my family? I never talk about that. Never.

And there I was spilling the beans with Elizabeth.

Who would have thought an uppity socialite from Midtown like her would get me?

Except she's not uppity. Hell, I saw her today. I admire any woman who can work. But it's more than her work ethic. Somehow, not sure if it's as clear to others as it's clear to me . . . but I see her vulnerable side. I saw it clear as day when her father was mentioned earlier.

Yeah. Her old man doesn't have the reputation of a softy.

I can't imagine what being the only daughter of Harold Banks is like.

But judging by what she said, it's not damn easy.

She wants to impress her dad.

And I want to help her. I want to shed this rough exterior and be the person she thinks I can be. And maybe even impress her a little in the process.

"I just shot you in the face!" Charlie whoops.

"I wasn't concentrated. Click restart. I'm going to getcha." I rumple his hair, and he groans.

"Fine. I'll get you," he mumbles, restarting the whole thing.

On first instance, back in Tim's Bar, I was blown away by how fucking stunning Elizabeth is in person. I'd heard of her. Seen her in the society pages. In person . . . all that beauty is fucking exponentiated to the tenth power. Gorgeous, shoulder-length dark hair. Wide green eyes.

More than ever tonight, my hands itched with the need to touch her. My tongue feels restless in my goddamn mouth with the need to lick her.

Not just because I know we'd be damn *good* together, if I can just be the person she wants me to be.

Because I see beyond those gorgeous dark locks and green eyes. I see something in her. Just like she saw something in me.

I LIKE what I see.

And I want it. Bad.

"I got you *again*!"

Giving up, I groan and toss the controller aside. "Yeah, I love you, too, brother."

"Why are you dressed all fancy?"

"Work."

"Work is here." He reaches out and taps my phone.

"I told you. I got a new gig. A good one. I'm not going to ruin it." Charlie's busy unlocking my phone.

"How many times have I told you that's private?"

Like any good little brother . . . Charlie ignores me. "Your subscriber list is up. When are we doing another video? Everyone's asking."

"When I'm done with this gig." I shrug then, adding, "Maybe."

YOUTUBE

Elizabeth

I have to send LB pics and a bio of our new model. He's asked me for it three times, each time with increasing urgency. That's what I opened my computer to do.

Instead, all I've been doing is sitting on the couch in my apartment, watching James's videos obsessively on YouTube, when he arrives the next morning at nine a.m.

I swing the door open, and the sight of him slams into me.

"Hey," I blurt out.

James Rowan is freshly showered. Hands in his jeans pockets. Looking as big or even bigger than before.

And for some reason, my heart gives an odd little skip of joy at the sight of him.

Trying to recover, I quickly step back to let him in.

"Hey, the suits haven't arrived—"

There's a deep, familiarly rumbly voice behind me, and he lifts his head to look past my shoulders.

At my laptop.

My open laptop.

My jaw drops when I realize I forgot to close the video.

"Oh." *Damn it, Elizabeth!*

Aware of James's sparkling blue gaze on my profile, I rush over to shut the laptop. "I was just . . . you know." I shrug.

He's slowly approaching.

"You haven't cashed the check yet," I say, trying to distract him.

"I'll get to it when I get to it, which will be soon. Don't worry. I'm still getting money from my YouTube views for what I need. In the meantime . . . thought we'd get started."

"Of course." I rummage through my desk. "I have my list. While we wait for the suits to get here, we'll start checking off a few things—"

"First things first."

He grabs my face and lifts it up at an angle so that our eyes connect.

He leans down and suddenly teases my lips apart with his own.

I inhale sharply when his tongue flicks over the tip of mine.

What the . . . *oh gawwwd.*

I grab fistfuls of his shirt and try to make the kiss go faster, suddenly wanting nothing more than this, but James slows me down. His tongue smoothing, calming.

I'm trembling head to toe as he leads the kiss. It's like he doesn't want to be rushed, like we have all the time in the world.

He peels his lips away from my wet ones and looks down at me with dark-blue eyes, sliding his fingers under the fall of my hair. He studies me for what feels like forever. I can see every dark fleck in his blue eyes as I study him back, unsure that this is happening. Here. In broad daylight. In NOT a dream.

He lets out a rough growl, my hair fisted in his hand as he leans back down again.

I shudder on contact, letting him seize my lips again. Fisting his T-shirt, harder this time. The heat of his mouth, the touch of our lips, I'm swimming in it. In him. He's so electric I gasp as the fire spreads through my veins, and this time I pull back too.

Our eyes meet again—hold. "What is that for?"

"For being irresistible."

"I shouldn't . . . ," I breathe out.

"Fuck this, I shouldn't have started it. It's in the contract. But I couldn't stop thinking of you last night."

Fuck the contract, I think, my eyes slipping down to his perfect pink lips, wet and red with the heat of our kiss.

He knows what I want.

"Give me one more, heiress."

He tilts my head back, parting his mouth wider, smothering my lips with his a third time.

I've never been kissed like this. Or kissed anyone back like this.

He kisses me as if this kiss is his whole reason for being . . . and me? As if it's my reason for existing.

His hand slides from my hair to grip my nape—and he devours me as I loosen my fingers and flatten them on the hard planes of his chest.

I can't get enough of him. The taste of him. The feel of him.

It's as if lately I've wanted nothing but to see him again. Pretending that I wanted to see him to change him—when I didn't realize until this very second that NO. NO. I was wrong. All I wanted was to kiss him.

He cups my jaw in his hand now, holding me still as he savors me. His stubble rasping against my cheek as he moves to trail a path of kisses down my neck, then back up. To catch my gasping breaths as he returns to kiss me.

I hear myself moan. Shaking from the heat of his kiss, and how much I want him.

When we pause, I stare at his mouth. His mouth that's red and swollen by how much we've kissed. Right here. Very un-Elizabeth-like.

I have to peel away with effort, panting as I wonder what got into him.

What's gotten into me?

HE did.

He has gotten to me.

He studies my lips with hooded eyes, his eyelids heavy, his pupils so blown up his eyes are nearly black.

My throat feels swollen and thick.

"Have a good day?" he asks thickly as he runs his gaze over my face.

"Yes. You? Beat anyone up?" My voice is just as thick and very faint.

"No. But it's still early."

"So it's . . ." I'm unsure. "*Not* a good day?"

"Oh, it's a good day."

I lick my lips, returning his devilish smile as I shake my head and try to recover.

"It really is," I admit.

Realization dawns.

We just kissed like crazy. During work hours. In my apartment. And if I had my way, I'd do more than that.

What the fuck is wrong with me? It doesn't matter if the contract will forgive me for having this fling. Sleeping with the face of our new line—what would Dad think of me if he found out? Do I really want to bring my whole future down because I can't keep my hormones in check?

I need to keep a distance from sexy devil James Rowan because of my dad. Because of me. Because I don't trust myself with him and he's so not what I need in my personal life.

"I . . ." His hands are still on my face. He looks at me like he wants me.

Like he knows I want him back.

"I haven't been in a relationship in a long time. Maybe not ever. Not really." I shake my head, forcing myself to step back as I try to explain. "See, sometimes it's hard to know what I'm worth to the guy I'm dating. Or why he's even dating me. I've never been . . . like this with a guy. Like I am with you. Relaxed. Able to let my guard down."

"Why? You're perfect."

"This isn't perfect to my dad."

"It's perfect. In any language, you're perfect."

I exhale as I walk around my desk, flushing in every part of me. "Well, now we want to make YOU perfect," I say, flushing when there's a rap on the door and Michael yelling.

"Honey, open up! I've got a ton of stuff in my arms, and I don't want to faint out here!"

James smiles, rubbing a thumb along his thoroughly kissed lips as he goes to open the door.

Jimmy

Michael and two of his assistants are setting everything up in Lizzy's spare bedroom. While Lizzy's pretending she didn't just kiss me right here.

Pretending I didn't catch her watching my videos just now.

That's okay.

Might have come on a little too strong over there.

But she looked edible when she opened her door. Her hair wet and tied in a bun behind her head. A little black dress hugging her form.

I didn't sleep for want of it.

So I just went in and gave us both what we wanted.

Now, as Michael's assistants go downstairs for another round of suits, I stick my hands in my pockets as I eye Michael.

"So, Mike," I say, clapping my hands as I circle him.

The fact that I call him Mike makes him beam.

"You mentioned something about some dude . . . some dude placing a bet on Lizzy's venture."

"Oh"—he waves a hand—"LB is always wanting to be sure Lizzy fails in her father's eyes."

"But you don't. Right?"

I gauge the guy, whether he's Team Lizzy or not.

"God, never! I adore Lizzy. She's smart, hardworking, warm, unlike that foolish, wicked . . . little bitch." He shudders as if merely thinking about the guy gives him the creeps.

"How much?"

"What?"

"How much was the bet?"

"I believe it was . . . 100K. Sicko," he mumbles as if to himself.

"So what do you say you get the guy to double up on his bet?"

He whirls from where he was organizing the suits by colors.

"Excuse me?"

"Get him to double up his bet to two hundred grand. Tell him there's an anonymous person wanting in."

Michael seems to be sweating from the excitement under his suit, licking his lips. "Oh my, I'm in love with you," he says, waving at his face. "Count on it, James."

"You two look cozy," Elizabeth says as she walks in. She halts, surprised to find us whispering behind the suits.

Michael's assistants stumble past the door, hurrying to continue with the setup.

"You know me, darling," Michael says, his attention back on Lizzy. "Always trying to offer drinks, dinner, or dick to the hottest man around."

I choke and slam a hand to my chest while Michael follows his assistants to the door and waves at me. "Don't forget your declaration of love," I tell the guy, meaning, *Don't forget our bet.*

"Never!" he replies with a nod that tells me, *I'm in.*

I smirk when he leaves, my gaze sliding to a suspicious Lizzy. I prop a shoulder on the wall, watching her watch me. "At least he didn't kiss me goodbye."

"Or good morning," Lizzy says, walking over to the suits. "Like me." She shuts her eyes and groans, then laughs, her cheeks coloring pink.

When she drops her hand, our eyes meet.

And I want to kiss her again—madly. Fully. Passionately.

Talk dirty to her.

Get her worked up over me, with me.

Get her under me.

I just watch her try to find words, swallowing as she sets a hand on a suit.

"So, can we . . . start over? Pretend that didn't happen so we can get back to business?"

She glances up at me. And damn me, just like the first time, I can't say no to her.

SUITING UP

Elizabeth

My stomach is tumbling.

Nervous because . . . um, the IRRESISTIBLENESS-of-him thing?

The delicious-kiss thing?

All that six-feet-plus thing.

Yeah.

He's just standing there, looking at me quietly. He said we can forget the kiss—but the look in his eyes. God, it's so primitive.

He seems pensive, possessive. Predatory.

"Hold it right there." I yank my phone from my back pocket and snap a shot.

James frowns.

"Exactly like that!" I say, snapping another one. Suddenly I can't help but take a few more.

When I realize James is just giving me a look, I lower my phone and think of how silly I'm acting.

"If you wanted a picture of me, all you had to do is ask. You don't have to go to all this trouble and pretend these are for the job." His blue eyes gleam teasingly.

"They're for the job, James," I groan, shooting him a little chiding look.

"Uh-huh. What do you *really* want to do with the pictures?"

"Post on my social media accounts after the launch," I tease. Really, what I need to do is send some pictures to LB to get him off my back.

"Will you tell your friends I'm your boy toy?"

"No, because you aren't." I'm frowning now, thinking of Jeanine.

"Not yet anyway."

"All righty then," I squeak, turning to the clothes.

"I bet you masturbate to them."

"What?" I turn around, shocked by his bluntness. Then again, I have to remember where I found him. James is a street guy. He brawls in the streets. He's lived near the streets.

The street lives in him.

"I'd do it." His gruff voice is sexy as hell.

"You'd masturbate to your own images?" I make light of it. "You give self-love a whole new meaning."

"You know what I meant."

I do, and that knowledge makes me very vulnerable. Because the thought of James Rowan pulling at his cock, breathing raggedly as he whispers my name? Well, let's just say that it gives me all the warm feels from my head to my toes. And the last thing I need is more warm feels about the guy.

"We're working." I point at the clothes before grabbing the first suit I see. While I unbutton the jacket, I watch him strip off his shirt.

Bad idea.

I glance away, out the window, as I extend the jacket out on the hanger. Then I sit down and start to craft a bio of James Rowan:

Atlanta native James Rowan is a true Renaissance man. Whether at the beach or in the office, he believes in living life to the fullest and will never resist an opportunity to make his mark on the world. Working hard or playing hard, he embodies the Banks image of strength, vitality, and power. That is why we have selected James Rowan as the new face of Banks LTD's exciting new line of menswear.

Hmm.

It'll do. I quickly send it off to LB, along with two of the pics I snapped, with *Presenting James Rowan!* as the subject.

James dresses without any other comments. Once I sense he's dressed, I turn and size up the man in the mirror. "Nice. Works for me. How about you?"

"Not my favorite."

At least he's honest. "Too bad, because it's one of mine."

"What's a suit like this cost?"

"Why? You get to keep the clothes."

"Just wondered. Maybe I'll buy one for Charlie."

Is he trying to get as much as he can from this arrangement, or is he genuinely interested in purchasing nice clothes for his brother?

"How about I throw in a gift card for Charlie?"

"Why would you do that?"

"Why wouldn't I?" I fish out another jacket. "I'll text my assistant now and have her email the code to Charlie. What's his email?"

James looks blank now. "I'll buy my brother's clothes."

"Suit yourself," I say, pocketing my phone and glaring at him. "And while you're doing that, you choose the next suit."

I want to see what he likes, what he'll choose. To my pleasure, he picks the next suit that I would've chosen.

"Do ya like this one?"

"Yes."

"How about the tie?" He chooses a bright-red one with royal-blue splashes.

"Definitely."

"And how about me? Like me too?"

"And we're back to this." I need to set some boundaries so we can get some work done. "You said we'd ignore what just happened."

"And yet here we are . . . alone in your apartment . . . just so you and I could be alone?" He's amused. His twinkling blue eyes always give him away.

"I DIDN'T . . . I didn't think of doing this here so we could be alone. I did it so that you wouldn't be exposed to the world before you were ready!"

My mouth dries as he sheds the shirt. My eyes fixate on his gorgeous chest and the matting of hair already growing back. The way he moves his long fingers, the way they work as he slides on and buttons the next shirt.

He closes the distance between us but doesn't touch me. Instead, he lets me long for his touch, and I do.

Long for his touch.

"I can stay professional, if that's what you want." His thick promise runs over the exposed skin of my arms like a caress. Like the caress I crave more and more every second.

"This line, it's important to me. It's everything." I want to tell him that my dad . . . that my dad is the only person that has ever truly loved me, and feeling his love—feeling his acceptance of me and his pride in me—is important to me.

"I get that, Lizzy," he says quietly. "But can't you have a little of both?"

I don't know how to respond, and so I let the silence envelop us. It's a safety net, a blanket of warmth and protection, because if I don't answer him, I don't grant permission or turn him away. We remain in this uncharted territory, and right now that's fine. The unknown may keep us trapped in dangerous waters, but I'm not in too deep. Not yet. But I'm afraid that soon this devil will have me drowning in him.

He clucks his tongue and checks out the next suit in the mirror. "Okay then. We'll play it your way."

"Perfect," I say at his back, now flooded with relief and surprised that I'm flooded with even more disappointment. "We have so much work to do."

Minutes fly by, and soon he's facing me again while he slowly fastens the buttons on a baby-blue shirt. He easily snaps on the cuff links, too, as if he's been dressing like this all his life.

"That's perfect. Matches your eyes." I force a smile but know the look on my face gives me away.

My cheeks feel warmer than usual, and the rest of my body is following suit.

His broad chest, cut abs, strong arms, and the way that shirt hugs all of this man make my stomach turn flips. He looks away right when I'm about to crumble, shrugging off the shirt and exposing his bare back.

"Okay, then," I say, twisting my hair into a knot as I watch him disrobe from the waist down. His cock is tight against his white briefs, and my mouth waters as I think about our questions.

"Eyes up, Miss Banks."

I swallow and try to think of anything but his hard body, his long and beautiful . . .

Clearing my throat, I somehow manage to snatch up the closest jacket and pass it over as I say, "This is our Banks Brunch Jacket. What do you think?"

He checks the collar and discards it, not even trying it on. "I like the solid black."

I watch him grab a plain white shirt and briskly button it, then shove on the jacket. I run my hands over his back to determine the fit as I circle him. "Move your arms."

He stretches them forward, and I admire the give in the material, the way it pulls nicely around his shapely shoulders, his broad form.

He smells good.

I'm surprised by how attractive the scent that clings to him is.

I peer around him. "You look great in this color."

"Black and white makes the sharp-dressed man?" he says, and rather than looking at himself in the mirror, he's looking at me.

"On you," I say, cursing my forwardness. If we're all business, I can't make comments like this. "Let's try the charcoal next."

He does. And rocks that one too.

We spend a couple of hours trying everything, from shirts to slacks to jackets, ties to cuff links to socks.

He's tried to flirt; I've tried not to notice and to simply focus on the clothes. He's now standing in a blue shirt that matches his eyes, and perfectly tailored black slacks, frowning at me as he buttons his cuffs. "You know, we can have fun with this."

"I'm having fun," I say absently, already selecting his next one.

"It doesn't have to be strained." He comes over and puts his palm on top of the shirt I was surveying, making me look up. He stares down the bridge of his slender nose and says, "I want you. I'm insanely attracted to you. And I mean to have you. How's that for an icebreaker?"

I gasp. "I, um . . ."

"Don't say anything. It's fine. But it's out there. It's out there, and I can still be professional, Lizzy." He waits, probably thinking I'll return the sentiment.

Instead, I'm melting.

Melting because of the way he looks at me.

Melting because he said he's attracted TO ME.

Melting because his eyes spin with desire.

Melting because I crave him like I don't remember craving anything before.

Not knowing how to deal with this, I thrust another suit forward, shoving it against his chest in a playful manner. "Okay, so you want to have fun. What constitutes a good time in your book?"

"You dressing up with me." He drags his thumb across his lip, thoughtful. "Maybe we finish here and go out for drinks. That would be fun. Right?"

I swallow. Of course that would be enjoyable, but it wouldn't be my smartest move to date.

"What d'you say, Lizzy?"

"We can't go out. Not yet. You're not ready."

"Okay. Let's pretend. Dress up to the nines and order in."

"As you can see, there aren't any clothes here for me."

"Ya don't have an evening gown hidden in your closet?"

"Maybe one or two."

"Go change. Hop to it. I'll wait here."

When I don't move, he adds, "We've been at this for a while now. Let me show you a good time tonight, and I'll be the perfect man for the rest of the duration."

"Why is this important?"

"Maybe I need to get you out of my system."

"And dressing me up will help with that?"

"Maybe."

"Okay, then." How can I refuse? I love dressing up in formal wear, and besides, we have a lot of things to practice, so I might as well look the part.

A minute later, I'm standing in my walk-in closet, thumbing through formal gowns, trying to find one that's elegant and stylish.

That's when it hits me. What will I wear for our big launch? Maybe I should decide now so we can see how we look together. We need to be perfect because on the night of our launch, we'll arrive *together*. We'll work the crowd *together*.

There will be a lot of togetherness in the coming weeks.

My body seems to like that idea and is far more sensitive now. What will this togetherness do for the rest of our relationship, not only in the professional sense?

We're about to find out.

I find a black-studded gown, one with a discreet slit to the hip. The low-dip neckline is stunning if flashing a bit of cleavage is the aim. It has a slender waistline and a snug top.

No, Lizzy, no.

Go for sexy, not slutty, something that leans toward inappropriate, yet pretty. No. Beautiful and classy.

I choose an open-back red gown dripping with sequins. Gentle curves with ample support cradle my chest and hips. The backless design leads to a V plunge and well-fitted gown, one that doesn't shift with the sway of my walk.

Super. I feel like a mermaid. Unfortunately, the design is so fitted that it looks as if it's been painted on.

One look in the mirror and I question my goals.

Bull.

I know exactly what I want. I'm sure of my goals. If not, I might as well take off the gown now.

I can't. I won't.

I want James to look at me as if he can't wait to strip away the fabric, tear away the design. I'd gladly toss the ruined dress to the side for one night of undefinable passion, one glorious night of James and Elizabeth, two people who are opposites but find the perfect complement in each other. Just one night. Several hours of pleasure-bound sex that ends in no promises, no expectations.

Snap out of it, Elizabeth.

Breathe in. Breathe out.

Daydreams and fantasies be damned.

I walk out into my great room.

"James?" Great. Where'd he go? "Are you hiding again?"

"I'm right here."

I jump at the sound of his voice and slowly turn to find him sipping a glass of wine by the bar, a glass of wine that seems to be quite intriguing, given the look on his face—only he isn't intrigued by the wine.

He's looking at me as if he can drink me in anytime he chooses.

He is eating me up with his eyes. His body is rigid as hell. His jaw is set, firm.

"What are you doing?"

"Looking at a damn fine woman. You?"

"Smooth talking your boss will not get you a free pass for drinking on the job!"

I approach the bar and pluck the glass from his hand. He's taken out my 1980 Chateau Margaux, which isn't exactly cheap, but maybe it shows he has some taste. Of course, my bar doesn't have cheap liquor. I glance up and notice that burning gaze again and promptly drink the wine. "But thank you." I set aside the glass. "For the drink and the compliment." I clap my hands. "Now, back to work."

"Believe it or not, I can work and drink."

"Good, because you need a lesson on how a real man drinks. None of that Montezuma shit from Tim's."

He holds up the glass of wine. "I opened this. It's not bad. Expensive?"

"Very," I tell him, going behind the bar. "But a Banks man will only drink wine with dinner. When you go out for drinks, you'll need to order a real man's drink."

"Tequila ain't a real man's drink?"

I shake my head.

"No wonder he doesn't like to fuck."

I smirk at him and say, "When you go up to the bar, you will order a Macallan 25 neat. Now, not every bar will have this scotch, but the ones on the fashion circuit will because they all know it's my father's favorite drink."

He raises his eyebrows. I take out the glass tumbler and put a splash in there. I've made this same drink about a million times for my dad.

He reaches over and grabs it, bringing it to his lips.

I shake my head. "Swirl it first a little."

He does, then looks at me for the go-ahead to toss it back. I nod.

"But don't chug it. Take a sip and kind of roll it around your tongue. Chew it."

He watches me as he takes a sip, doing exactly as I told him. When he swallows a bit too soon for my liking, he says, "What? Did you want me to gargle too?"

"How was it?"

He shrugs and peers deep into the glass. "I guess it'll do the trick. But I'm a tequila guy. How much would this run you in a bar?"

"Two hundred. Maybe more."

If he's impressed, he doesn't show it. He simply says, "Better not let it go to waste," and then chugs the rest of it.

Sigh.

I reach into the humidor, where I keep a stash of my father's favorite cigars for those rare, once-every-few-months evenings when he comes over for dinner. I offer the open box to him.

He shakes his head. "Quit smoking when I was eighteen."

"To smoke is human; to smoke cigars is divine." I take one out, open his jacket, and stuff one in the inside pocket. "That and a glass of scotch is a singular after-dinner pleasure, mellows you out."

"I'd rather just fuck." He shrugs. "Cheaper?"

I give him a look and shake my head slightly. "James," I say, groaning.

"Then after you," he says, sounding disappointed as he puts his hand on the small of my back.

I take one step, then stop. "That's not how we enter a room."

He cocks a brow. "Why not?"

"It's too personal."

"Putting my hand on your back is personal?"

"Yes. When we enter the ballroom, you'll need to hold out your arm and offer it to me like this." I show him a gentleman's gesture. "I'll accept, and you'll lead me in. We'll be greeted by reporters, bloggers, all sorts of people who will be there to learn more about Banks LTD and the new line. Most importantly, they'll be there to meet you."

"If you're wearing that dress . . ." He lets out a whistle, eyes sparkling. "They won't see me."

I blush, and my body reacts with pinging nipples, tingling thighs, a tighter stomach, and clenching inner muscles. Damn traitorous body.

I sigh and hope it doesn't sound like one of those dreamy little sighs.

"You like it when I compliment you, Elizabeth?"

I don't know what's worse. When he calls me Lizzy. Or when he calls me Elizabeth.

"I like complimenting *you*. And you look very nice in charcoal." I try to switch topics.

"You look lovely in red."

God help me.

"Thank you." I want to tell him that he should be gracious as well, but manners will come later.

He tilts his head up and holds out his arm. "It's good to see ya tonight, Miss Banks."

"The *ya* must go," I tell him, hoping to keep our practice run in a positive light. "Use the traditional *you* wherever possible. In fact, working on vocals and vocabulary is next on my list. But first . . . dining etiquette."

He roughly pulls my arm through his. "So we walk together. Like this?"

"Yes." I'm breathless again.

I relax until his free hand strokes mine. As we walk, my body reacts to him, and every nerve ending feels alive and wired.

We stop in front of the mirrors.

"Now what?" He grins at our reflections. "Do we strip off here and try something else or . . ."

"I'll stay in the red dress."

James runs those twinkling, mischievous blue eyes all over me. "You really do look great in red."

"Thank you." I like that he likes it, but I'm trying to keep it together. "You can try another suit."

"How about I just try you on? We'll be a good fit. Promise."

I swallow, laughing because I can't help it.

Smiling, he leans forward. I'm a breath away from his lips.

"You're tempted." His words a dark, tantalizing murmur.

I *am*. I shake my head anyway.

"You are." He nods at my chest. "Those beaded nipples?" He kisses the corner of my mouth. "Say otherwise." He holds me at arm's length. With the distance between us, I look down, and he catches me. "And when you do that?" He grins. "You send mixed signals." He gives me a saucy look. "I like it."

"You can't keep doing this. We . . ."

"Feels right to me."

He has a way of turning everything around, and I can't win. There's no point in trying now. I'd only back myself into a darker corner.

"Feels right to you too. Your little fists balled at your side? That's because you want to stop yourself from touching me. Those legs, that hint of skin showing when the dress shifts? That's for me. Nobody else is here." His voice is dark with desire. "All of it—this—is all for me, Lizzy."

I can hardly talk now.

"I think maybe I chose the wrong dress," I say, feeling light headed. "I'll be right back."

He grabs me before I can get away. One hand slides up my face. The other drags up and down my torso. Now it's anybody's game, and somehow it's turned into a very provocative, and quite thrilling, inappropriate game. "I guess we're all finished today."

"With business."

"I see." I'm supposed to be in control but can't find it. In James's arms, there's no control to be found. "So you liked the designs."

His eyes dip lower. "Yours."

"Not mine," I say, already aware of his tightening grip. "I want you to like what *you* wear."

"I'd be happier naked." He grins. "YOU would be happier naked."

"Well, we can't exactly work in our birthday suits."

"Trust me. We definitely could."

Pull. It. Together. Banks.

"Tell you what. We'll finish here tomorrow. Feel free to change back to your clothes." I point to his street clothes. "Meet me in the dining room. The next lesson is one we need to master as soon as possible."

"I don't need you to show me how to eat, baby."

"Wanna bet? Don't call me baby."

"How about you let me take you out again. On a date?"

"We're not . . . we can't go on a date."

"Oh, we will. Baby."

"Dream on, Devil," I toss back as I head down the hall to change, taking care not to steal a peek behind my shoulders at his gorgeous body as he changes back into his street clothes.

DINING ETIQUETTE

Elizabeth

I'm glad we'll be dining now so that he can't be looming so close to me, unsettling me.

I think we're both a little pissy because we'd rather be doing something else.

Each other.

"Sit." I pat the back of the white parsons chair, and right as he starts to sit, I move the chair. Revenge for him teasing me like crazy just now.

He loses his balance but catches himself before plummeting to the floor.

"What the . . ."

"A gentleman always offers a chair to the lady at his side, and he never sits before all ladies have been seated." I notice he's not paying attention. "Need a demonstration?"

"How hard can it be to hold out a chair?"

"Okay, then." I wait. "Well?"

James rolls his eyes and stands to full height, exasperated as he pulls out and holds the chair for me. I slide in front of it and wait for the chair to be scooted forward. As soon as it is, I sit . . . and immediately fall to the floor.

"What the hell was that?" I glare up at him.

"Fair play." He laughs as he reaches for me.

"This isn't funny, Rowan!" My ass aches.

"It's hilarious, if you ask me." He winks. "How's it feel when the chair is pulled out from under you?"

"I was trying to teach you a lesson."

"Ditto, baby."

"I don't need lessons in manners." I glare up at him. "*You* do."

"Clearly." He's mocking me with his stiff upper lip. "For future reference, you can let me know what's expected. There's no reason for etiquette lessons to become more dangerous than ice hockey."

"Says the man who didn't find his ass against a hard floor."

He offers to assist. "Shall we start again?" I place my hand in his. He hauls me forward with so much force that I land against his chest with a thump.

He brackets his arm around me and holds me close. "See? That wasn't as bad as you first imagined. Was it?"

"James, you use every opportunity to come on to me."

"I thought that was part of my charm."

"You aren't paid to think," I say, my ego terribly wounded because he used my tactics against me. Then again, maybe I shouldn't use tactics. Maybe he's right. Perhaps all I need to do is make a request.

It would definitely be much easier if he followed a few!

"Let's try this again," I say, backing away from his embrace.

"Shall you have a seat?"

"What?" I croak. "No." I hold up my hand. "You're trying too hard to be proper. Don't say *shall* unless it suits."

"And when does it suit?"

"Whenever it sounds natural." I think. "Like before, when you said, 'Shall we start again?' That was okay. It's not the norm, mind you, but it wasn't one of those in-your-face attempts to sound like a polished gentleman. In today's world, we all hear 'shall we' from time to time, but it's rare when it's used for anything more than a gesture to suggest walking forward or ahead of someone."

"After all that? I won't make the same mistake again." He looks frustrated. "I'll try not to sound too stiff."

"Very well."

He thins his lips and stares at mine.

"What?"

"You just said . . ." He shakes his head. "Never mind."

"What?"

"You sounded stiff."

"My peers expect me to be stiff in social situations. I was raised by traditional au pairs and American nannies."

"So you can get away with it."

"Right. But I guess you should, too, because you're supposed to be THE Banks man."

"I'm an improvement on the Banks man," he says. "I fuck."

I blow out a hard breath and go to the bar for wine. "I need a drink."

"Thought we weren't drinking on the job."

"We are now."

"So basically as long as I play by your rules, we're all good."

"You're catching on." I place the bottle on the table. "Now, where were we?"

"I was about to offer you a chair."

"Right." I glance over my shoulder before sliding between the chair and table.

James holds the chair out for me and leaves me there as soon as I sit. I immediately stand again.

"Now what?"

"You should keep your hands on the chair until I'm seated and lightly scoot the chair forward before joining me at the table."

"I'll remember that."

I remain standing.

"Really?" He exhales and rakes a hand through his hair, eyes flashing dark blue in exasperation.

"We have another twenty or so minutes before the food arrives."

"Or we could both be seated and enjoy each other's company."

"James."

He releases a ragged breath. "Please be seated, Lizzy." He pulls the chair out a little more for me.

"Thank you." I'm pleasantly surprised when he scoots my chair close to the table as I'm seated and then waits until I'm comfortable at the table before taking his seat across from me. "See? That was perfect. Right?"

"Of course it was." He looks at the silverware, jaw clenching. Obviously still irked about all this. "And what the hell is all this?"

"A place setting."

"We couldn't use one fork, one spoon, and a knife?" He picks up the butter knife. "And what's this? A tool to use in case we need to discreetly remove a piece of lint from the tablecloth?"

"It's a butter knife." Is he serious? I try to read his expression and decide he is. "Would you like to pour the wine?"

"Sure." Reaching out, he places the bottle under his nose and sniffs. "Smells fine." He pours himself a full glass, then pours mine.

I watch with my mouth open, then make a note to work on wine selection at another time.

He lifts his glass. "A toast."

"I can't wait to hear this."

"To the woman who hired me. May she change me into a better man."

I lift my glass and then pause, noticing the challenge in his eyes.

He drinks, then asks, "What?"

"I don't want to change you into a 'better' man, James. I . . ."

"It's okay." He refills his glass. "Don't feel rotten about it. At least you have a reason for wanting to change me." He drinks. "Most women want to change their men for personal reasons. This is professional. Strictly professional. All for the job. Right?"

Right.

"James . . ."

Before I can say anything, the buzzer alerts us to our arriving takeout.

"Saved by the bell," he says, holding up his hand to stop me from leaving the table. "Please. Stay seated. I'd like to eat sometime this evening, so I've got this." As he walks away, he adds under his breath, "God knows if you get up from the table, it could be hours before we get to eat our meal."

"Dinner is served." He grins when he returns. "Where do you want these?" He lifts two white bags.

"Anywhere on the counter is fine. I can transfer everything to the serving dishes."

"You don't need to go to that much trouble, heiress."

"Sure I do," I say, on my feet already. "Only the best for you."

"Or is it for you?"

"For us," I assure him, hoping we can have a relaxed dinner.

"That table is kind of intimidating."

"I'll walk you through it."

"Do."

"What?" I stop unpacking the containers.

"Do be so kind as to walk me through it now. Before we eat."

"Wouldn't it be better to . . ."

"No." He shakes his head and steps aside with his arm out. "After you, Miss Banks."

We return to the dining room, and he immediately asks, "So what do you want me to know?"

"It would be easier if we had our food."

"Dinner is the trial run. I want the basics. Give me that much, and then you can give me a fair chance to show you I'm a fast learner."

"Are you?"

He grins his devilish grin. "Never heard any complaints."

"And there he is." I laugh. "Good to have you back."

"Honey, I didn't go anywhere. You want to be respectable. I respect that. Let's get to it. I'm hungry." His phone beeps, and he checks his message.

"Are you expecting an important call?"

"No."

"Good to hear. Silence your phone before you sit down at any table."

"Okay." He does. "And then what?"

"Napkin in your lap. The old rule of thumb is to do this after the hostess does it, but it's perfectly fine to do it as soon as you sit down."

He tosses his napkin in his lap. "Now what?"

I cringe when I notice his elbow on the table.

"Something wrong?"

Noticing the irritation in his voice, I try to take a gentle approach. "You don't want to put your elbows on the table before the meal. It's too casual and inappropriate."

"Elbows. Got it."

"After dinner, it's okay to be casual and rest an elbow on the table. Some men even lean in and talk to their female counterparts, and that's acceptable. Before we eat, however, it's not."

"I'm with you." He forces a smile. "Let's do this quickly so we can move along to the meal."

"Right." I tap the table. "Next. Let's look at silverware order."

"Looks like a perfect setting for wasted time."

"It's more like a perfect place setting."

"Or a table with too many glasses, plates, and silverware." He looks up at me. "Do you really think this is necessary?"

"It will be." I know he's frustrated, so I offer quick tips. "Use forks with your flat plates. Use spoons for anything served in a bowl."

"So I'm supposed to use all these forks for one plate?"

"No. I'm getting to that." I take a breath. "Okay, the best way to explain this is to work from the outside in. You'll cut with your dominant hand, set down the knife, and take a bite. If something is too far out of your reach, ask for someone to pass it. If someone asks for the pepper, pass the salt and pepper."

"But if they asked for the pepper, then they only want the pepper."

"Maybe, but it's still proper to pass both."

"I see." He looks bored. "What else?"

"If you leave the table during the meal, quietly excuse yourself. Place the napkin to the left of your plate. Leave without announcing your reason."

We go over a few other tips, and James finally announces, "I'm hungry. Let's eat."

He abruptly stands before I can move aside. He goes one way, and I go the same. He veers to the right. I veer to the left.

We smile at each other. We're locked in this tense, unspoken moment.

"Now what, heiress?" He rests his hand on my waist. "The proper thing to do here is what?"

"I, um . . ."

He moistens his lip, and I can't help but watch that naughty tongue, that slow and decadent swipe.

Is he thinking about kissing me? Do I want him to think about kissing me?

Hell no.

I want him to kiss me.

"I'll move out of your way," he says, stepping aside.

"Thank you."

"After you." He holds out his arm.

I exhale, running a trembling hand down my sides as I step forward.

Once we return to the kitchen, he stands out of the way and watches me as I fill the dishes in silence. "Do you mind taking the salad to the table?"

"My pleasure." He accepts the large serving bowl, and when our fingers touch, our gazes meet. "Lizzy . . . I . . ."

"What?" My body is on fire. My hands are tingling. My breathing is sort of labored.

He meets my gaze. Swallows. "I won't let you down."

"Thanks."

He nods and disappears into the dining room. And for the first time since we've started working together, I wonder what it would be like for him to hold my hand across a linen tablecloth during a candlelit dinner.

What it would be like to date a guy like him, a guy who's unique, not concerned about appearances but only about himself, what he wants, what's fun and feels good.

I take the daydreams a step further and imagine a quite forbidden fantasy, one that includes James taking me out on the town and kissing me good night.

Unfortunately, my fantasy wouldn't end with a kiss good night and a promise to call. This fantasy, this illicit dream of mine, would end up with a kiss goodbye, long after the deed ended and the forbidden had been thoroughly explored.

James and I wouldn't part ways until the wee hours of the morning. If we parted at all.

BEHIND THE WHEEL

Elizabeth

The next three weeks, we work on everything.

First, vocals. The *ya* definitely has to go.

Next, more manners. *Please* and *thank you* and all the manners of a gentleman.

Then, I teach him to dance. And get stepped on like crazy.

And finally, I make him watch some etiquette videos while I organize the suits that we'll be taking to our visits with the department store buyers.

By the end of it all, I can sense James is restless and exhausted with all the things he's had to learn, and so am I. A part of me wants to beg him to take me out again, but I dread what that could lead to. That he'll feel it's like a date. So I resist. But then it occurs to me that we definitely need to try this one thing. "Do you know how to drive?"

Now that I think of it, I've never seen him drive an actual car in any of his stunts. Only motorcycles, Jet Skis, and other crazy engine things. James raises his brows at my question, which I take as a possible no.

"Let's go. I'll teach you. Let me drive my car to the outskirts of the city so that you don't hurt anyone. And for the well-being of my car," I tease as I grab my stuff to leave.

We drive in silence as the sun sets, and by the time I reach decently empty roads, it's dark.

"So." I park on the side of the long stretch of road. "You can do this. Can't you?" I ask, suddenly nervous.

His whisper is gruff in the dark. He sounds a little amused. "Do you doubt me?"

I hesitate, not certain I trust the guy not to do something crazy with my Audi.

He shoots me a daring smile and opens the door, and before we know it, we're switching seats. And Devil is settled behind the wheel of my car.

"Okay. So this is an automatic, so it's much easier than when I started learning on a manual—"

I trail off when he leans over, the clothes rustling in the silence of the car as he slowly takes my seat belt and draws it across my chest with infinite slowness.

I go breathless. The silence is a little deafening, when suddenly I hear the audible click of the belt—his hands lingering on my hip. Our eyes holding as firmly as the seat belt just latched on.

It's an effort to get my windpipe to start working normally again. "Anyway, as I was saying, you just need to press the ac—"

He straightens, and as I'm explaining, he shoots me a questioning look—"Like this?"—and rams the car so hard and fast I hear a screech on asphalt as we roar onto the road.

He sinks down into the pedal, sending the car tailspinning with a deep and joyous "whoo!"

"What are you doing! Are you insane?"

"A little bit. Hang on."

He winks, and I shouldn't be flushed, or scared-laughing either. But *I am*.

I sink my nails into the sides of my seat and can't believe how . . . exciting this is. When have I driven my car LIKE THIS?

Never, not in my dreams.

But this guy is driving my car like he stole it, and my heart is pounding like he stole me right along with it, and I didn't even need coaxing because I was only too willing to go.

Damn this guy. He makes me want to dance. To unbutton the top buttons of my top. Take it all off. Strip to my undies, run down the highway, and laugh until I almost need to run to the ladies' room to pee because I'm laughing so hard.

I always thought that was ridiculous. That people who needed huge thrills and crazy things to make them happy were missing something. I realize it's not about missing something; it's about the experience of things. The way things make you feel—excited, or scared, or daring, or courageous. Being with Devil makes me feel all those things.

We hit an area of the highway where it's raining, and suddenly the rain is coming so hard that it's difficult to see.

"We should stop somewhere!" I yell through the sound of rain pounding on the windshield.

"Yeah, I know where. I'm hungry."

"You're always hungry." I groan, rolling my eyes and peering out through the pounding rain.

Rain pounds into my windshield as he parks in front of a one-story, old-looking bar. Only half of the sign is lit, spelling out "WHERE BA" where it should read "NOWHERE BAR."

Devil raises his brows as he comes around the car to help me out, holding a folded arm above my head to shield me from the rain.

Slamming the car door behind me, I duck under the protection and try to leap over the puddles toward the door, laughing when we reach it, and James shakes the rain off his hair.

We hurry inside.

There's a pool table at the end. An old jukebox. A few high tables. And a bar.

"I don't think there's anything to eat here," I warn as I head to the bar, determined to get something into my stomach, even if only some olives or peanuts.

James takes a seat next to me and holds out two fingers. "Tequilas." And at my surprised, questioning look, he only grins.

Jimmy

"Your turn. Truth or dare?"

"Truth."

"You always go for truth."

"Because I'm afraid of your dares," Lizzy shoots back at me.

"Fair enough." I narrow my eyes, letting her squirm as she wonders what I'll ask. "First kiss. Where, when, and rate it from one to ten."

"Back of my date's car. Party at Sylvia Hollis's place. I was fifteen. And one to ten? Zero." She groans, and my eyes fly up in surprise.

"That bad?"

She nods. A perfect cherry-red flush on her cheeks. Damn, she's so cute I can't stop grinning. Somehow glad her first kiss wasn't all that great. Thoughts of taking her to the back of her Audi and giving her a memorable one spin through my head as she cocks her head and sasses out, "Your turn. Same question."

I shift in my stool. I'm sitting legs splayed wide, facing her, one arm draped on the counter as I thoughtfully tap my fingers on the cracked wood. Memories of getting it on with a busty redhead much older than me in a dark alley flit through my mind. Not really one for Lizzy's precious ears.

"Can't remember."

"Oh, you totally can," she says, shaking her head and pushing a tequila shot my way.

I laugh and toss it back, setting it down empty. "A gentleman doesn't kiss and tell."

"You're no gentleman," she scoffs, rolling her eyes teasingly. "Not yet."

I like this Elizabeth.

I like her a lot.

Her scarf's all skewed on her throat, exposing that lovely neck. Her hair's tangled; her makeup's run from the rain. And she looks adorable.

So loose I want to drill into her. Figure her out. Find out everything there is to know about her. I motion with a jerk of my jaw. "You're up next. Truth or dare?"

As if noticing the challenge in my gaze that dares her to go for the unexpected, she surprises me by blurting, "Dare."

My brows fly up in surprise. I lean forward, unable to resist tucking a wet strand of hair behind her ear.

"Dare you to take a snapshot of you right in this bar and text it to good ole Daddy."

Judging by the widening of her eyes and slightly hanging jaw, she's not taking. "Damn you," she hisses, the cherry-red color back in her cheeks as she shoots me a playful glare.

"No?" I give her a moment to retract her cowardice, and when she can't, I use the back of a curled finger to shimmy a tequila shot all the way up to her side of the bar. "Drink up, baby," I croon.

"Thanks a lot, Devil," she mumbles, tipping the glass back and downing it in one gulp.

Oh, I think to myself, grinning like a Cheshire cat in my mind. *Don't thank me yet.*

Elizabeth

We've been playing truth or dare for a while. I can't even remember how many shots I've had. And if James really did say that he's slept with over fifty women. FIFTY! He couldn't even remember the exact number. I'm woozy. And a little jealous. Maybe more than a little—more like a lot.

I can't help but swoon a little while I stare back at those devilish blue eyes as he asks truth after truth, dare after dare.

I'm dizzy, and I'm not even standing, and he's all to blame.

Suddenly in the background, someone's working the jukebox. And the song "Get outta My Dreams, Get into My Car," by Billy Ocean, starts playing.

"Oh! I love this song!" I cry, leaping to my feet and heading to any vacant place where I can dance to it.

I raise my hands and lock them at the wrists above my head, twisting my head side to side, my hair flapping, my hips swaying, the song playing.

We're pretty drunk at this point, both of us.

While I'm dancing, Devil is somewhere in the bar, with a thousand girls whooping as he twirls on his back on the floor like Michael Jackson.

When I see him, I stop dancing altogether. Everyone is cheering and clapping. When he leaps to his feet, I'm genuinely feeling hurt that he's never told me this about him.

"I didn't know you could dance like Michael Jackson."

"That makes two of us." He smirks.

"What?" I laugh, and he pulls me away from the crowd to shield me from the chaos. "Want to head home now?"

I nod, grabbing a tequila shot from the counter as a memento. I guzzle it down.

"Hey, bitch, that was my drink!" some burly dude calls out.

Suddenly James is pushing me behind him and confrontationally pushing his chest out. "Who the fuck are you calling a bitch, motherfucker?" James pushes him.

The guy stumbles back.

"Apologize to my girlfriend. It's a fucking honor to buy her a drink, buddy. Now thank her for letting you," he growls, pulling him up by the shirt and forcing him to look at me.

The guy blinks confusedly. "Heya, ah, thanks for letting me buy you a drink . . ."

"See?" He slams a bill onto the counter. "But that one was actually on me." He walks in my direction, taking me by the elbow as he leads me out of the bar.

I'm laughing hysterically as he guides me to the car, blinking up at the dark skies and realizing it's still raining, though much more lightly now.

As James unlocks my Audi, I hear myself fumble behind me for the door and swing it open, falling into the back seat.

I grab a bunch of his shirt and pull him close until our lips fuse. He pulls the door shut behind him and shifts us until he's on his back, pulling me over him on the back seat. I straddle him, but since he's lying down, I fold over and rub myself over him. Kissing him like I've never kissed in my whole life. Not drunk, not in high school, not in my wildest dreams have I kissed anyone like this.

I feel young and perfect, like it doesn't matter that I ripped my scarf while I was dancing. Doesn't matter that my hair is a tangled mess behind me from the rain, and it definitely doesn't matter that my lips are swollen and my lipstick smeared all over my face because of HIM.

He shoves my skirt up and pulls off my top until a gust of air hits my skin.

I catch my breath as he eases back—tossing the garment behind him. Eyes narrowing as he looks up at me. Partly dressed, swallowing nervously.

"Do you know what you've gotten yourself into, Elizabeth? It's about to get rough for you, baby."

"Just kiss me."

I pull him up by the face, and his mouth crashes against mine, and he tastes sinfully good. My body buzzes as I press closer, my breasts squished against his hard chest as his tongue slips into me, over and over.

I feel his fingers grip my ass as he sits up and devours me. They tease up and down the crevice of my butt, and I moan against his mouth because I can't get enough.

I rub myself against his erection. Only my panties and his jeans separating us.

He growls into my mouth, still busy caressing my bum, my back, my breasts. I think he wants me to rock against him.

And so I do.

He wants me to let my hair down.

And so I have.

I gasp and peel away as I look at him. His mouth spreads into a full-fledged naughty smile, the kind that makes me ache and burn, the kind that dares me to kiss him.

And so I ease back down to him.

And I do.

PHONE CALL

Elizabeth

Saturday morning, I wake up fully dressed in my big king bed, with nothing but a pounding headache for company.

I glance around in confusion, feeling for my clothes and then searching for Devil in my room. He's not here. I click the remote of my drapes and as they open, squint against the sunlight, finding two aspirin and a bottle of water on my nightstand.

My stomach knots up as I wonder if something happened last night. What's the last thing I remember?

I strain my mind, and like petals, the memories start falling on me.

Dancing like a maniac in some seedy bar.

Pulling James into the back seat of my car, kissing him like crazy.

James kissing *me* like crazy. And then . . .

Did I pass out?

I feel between my legs, but I'm not sore at all. But then I touch my mouth, and I almost wince. So . . . looks like we didn't have sex. I would REMEMBER that.

Only kissing. Lots of yummy . . . out-of-this-world . . . kissing. Touching. And then . . . did I pass out . . . ? Then Devil drove me home, and probably . . . Devil tucked me . . . *he tucked me in bed?*

I call Jeanine.

"How's it going, chipmunk?"

"It's, ah . . . it's going well."

"He learning a lot? That sexy manbabe of yours?"

"Yes, actually!" I say. "And so am I!"

"Like what his manhood feels like buried deep in your nether regions?"

"No," I say, blushing. "I'm not. We're not . . ."

I can't even begin to finish that. Because last night, *we almost did.* Maybe. What do I know? Things were heading in that definite direction before I . . .

Ugh. Who knows what I did?

"What are you waiting for, love? I hadn't heard from you in a while but figured you'd be busy getting that man in line, and in your pants."

"Oomph," I cry, settling back on the pillow with a sigh. "I'm not . . . it's not like that, actually."

"How so?" She's curious, and I dread telling her that James Rowan is not the piece of garbage she thinks he is. He's complex and intelligent and funny and . . .

She'll never understand.

I don't even know how to put into words how James . . . gets to me.

Every part of him gets to me.

I skim into the future and realize that Jeanine will think I'm a complete crackpot. Then she'll warn me that James is and can only be for a quick fuck, because my dad'll never approve of anything more.

Silence.

"Elizabeth." She sounds concerned now.

More silence.

Then, "Shit. I have just gotten my new opening statement for tomorrow. Let me call you back tonight?"

"Yes, perfect." Exhaling, I hang up.

While I'm dropping back in bed, my cell phone rings again. And I don't have to check the number because Jeanine is the only person I know who'll be up this early. "Ah, so you couldn't wait until tomorrow. You want to talk about HIM now. Okay, so here it is. Are you ready for it? Jeanine, yesterday . . . god, I almost screwed his brains out in the back of my Audi. He kissed me, a kiss to put all kisses to shame. And I wish I hadn't been so drunk—me? Drunk, YES! I was so drunk, but I wish I hadn't been so I could have just moved forward with this. Gah, all this time teaching him to be a gentleman, he left me here in bed with aspirin and a glass of water at my bedside when all I wish was to wake up to all six inches of him beside me. I swear next time I'm going to just go for it and ride him like an award-winning cowgirl at a damn rodeo. Just like you said I should do. Unfortunately . . . right now, all I have is my vibrator." I sigh. "God, I've got it bad for this guy. Maybe I'll tell him tomorrow."

"Why would you wait for tomorrow when you've said everything I needed to hear today?"

Oh. Myyyyy. God.

I gulp, stare at the phone, and then do what every red-blooded American woman would do. I hit end and wish I could take it back. Not the "end-call" part but the "babbling my truths" part.

I leap out of bed, and for the next five minutes, I pace. I pace because I don't know what to do.

I could call Jeanine, but then I'd feel guilty. She's about to try one of the biggest cases of her career, and the last thing she needs is me blabbering about James. Then again, I could call her anyway.

OR—I could call James, tell him that I was in a dead sleep, having the strangest dream EVER, and *just guess* who was in it?

Would that be cool?

Fuck no. No. And no.

He wouldn't believe me.

It's another ten minutes before he calls back. I reluctantly answer. "Hi, you."

God, he is SO sexy.

"Hi," I answer grudgingly.

And I'm so not.

"What's up?"

"Not a lot." Just kind of walking the carpet. "What about you?"

"Oh, you know, I'm just hanging out, waiting for the call."

"What call?"

"It's really more of a summons. Seems a woman plans to use me for sex, and I'm not sure what all 'fucking me out of her system' entails, but I'll definitely need to be present for the act itself, so yeah, I'm just waiting here by the phone."

OH MY GOD. I'm dying. I'm so, so dying.

"Look, James, I didn't . . ."

"Oh, I think you did."

"Well, I mean . . ."

"You did. And you know what? That cowgirl at the rodeo is sounding pretty damn good right now."

Deep breaths. "Yeah, I guess that's pretty much etched in stone now, huh?"

"So were we ever gonna discuss this?"

"You knew. I mean, you know."

"I do now." There's this guttural edge to his voice. "Lizzy?"

"Yes, I'm . . . I'm here."

"Want me to come over?"

Of fucking course. "No. No. Not at all. It's like nine in the morning."

"And here is where you tell me that all good little girls like spending their Saturday alone in their beds."

"Yes."

"After what I heard? Lizzy, you are not a good little girl."

"I have to go."

"Lizzy."

"James." My mouth dries, and I stare down at my trembling hands. I want this guy. I want him so much that I'm scared to want him. "Not today. Okay? Let me have the day and, um . . ."

Maybe I'll practice with my vibrator so I can perform well? What the fuck am I supposed to say now?

I don't say anything, and the silence stretches.

Finally, he says, "I'll see you Monday. Nine okay?"

I release an exasperated breath and relax. "Let's make it about five p.m. I need to head to the office because my dad should be back, and I need to check in on Michael and see if the suits are ready for our travels."

"All right then. Monday at five. Sweet dreams tonight, baby." I breathe out another sigh of relief, thrilled that he doesn't mention the vibrator.

"You too, Devil," I toss out as lightly as I can, ending the call and groaning back into my pillow, partly wanting to suffocate myself with it. I'm going to need to buy extra batteries for my vibrator this weekend.

♥ ♥ ♥

Sunday night, after watching YouTube videos almost as much as I was working scheduling meetings with our store buyers, I shower, slip on my robe, and head to bed. That's when I spot the envelope James gave me when we made the deal. Crinkled all over and folded in half as it lies on my nightstand.

I pull up my duvet cover and slide under the sheets, giving it another curious look. Trying to ignore it, I prop my pillow up, grab my TV remote, and look at the envelope a third time. Sighing, I set the remote aside.

Then I take it in my hands and turn it around, wondering what it could be.

I decide he never told me not to open it.

In fact, the seal is already open.

So I decide to take a peek, flipping the flap back and pulling out what seems to be a photograph. It looks old, slightly yellow, and worn at the corners.

It's a picture of a family, one with a teenage version of James, a girl who looks just like him, and a little toddler next to a beaming pair of adults. The perfect family.

Without a doubt, he has a sister, good-looking parents, and a kid brother who clearly admires him.

Had, I think with a pang as I remember what he told me.

It was an accident. *He LOST this family.*

And this is his most precious belonging . . . their last image together? Maybe the only image of them together that he has.

I picture him moving on his own, taking care of Charlie, doing anything possible to succeed and get ahead. Then I think of how punctual he now is, how he does everything I ask him even when it's difficult and driving him crazy. I admire his dedication and how he's able to keep that sense of humor after all he's been through.

I lost my mother. But my mother gave up on me. James's family hadn't . . . and he lost them all except Charlie.

I put the photograph back in the envelope and glance at my phone, tempted to reach out to him.

And say what, Lizzy? "Did you like the cologne?"

We went shopping what feels like ages ago. I used my plastic and bought him articles that we, at Banks, don't have. Designer shoes. My favorite men's fragrance. The coolest Ray-Ban shades. And a pair of silk pajamas, like all gentlemen should wear.

James grimaced at the pajamas.

"I won't use 'em," he assured me.

"You will. They're silk, and they're delicious."

"Not as delicious as sleeping without a stitch." He smirked at me playfully, that devil's gleam in his eye.

I huffed and turned away to hide my flush, and now I'm wondering if he's wearing them—or if he's wearing nothing at all. At least the bottoms?

About that time, Dad calls. "I hear things are progressing with the new guy."

"Yes."

"LB sent me the brief you gave him. He looks good, if a little mysterious. What's his background?"

"Um, well—"

"LB says he hasn't met him in person, though, and you've been working from home. Any reason you can't work at the office?"

LB.

UGHHHH.

Ratting on me to my dad. I know LB wants to be CEO. I know he's desperate for me to fail at this. But I also know that this project is *my* baby, and I'm protecting it at all costs.

"I've checked in a few times," I say defensively.

"Remember we're a team at Banks Limited. And whatever reason you are not sharing yet fully with LB . . . I hope it's not personal. Don't get too attached with your project or your model, Elizabeth. We form professional relationships. Keep your personal life away from the office."

I clear my throat. "Of course, Dad." I glance at the calendar on my phone. "How's Minnesota?"

"Cold."

"When will you be home?"

"I might head over to China to meet with some of our fabric representatives."

"Oh." I'm disappointed but don't show it. "Okay, so then we're good to go with the new model?"

"Introduce him to LB," he says. "He'll give you the final say-so."

Oh, hell.

"But—"

"Lizzy, I don't want to hear it. If I head to China, I'll be there over a week. I'm probably going to be cutting it close for West Coast Fashion Week. LB can make the assessment."

I frown. No, he can't. He's been taking bets as to whether I can pull this off. I could present Prince Harry to him, and it wouldn't be good enough. LB simply has to tell my father that he's a mess, and the plug will be pulled. Game over.

So the name of the game now? Keep LB out of my way, as much as possible, for as long as possible. It's not much longer now anyway.

I decide to change the subject. "And are you taking your meds?"

"I am. Thank you for taking care of your dad. How are *you*?"

"I'm good, too, Dad."

"All right then. Take care."

The line goes dead, and as soon as I hear the tone, I curl up on the bed and imagine that we're still talking. He tells me everything that's going on in Minneapolis, and I tell him . . . ask him. For fatherly advice. Not afraid of being judged. Simply wanting to know what he'd say to his daughter, if he truly loved her and she were falling for a guy so different, so exciting, so wonderful she can't even resist.

But of course I can't ask him that.

Dad's already said goodbye, but in my mind, the conversation lives on.

Like it or not, things haven't changed much. I'm approaching thirty, and I'm all alone. Living the independent career woman's dream. And still dreaming of more. And dreaming, not for the first time since he came into my life, of a lone dimple and gorgeous, intense eyes that tempt me to take a risk on something other than business. Something more precious and personal than that.

I end up calling him less than an hour later. "Have you cashed the check yet?" I ask when he picks up the line.

"No, but I will. When I've made sure I've delivered what you want." His sexy, gruff voice melts me.

"So I can give you back your envelope."

There's a silence.

"I peeked at it," I admit.

"Somehow, that doesn't surprise me."

"Please don't be mad at me."

"I'm not mad. You're a curious little kitten." I can hear the smirk in his voice, and my stomach warms.

"Well . . . it's a beautiful photo," I admit. "And I've been watching your videos. And . . . you're a brave guy."

"Or stupid. Take your pick."

I laugh and chidingly say, "You don't mean that."

I hear a low sigh as if he's shifted positions. "I'm lucky. Still got Charlie."

I nod. "And me," I add, then realize what I said and clear my throat. "Anyway. Cash the check, James. And I'll see you tomorrow."

"Heiress?"

"Yes?"

"Dream with me."

LUCK: WHEN PREPARATION MEETS OPPORTUNITY

Jimmy

At four p.m. on Monday, I'm at the drugstore—getting prepared. I couldn't sleep, went to bed with a hard-on Saturday AND Sunday. Woke up with a hard-on—TWICE too. This woman is driving me crazy.

After so much work to get Lizzy all lathered up and wanting me, the last thing I want is to not be prepared.

But fuck me. Who knew choosing condoms would be worse than choosing a tie? I stand in front of multiple shelves lined with all shapes, brands, and prices. I never really took the time to evaluate all the options. But those ribbed ones they pimp for her pleasure? Well, her pleasure's a priority. Obviously, I'm tempted.

I'm definitely on the wrong side of town, I think, watching as a prim and proper lady passes me for the fourth time.

Seems these people pay for choices. I search for the Hotman brand and grin when I spot it. Of course it's one of the cheapest, but reliability is important.

Here comes the lady again.

I can't resist the opportunity to tease her. Poor thing looks like she needs to get laid.

"Can I help you make a selection?"

She pales as she holds her head higher.

I shake the Hotman box. "I like these. They're comfortable, easy to slip on, easy to use. Dependable for those long-lasting rides." I toss them in her buggy and grab another box. "Trust me. He'll like 'em."

She never says a word. Horrified, she turns on her heel and wheels away. I try not to laugh because she reminds me of Lizzy, and I smile a little.

I'm checking out when my phone rings. "Maria?"

"Yeah. It's me. Jimmy, you need to come home."

♥ ♥ ♥

I've never been this pissed off or scared shitless before.

The cab sped through Midtown and raced for my house, but I still had just enough time to dream up a dozen scenarios.

As soon as it stops before my place, I shove him a twenty and bound out of the car, up the front steps, and straight into our cottage-style house. "Where is he?"

Maria points to the bathroom.

"How bad is it?"

"He was jumped."

My heart sinks, and I fly down the hall but bump into the locked bathroom door. "Charlie?" I knock. "Open up."

"I'm fine, Jimmy."

He doesn't sound like it. His sniffles fill the air, and my stomach tightens.

"What happened?"

He swings the door open, and I can't stand the sight of his battered face, split lip. What the fuck? He's barely a teenager. My blood is boiling now. It's too much to handle, but I know he fears telling me about it, so I try to make light of the situation. "How's the other guy look?"

He scoffs and pushes by me. "I didn't get the first swing!"

Oh, and that just pisses me off. I spend another minute or two finding out the details, then march through the house again. Before I leave, I grab a few crumpled bills from a tin in the kitchen cabinet, then look at Maria and say, "If I'm not back in two hours, get him out of here."

She nods. "Be careful, Jimmy."

I send a text to Lizzy so she's not expecting me and then head to Tim's Bar. Thanks to Luke, I already know the gang is there. They're trash-talking Charlie, a little thirteen-year-old, and don't even see me enter from behind.

Luke nods. I throw down some cash to cover the forthcoming damages. Then, I turn to the guys who are old enough to drink and too old to be taking down a boy not yet fourteen.

"Which one of you pathetic *men* want your spanking first?"

HOME

Jimmy

Charlie wants to know what I did to those fuckers the moment I walk in.

Simply tell him, "I gave them a couple spanks. In their damn fool faces."

I grin, and Charlie, though he worries he'll lose me one day, nods and exhales.

I want him to forget this whole damn day ever happened.

Need to feed the kid.

Plump up those scrawny bones so he doesn't invite assholes to rough him up so easily anymore.

I'm throwing together a quick box meal when Charlie says, "There's a badass convertible in our driveway."

"Don't open the door." Quickly, I sprinkle bread crumbs on top of a chicken mixture before popping it in the oven. "Did you do your homework?"

"Scouts don't have homework this weekend." He holds down the blinds and looks at the driveway again. "If you're smart, you'll open the door. That badass car has a badass bitch sitting behind the wheel."

"She's not a . . . what's with the language, kid?"

"Uh-huh." Charlie laughs. "Somebody's lovesick."

"Not lovesick."

I clench my jaw at the thought.

"You've been listening to Darren too much," I scold. Maria's husband. "Got your stuff together?"

"Yep." He grins. "Gonna go out there or make her come in?"

I peer outside.

As I watch her leave her car, I have to admit. This is nice. Great, actually.

I'm glad she's here.

As soon as she knocks, I swing the door open and grin down at her. She looks nervous and out of sorts, like she's not sure if she's overstepped some imaginary boundaries.

"You're a long way from Midtown."

"Yes, well, I got your text, and I worried. Is Charlie okay?"

"Yes."

"And . . . you?" She seems flushed, hesitant as her eyes scan my whole face like a minefield.

"I'm fine. Perfect. Not a nick." I aim at my face, winking.

Her lips curve, and she shakes her head. "I didn't ask because of that," she says but seems relieved to see that I'm well.

I eat her up with my eyes, and it's intentional as shit.

If she didn't look so good in a skirt and blouse, I'd haul her off to my bedroom and insist that she throw on one of my T-shirts and get comfortable. She looks like she doesn't belong here, and yet she's so girl next door. Maybe it's the innocent look that makes me crazy.

Or maybe it's just the sexy woman who causes me to lose my mind.

I move aside. "Would you like to come in?"

"Sure. I thought you'd never ask," she teases, stepping inside. "You have a really nice place." She turns to the kitchen, inhaling like she's just stepped inside her grandma's kitchen. "You're cooking something with panko. Aren't you?"

"Yes. Want to stay for supper?"

"*Supper* sounds great," she says, grinning down the hall at Charlie.

"You can stay," Charlie says, reaching around me to shake her hand. "I'm Charlie. I'm this one's brother."

"Nice to meet you. I'm Elizabeth. My friends call me Lizzy."

"Great, Lizzy," he says, suddenly peering out the window and waving. "Hate to rush, but I'm headed to a campout, and my ride just got here." He grabs his jacket.

"Hey, tiger, what about your dinner?" I glower like some pissy French chef who thinks the world revolves around his dishes.

"I heard about that," Lizzy tells Charlie about his campout.

"SWEET." Charlie shoots her a grin before he turns back to me. "If he's talking about you to me and me to you, I'd say you're pretty high on his list of priorities."

"Okay. Let's not keep your ride waiting, kiddo." I use his shoulders to steer him outside.

"Later!" We give one another high fives, and he's on his way a minute later.

As soon as the door slams, Lizzy says, "Charlie seems like a great kid."

"He is . . ." The kitchen timer goes off. "*And I guess* dinner will be ready in five?"

I frown because it's too damn late for Charlie to eat some, and Lizzy laughs.

"I'm sure he'll get some food in. Boys that age always do," she says, as if reading my thoughts. She follows me to the kitchen. "Need some help?"

I suck in a breath and turn to find Lizzy standing at the table.

The French chef is suddenly gone. I feel damn young and awkward, like I'm younger than Charlie and have never had a girl I liked look at me quite like Lizzy is looking at me now. "I've got this." I fake confidence. Fake it till you make it, right?

"If this is too much, too soon—you know, after our embarrassing . . . morning . . . I can go home?"

I shoot her a look that tells her I think she's insane.

And hot.

And insane.

She's noticed her effect on me. *Chill, Jimmy. I mean James.* Yeah, *James.* James is chill. James has got this. "Go home? Are you kidding? While I enjoy one of the best boxed recipes ever created on my own?"

"Well, when you put it like that . . ."

I sit down and wait for her to do the same. Damn. Where are my manners? I scramble to stand again and hold out her chair. "Have a seat."

She flushes, as if embarrassed about my blunder.

My hand brushes against her neck, and she jerks. I see the goose bumps scatter across her neck, and I want to kiss her there, kiss her and whisper sweet things that I know will get her going, set her off. Maybe I could start by telling her that I'll never fuck up and be ill prepared again, tell her that I'm now good on the condoms, lube, whatever the hell she wants.

Too much, man. Chill.

She primly unfolds her paper napkin and glances around the kitchen. "You have a lovely place."

"It's home." I sit opposite her. "Hope bottled water is okay. I didn't take you for a beer drinker."

She eyes my water and shakes her head. "I'm fine."

Damn her for removing her jacket.

"You are *very fine* and so much more." I'm grinning, loving the blush that keeps reddening her cheeks.

"I'm impressed you cook."

I affix my napkin to the collar of my shirt and love it when she looks appalled. "We make do on this side of the tracks," I tell her.

"Don't do that." She studies her fork before using it. After a moment of silence, she says, "Never be ashamed of who you are or where you come from."

"Says the woman who's trying to change me."

"Change you? No. I'm working for gradual upgrades. That's all."

"I'm not an automobile."

"That wasn't an insult."

I laugh. "'An upgraded model' insinuates that only a tweak or two will be needed to achieve perfection."

Silence.

"How long before I'm perfect?"

"You almost *are* already," she says.

"Okay," I say, laughing. "Tease me now, and see how far that gets you later."

"I'm scared," she says, shuddering.

"You should be." I've walked around with blue balls while imagining what that tight little pussy might feel like clenching around my cock.

I pretend to be interested in my food but can't seem to eat when all I want is to take this girl to my room.

She.

Rocks.

My.

World.

"Why didn't you let me come over Saturday?"

"Maybe because . . ." She looks at me. "You scare me."

"I won't hurt you."

"I know you deliberately wouldn't. But this is messy. My dad hardly ever approves of any man I bring home, and bringing you—"

I wait for her to say it. That people on this side of the tracks will never be good enough. She doesn't, though. She just freezes, as if she has no idea how to continue.

"Do you always jump when your dad says?"

"Most of the time."

"Do you jump for anyone else?" I ask.

"No," she says quietly.

I'd like to change that. I will change that. "Would you jump for me, Elizabeth?"

"Excuse me?"

"I think you would," I whisper, smiling to myself when she has no response.

She's silent.

We eat our meal with polite conversation, a bit of business, and a lot of flirting.

While we're doing the dishes together—which is kind of cool—she talks about a few shows that we'll be attending, the first one at the end of the week in Los Angeles, then asks if I have a passport.

"I always hoped to do some overseas stuff with my YouTube channel, so I have one. I just haven't used it."

"Like what?"

"Are you making fun of me now, Lizzy?"

"No. Really! I'm interested. Like what?"

"Like . . . jumping off the Eiffel Tower?"

We laugh.

"What's your dad think about you traveling with me?" I ask.

"He won't question it. It's business."

"I'm not the kind of guy a wealthy businessman hopes to find at his daughter's side, much less in her bed."

"You're not in my bed."

"Maybe not yet, but that's what I'm aiming for, and I always hit my mark." I put away the dishes and turn to face her. Butting my hips against the kitchen counter, I cross my arms and say, "When we stopped in the back seat of your car . . . I'm surprised we could both do it. But I'm not up for either of us stopping again."

She waves her hand in front of her face, blushing.

I know Elizabeth's type. It took a long time to get her to a place where she trusted me enough to touch her, see her. It could take twice as long to get there again.

Either way. No matter how long it takes. We're still a done deal.

My hand is in hers, and I'm leading her away from the kitchen before I realize that our hands are still adjoined, our fingers laced together.

"I guess I'll go." She thumbs the air over her shoulder. "Walk me to my car?"

No. I'd like to see her sprawled out on my bed, waiting for me, watching me as I fuck her. But that's not going to happen. Not yet. "We could hang out here."

"I can't stay with you."

I narrow my eyes. "I didn't ask you to stay. I suggested that we hang out awhile. I can mix up an appletini. Isn't that classy enough for you? Maria keeps a bottle here somewhere."

"I think . . ." She glances around at our small living room, the one with a lone sofa and beanbag. "Maybe we could do it another time?"

"Because we have work to do?"

"Yes. The photo shoot starts early tomorrow, and we need to be ready for LA."

"Yeah." I stuff my hands in my pockets and wait a minute, in case she changes her mind.

She doesn't.

"Okay then, I'll walk you out."

"James?"

"Hmm?" I turn too quickly, maybe hoping that she's changed her mind.

"I'd love to stay if we didn't have so much work to do. Maybe another time?"

I approach her slowly, then tuck a lock of her hair behind her ear. "I'll ask again, then."

"So are you going to show me around?"

"No. Not today." I don't want her to see my clothes piled in the corner, my unmade bed. "But if you're free for a few hours tomorrow after the shoot, I'd like to take you somewhere." I lean forward and look at her.

She glances past my shoulders at my room.

For a minute, just one glorious sixty-second set, I watch her as she looks around at my meager belongings. My shelves are lined with sports trophies and other youth memorabilia, a few favorite Harry Potter books—not that I was a fan, but I read a few—and family photos.

I like that she's here. I could get used to this.

Don't know that it's smart of me to get too used to the idea of seeing her here.

But I'm a fool who thinks he can cheat death every single time he does a stunt.

So there you have it.

And when she finally consents to my request, I'm like a man who's just hit it big.

PHOTO SESSION

Elizabeth

"Well, I don't know what to tell you, LB," I say into the phone as I pace the hallway.

"I don't understand why you've been so busy that you couldn't just bring him by the office," LB says.

"I just ran out of time. I had a lot to do," I explain, peeking into the studio, where James is with the photographer. "If you really want to see him, come down to the studio."

"I can't. I have far too much to prepare for the New York show."

I knew that. "Well, that's too bad. But trust me. It's under control. Everyone will be dazzled at the New York show, including those who can't seem to believe I've got what it takes for this show to be GOLDEN," I say, hinting to him that I *know* he's betting on me to lose. What an asshole.

I end the call and push open the door.

"One more, Mr. Rowan," the photographer calls.

We're having the photo shoot for the ad campaign for the line, and James looks amazing. Sexy as hell. I'm nearly drooling. I already know these photos are going to slay. I can just imagine the traffic jam they'll cause when he's on the side of a building in Times Square.

But we've been doing this for hours. James looks exasperated, pulling at his tie as if giving up and striding over to where I stand to the side.

"I'm not Mr. Rowan," he growls at me. "I'm losing my mind here."

Desperate to get out of here, too, after the long day, I grab him by the back of the shoulders and steer him to the mirror, peering from behind his large frame to meet his gaze in the reflection. "Look at this man. Is he not Mr. James Rowan? Jimmy to his friends? James . . . to Elizabeth?"

His smirk appears. He slowly starts to turn, his blue eyes seizing mine. "And to Lizzy?"

He's challenging me.

Boy, does this man like to challenge me.

I peck his lips, quickly, then fall back and smile calmly as if I peck all my models on the lips. Right.

"You're my manbabe," I whisper cheekily, "but nobody needs to know that."

Grinning ever so slowly, he says, "That makes you *my* babe," and heads back to the stage, making the photographer literally squeal in joy as James Rowan faces him with a devil's smile.

And then I whirl and see Jeanine standing in the doorway, grinning at me.

Jeanine is blonde and curvaceous to my dark and slender, but we've been like two peas all our lives. She and I used to joke about being two rich and spoiled bitches. If there's anyone who knows how to flaunt her wealth, it's Jeanine.

"My, my, my." She's grinning like the cat who ate the canary at James while she comes in and gives me a quick hug. "Oh my goodness. You did it. He's hot as hell."

I nod, smiling at him, wondering if she saw the kiss as we watch him posing for the camera.

"So I guess considering how cozy you two look . . . you took him to bed?"

I shake my head. "No. We're not."

"God, Lizzy, are you crazy? Just for a little playtime? How can you work with him day in and day out and not want to tap that?"

She's looking at him as he poses and gnawing on her lip like she wants to take a bite of him.

"I'm not," I tell her. "Like I said, this is business. I need to get the launch right. I can't think about that."

"Hell, that'd be all I could think about, next to him. You think you can introduce us?"

"But you've already met . . . ," I start, my head suddenly filling with sheer terror. Jeanine was the type of best friend who usually always got the guy, while I was the cute and single wingwoman. She consumes men, and easily.

What am I, jealous?

I'm so lost in my thoughts that I don't notice until James has sauntered up behind me and Jeanine extends her hand. "Oh, hi, James! So nice to finally meet you in person!" she gushes.

"So this is the best friend with the killer contract," he says with a low, assured voice. And he takes her hand gently and bows like a regular gentleman.

"James. Meet my best friend, Jeanine," I say, trying not to be bitter.

I can just about see Jeanine swoon. Because he might as well have been James Bond.

And that is my first hint.

My first hint that I'm in too deep. And I've created a goddamn monster.

♥ ♥ ♥

After enduring my best friend throwing all her flirting ammunition full bore at James, we head down the elevators toward a conference room to go over the details.

"We've got flights leaving out of Atlanta tomorrow," I say to him, my voice clipped. "The aim is to get every single store buyer to stock us."

"Something wrong?" he asks me.

"No," I say. There shouldn't be anything wrong. Jeanine stopped short of flashing him her boobs, and he remained friendly, but he didn't flirt back. Well, not really. With a man with such a penetrating gaze and raw sensuality, even innocent chatting feels like a flirt.

I shouldn't be feeling like this.

Like I'm about to lose something close to me. Something I can't bear to part with.

"Don't worry, Lizzy." He sounds confident. Almost more confident than I am. "We've got this."

I'm amazed how easily he can step in and out of my world. He already looks like he was born in this one. "Oh. I know. You do."

"*We* do," he repeats with that lopsided grin, making my heart melt a little. "So that was your best friend, huh?"

My stomach drops. "Yeah. We've been best friends forever," I say. I take a breath, knowing I should address the elephant in the room. "She really thinks you're something."

"That so?" Either he doesn't believe it, or he doesn't care. And there are few men who don't care where Jeanine is concerned.

"Yes."

I wait for him to say more, but he doesn't.

After we take a table in the empty conference room, we spend some time reviewing possible interview questions and how I'd like him to answer them. Then I hand him a tiny wrapped box. "This is for you."

He looks at it before pulling off the ribbon. He opens it to find a brand-new cell phone. "What's wrong with the one I have?" he asks.

"You can't have that anymore. A person's phone is a reflection of him."

He lifts up his old dirty phone with the cracked screen. "So the old me was broken and dirty?"

I shake my head. "That one is Jimmy's. You need James's phone. Be sure it's ready for LA."

He opens it and looks at it. It's sleek, shiny, sophisticated. Everything James should be. He nods and turns it on, then starts to play with it. "Thanks."

We wrap up the discussion when Charlie calls on his old phone to tell James about his school day. James looks proud, and I'm too curious to ignore the pang in my stomach.

I don't know why, but I feel thirsty for him. For more. To know every little thing about him. "Good news to share?" I ask.

He shakes his head. "Nah. It's nothing."

"Didn't sound like nothing. Tell me."

He shrugs. "Our minds should be on other things."

I face him. "We can talk about things other than work."

"All right. He just did well on an honors math test today." He shoots me a naughty grin. "Tell me something I don't know."

I think for a moment, trying to come up with something non-work related. But sadly, I have nothing. Everything in my life has been attached to Banks LTD, ever since I was a little kid. I have so much riding on this even James can't possibly fathom. "I've always dreamt of being the company CEO."

"After tomorrow, maybe that will happen."

"Dad isn't a man who'll hand over the company reins unless I deserve to hold them."

He searches my eyes. "This launch is really that important to you?"

"Nothing else matters. If I don't make the line wildly successful, then it's a failed effort, as far as I'm concerned."

"You or your dad?"

"Both, really. He'll want to see the numbers, and I want them to exceed whatever expectations he has."

"That explains why you've set your goals so high."

"They can always be higher," I say.

"Trust me, sugar—they're high enough."

I freeze. "Sugar." I swallow. "No. Just no."

"What's wrong with *sugar*?" He laughs. "Would you prefer *honey*?"

"I'm not a staple food." I point to the door. "And let's step aside to look at some of our trip details before we go."

He pops a kiss on my lips. "If it's really my choice, then I choose *sexy*, and you damn sure better answer when I call."

THE HILL

Elizabeth

It's the night before LA.

The night before I unleash my creation upon the world.

My heart skips as I see his large form step out of his house. He jogs over to my Audi and opens the driver's side door, motioning me toward the passenger side. "Scooch."

I wrinkle my nose. "Scooch?"

"Yeah. Like, get your ass over to the other side. I'm driving."

I frown at the gearshift and console in the center of my car. It'd be much easier to just get out of the car and run to the other side. I'm wearing a short skirt, after all.

But what the hell.

I lift my legs out from under the steering wheel and, not very gracefully, "scooch." He watches my legs the whole time, licking his lips as if he's hoping to get a peek. Then he slides into the driver's seat and pulls out of his driveway like a bat out of hell.

"So where are we going?"

"I want to show you something."

"What can you possibly show me in Atlanta after dark?"

"You might be surprised," he says, shooting me that wicked smile again. "Are you game?"

"Not really, but you seem determined, so I guess we'll do things your way."

"Smart lady." He winks. "Glad to see you're paying attention."

"But only tonight." I narrow my eyes. "Tomorrow, we're up bright and early to fly to the West Coast show."

"Deal. Now, step out of your little 'I'm special' box, and hang on for the ride. You'll love this."

He accelerates and weaves in between a couple of semis before taking off like a man who knows how to get what he wants.

I can't help but wonder if he wants to impress the girl or lay down the woman, but either way, I trust him. I just hope that trust doesn't land me in a heap of trouble.

It easily could.

I feel comfortable with this guy, more comfortable than I feel with CEOs and millionaire types. I love that James doesn't look at money as if dollar signs should be worshipped on the altar of success. It's definitely part of his charm. Money is a means to pay his bills, and nothing more. I've never known anyone who didn't care about managing and accumulating wealth.

Then there's Charlie. How many young men would take on their kid brother to raise? Not many.

Men in my crowd would've hired a team of nannies or unloaded the kid on a family member. Not James.

He's such a good person. Maybe I've suspected as much from the start. I saw glimpses of his character even when he was fighting at Tim's Bar.

James is the kind of man who might go in for the kill, but he won't take it. He might rough someone up, but only if few other options exist. He could've taken advantage of me that first night but didn't.

He's rowdy, but he's also honorable.

All in all, he's more upstanding than anyone I've ever known, so that's something to build on. Right?

I glance at him. He smiles at me.

There's only one way to find out.

An hour later, security clears us at a checkpoint and waves us through.

"What is this place?"

"A studio."

"Of course it is," I say, laughing.

"I may be an amateur in your book, but some of my stunts happen at fifteen thousand feet." He points to a building. "I've been up there many times."

"You work here?"

"I do. Too much time between jobs, though, so my channel was born."

As soon as I see a guy leaping off a building, I panic. "But you can't . . ."

"I have and could again . . ." He parks the car. "But won't while I'm on your payroll."

Suddenly, I don't want him to risk stunt work again. A young guy with an everlasting death wish tumbles off the side of the building while a director waves his arms and shouts, "No. No. No. Not like that."

"Come on." He takes my hand. "I want to show you a surprise."

Surprise? When did he go from "showing me something" to "surprise," and what does this all mean?

Calm down, Lizzy. He isn't taking you to Disneyland or an X-rated couple's retreat. I grin because I like the idea of the first, while James would probably enjoy the latter.

What is it about opposites and attractions?

I follow him until we reach a couple of golf carts and four-wheelers located at the edge of the parking lot. "Hop on."

"I'm not an adrenaline junkie."

"Ah, come on. Live a little."

"Look what I'm wearing. Would you?"

"Sit sideways." He grins. "Or just hike up your skirt and slide in behind me. I won't look."

"Liar."

"Tease."

He boards the ATV and starts it with ease. "If you don't get on, then I've wasted your time bringing you out here." He shoots me a daring look. "You don't strike me as a woman who likes to waste her time."

I stare into the night wondering what he could possibly want to show me *out here*. "My life is in your hands." I climb aboard, straddling the seat behind him.

"And I take that shit to heart," he says, pulling my arms tighter around him. "Relax and enjoy the ride!"

He guns it, and I feel like I've lost all control, and I can't help but wonder if that's his motive.

We reach the top of the ridge, and he steers the ATV down a rugged terrain. To the left is a cabin, but to the right is what I'm sure he wants to show me . . . Atlanta at night.

We stop, and his back stiffens when he glances over his shoulder. "Worth it?"

"This is incredible." I want to sit right here and drink in the view, the flickering beauty of Atlanta's skyscrapers and awesome beauty without the noise so typical of our overcrowded city.

"Wanna take a walk?"

"Now? Here?"

He chuckles. "I'll protect you."

"Okay." I slide back but don't get off. I'm not sure what's on either side of the ATV.

"You'll need to slide off first."

"I can't." I tremble a little. "I don't know which way to go."

"Don't be afraid."

"It's not exactly fear. I'm smart. I'm not about to get off this thing if I don't know what I'll find under my feet."

"Hang on to me."

"Get off first."

He snickers and then somehow manages to turn. We're face to face. "How much fun would that be?"

"I meant . . ."

"I know what you meant." He holds my chin in one hand while crawling his fingers up my bare thigh.

I slap my hand over his wrist. "Don't."

"I was going to help you pull down your skirt." His eyes search mine.

"Oh." And I swallow, suck in a deep breath, and maybe even wish he'd had other ideas.

"You sound disappointed."

"You're teasing me."

"I don't tease, sweetheart."

Clearing my throat, I use his shoulder in hopes of leveraging my position so I can give him enough room to move freely.

"This is so beautiful," I say, very much aware that he's not making an effort to leave the seat.

"Best view in Atlanta." He's consuming me with his eyes, seemingly unconcerned with the city lights.

"I bet you say that to all the women."

"I've never brought one up here."

For some reason, I believe him, and that makes me feel very vulnerable.

"Well, maybe you should."

"I'll see how this goes and decide from there."

"How what goes?"

His gaze darkens, and he looks at me, his voice quieting. "This." His lips devour mine as his hands cradle my hips. He quickly lifts me to him, forcing me to part my legs and straddle him.

I'm undone. I wrap my hands around his neck. Wanton, aching, wanting him. This daredevil, the guy that does stunts for a living, my first stunt—the first risk I've ever taken in business and maybe even in life as well.

I'm shivering when I pull back, meeting his gaze. Dreading getting attached to him, knowing that it would be only too easy to get attached to his cool, fun attitude and charming, blunt personality.

"James, this isn't a good idea." I lick my lips, shaking my head.

"Let me change your mind, Elizabeth." He pulls me back slowly to him, then kisses me like he's probably kissed plenty of women but in a way that feels like he will never kiss another. His mouth trails to my cheek and up to my ear, down to my neck, and across the low dip of my neckline. He groans as he's tasting me. As if he's as undone as me.

I'm breathless, arching against him and wanting . . . needing . . . so much more than a kiss that could lead everywhere. If I don't stop him now, stop him with a kiss, a kiss that could lead . . . every . . . fucking . . . where . . .

I gasp, realizing I'm squeezing his thighs with mine, spread wider by the breadth of his body.

"That's it," he whispers on a hiss, rocking steadily against me.

My hands are in his hair. His fingers. Oh my lord, *yes*. His fingers climb higher and higher.

His thumb eases against my panties. He rubs the pad back and forth as he holds my head in the palm of his hand, kissing me until I can't breathe. I can't think.

I don't want to fucking think.

I just want to feel. *Need* to feel his hands and lips all over me.

He buries his mouth in my cleavage, rubbing his face against me as he works my shirt up and kisses my breasts, moaning then as he dips his finger under my panties and rubs my sex. He coaxes me with his kiss and compliments. Tells me how much he wants me, how much he wants to please me.

I drink in the pleasure. I drink it in because when his fingers drive inside me, I'm so fucking ready for him *and this*.

His fingers pump and stroke, in and out, back and forth.

I. Am. Dying. Here.

His hot breath is against my ear. "Let go, Lizzy. Let me watch you enjoy me."

My hands are on his shoulders. My head drops. My mouth opens.

It's all I can do to keep from coming, to stop myself from riding out the pleasure, that earth-shattering orgasm that I somehow manage to resist. But resistance is only a mere stepping-stone in the wrong direction because I'm still a short breath away from the most tantalizing and reckless pleasure that I've ever known.

When I scream out in pleasure, it's like the night awakens with the energy passing between us. Our shadows rock back and forth as he stays with me, holding me against him as he thrusts his hand against my body, bringing me pleasure and wreaking havoc on my brain.

This man could destroy everything I've ever worked for.

He could take my heart, walk all over my spirit, dampen my dreams, and yet all I can do now is ride out the pleasure, scream into the night, and enjoy this moment because while that's all it is . . . just a moment . . . it's the first time in my life that I've felt unabashedly free.

I'm gasping as I recover, my fingers clutching his shirt, his scent all over my nostrils. Even the scent of me, on his fingers, as he eases back and uses his thumb to tuck my hair behind my ear.

"You okay, Lizzy?" He's wearing the most gorgeous smile.

My vision is blurry.

Emotions overcoming me from the release of all my pent-up frustrations.

I nod. My windpipe feels a little funny. Closed and tight.

I see him shove his fingers into his mouth and lick me off him, still smiling, his blue eyes brilliant in the darkness. "You need to let me do that again very soon," he says, and I briskly turn my head away to silently stare at the city just to keep him from noticing the tears in my eyes.

I don't know what it is about this guy that affects me so much. Maybe it's because he's daring, unique, and not afraid to be himself. Or maybe because my whole life I've tried to be perfect and never really bought into the act. And yet when I'm with him, I don't feel like I have to play at anything at all. I can simply be me.

He makes me feel like Lizzy, young and carefree, the girl that doesn't need to be perfect . . . that is perfect just as she is.

James slips his arm around my waist and looks out at the city with me, and I set my cheek on his shoulder while I try to summon myself back from whatever parts of the universe he and his hot kisses and irresistible charms just scattered me.

And I whisper, "Very soon, Devil," in answer to the provocative proposal that he made just minutes ago, and turn to meet his devilish smile with one of my own.

♥ ♥ ♥

We get back to his house really late, when all the windows are dark. "Is Charlie home?" I ask.

He nods. "Maria's staying over in the guest bedroom."

That's my cue to drop him off and leave. I've overstayed my time with James, and now I'm just traveling farther and farther into dangerous territory.

Still, when he says, "Come in for a minute," I'm powerless to do anything but that.

When we creep inside, he goes down the hall and checks on Charlie. It makes my heart feel soft and warm to see the way he looks in on his little brother. "What?" he asks when he sees me staring.

I shake my head.

He takes me to the overstuffed couch in his living room, in front of a television covered in video game boxes. I sink down next to him and lower my head onto his shoulder.

"Charlie's a good kid," James says after a moment. "He just wants to be liked. He wants to be accepted. My aim is to get him into a better school. Give him a kick-ass education. Get him out of the slums."

I smile, my heart reaching out within my chest with greedy, grabby hands toward him. "You're raising a good kid, James."

"I think about that. All the time. What my parents would say." He presses his lips together. "Because when they were alive, this wasn't the way my life was headed. We lived in the suburbs. I was thinking of college but not too keen on that. Maybe military. But I was a kid. I had time to figure things out. Fuck up all I wanted. My dad kept saying that to me. 'You're young, kid. You'll get it all figured out.' And then we left for vacation one week, and it all changed."

"Car accident?" I ask gently.

He shakes his head. "My grandmother died that winter, and we were going to stay up at her old cottage on Lake Sinclair while we got it ready to sell. We were staying there, and Charlie was crying. My parents and Leanne—that's my sister; she was thirteen—were tired from the drive. I was a typical eighteen-year-old and didn't go to sleep until two in the morning most nights, so I took Charlie outside to play for a few hours and check out the area. He was barely going to turn four. When we got back, I tried to wake up my mom because I couldn't find Charlie's sippy cup in all the boxes we'd brought. But she wouldn't. Then I tried my dad. I thought they were just really tired. Leanne . . . I checked in on her, and she was sleeping too. It took me a while to realize it was carbon monoxide."

"My god, James."

"My family . . . we don't talk about the accident, Charlie and I. I don't even know if he really remembers what happened. It's been . . ." He scrunches his nose, his expression thoughtful. "Fuck. Almost a decade now? And we still don't talk about it. I realized soon into mourning as you wait for the pain to go away that it never fades away, that distance from what happened is the only way you can bear to go on. It's not that

I don't remember—it's that I try to leave the past in the past and look at what I have. Charlie. My business. Some good friends. Maria. Luke." He looks at me. "You."

The way Devil says *you* makes my whole body grip with longing.

"I'm sorry for what happened. You were young, still."

"I can't complain. Some people have it worse."

"Some could say that you can also view it like some have it better, and think of yourself as having it worse."

He laughs and shakes his head. "Now, baby, that's not a winning attitude. Is it?"

I laugh. "I know it's not, which is why you're so irresistible. Because of . . . you."

I pause, then push my chair back and head around the table. As if sensing my intentions, James pushes his chair back and makes room for me, seizing my hips and drawing me sideways on his lap. A nice little hard bulge greets my bottom as I sit. I walk my fingers up his chest, keeping my voice low so that Charlie doesn't overhear. "You're sort of . . . irresistible," I admit, stroking my fingers down his clean-shaven jaw.

He raises his hand and strokes his thumb down my cheek, the touch exquisitely tender, even though the gleam in his eyes is fierce.

"Want to spend the night here?" he asks quietly.

"Charlie . . ."

"Charlie's asleep." He grins wickedly. "Maria's probably binging on Netflix. And me . . . ?" A heavy silence before he starts to nod meaningfully. "I'm available. Very, very available for the likes of you, Miss Banks." His voice drops.

"James, I don't know . . . ," I hedge, my heart skipping.

"You do know, Lizzy. And if you don't, then *I* know. I know what you need. I think you need *these*." He slides two fingers into his mouth and pulls them out with a pop. Then he wiggles them, slowly giving me a roguish grin. "Inside you." The gleam in his eyes darkens as he looks into my eyes, then greedily surveys my mouth. "Three minutes with my fingers inside you and you'll be screaming for mercy, and you know what . . . ?"

He seizes my chin, holds my face still, and leans forward.

"I'll give you none." His lips smother mine—take mine, possess mine. My arms wind around his neck, and his hands are covering my whole ass, squeezing my cheeks as his mouth claims mine.

It takes every ounce of my power to pull away from him. "I can't, James. I shouldn't have let it go as far as it's gone. Tomorrow . . ."

"Tomorrow what?"

Tomorrow, everything will be different. Tomorrow, he won't be just mine. I look into his eyes, wanting him to calm my fears, but I can't tell him this.

"We just have a big day ahead of us," I say, and it takes every ounce of my resolve to untangle myself from the heaven of his arms and push myself to my feet. I grab my keys. "Good night, James. I'll see you tomorrow."

WEST COAST

Lizzy

It's the big day. The West Coast Fashion Week starts tonight, and James and I have seats together for the plane ride out to Los Angeles. I can't remember being this excited about a trip before.

James takes my handbag and shoves it into the compartment above our heads, then settles down next to me.

The air shifts in temperature, or maybe it's just me, warming because he's so close.

A whiff of the Tom Ford cologne I bought him reaches me. It's a struggle not to lean closer and take another, deeper whiff. It's my favorite cologne. But somehow, on *him*, it's even more sexy and seductive.

He buckles his seat belt, his shoulders bumping mine. James is wearing black slacks and a plain white button shirt. The top two buttons unbuttoned. He looks like a businessman—clean shaven and beautiful, fit and young—but it's those twinkling blue eyes and that dimpled smile that always get to me the most.

"What are you watching?" I ask him as he plays a video on his new phone.

He angles the screen in my direction. "Some stunt videos that I did that I never uploaded. Thinking of editing a few and loading them up, you know, once our contract is over."

He winks playfully.

Curiosity pricked, I feel myself smile and edge closer, curious. I watch the video with him.

James is wearing a wet suit on board a Jet Ski. I assume Charlie is on the shore, filming. When the camera zooms in on James, the view is fuzzy. James seems to say something, but he's too far away to hear clearly. Instead, I listen to Charlie's voice in the background.

"What?" Charlie's yelling at him.

James cups the side of his mouth, his deep voice carrying through the wind. "Don't get too close to the bank, or you'll fall on your face! You got a clear view?"

Charlie starts answering, but the camera shifts away in a jerk. We're suddenly staring at a view of the sky, and I hear Charlie curse in the background.

I start laughing when it hits me.

"He fell?" I ask James.

I can hear the motor of the Jet Ski coming closer and suddenly James's voice. "You okay, buddy? I'm supposed to make a fool of myself, not you, buddy. Come here." I hear shuffling as James helps Charlie to his feet; then James peers into the phone and taps the screen, blue eyes squinting. "Still working. Damn, Charlie, you—" He turns it off.

"I can only imagine all the adventures you guys have had."

I can't help but giggle.

Lifting my eyes to find James watching me intently. Has he been watching me all the time I was watching the video?

He's smiling to himself.

He reaches out to brush a strand of loose hair behind my ear, then drags his thumb down my jawline to brush fleetingly across my lower lip.

"I like it when you let your hair down," he husks.

We're taking off now, and I'm breathless under his touch.

"Literally? Or figuratively?"

"Both." We both seem to adjust to the plane taking to the air, and then James asks, "Want to see one where I ended up with a broken wrist?"

"God no!" I gasp. He's already searching through his videos.

"Let loose. Have some fun, Elizabeth."

"I *have* fun. *Safe* fun. You're crazy, James." I peer at the screen. I'm partly wanting to watch only because he seems to want to show me—and I'm partly dreading it.

I can't pretend that I don't love seeing videos that nobody but him and Charlie have seen.

I can't pretend that it's not crazy exciting that this guy fears nothing, won't hesitate to take a bet.

I'm not sure he even took these bets for the money.

James likes a challenge. And I wonder if he slowly works past every obstacle in his way and goes for what he wants—just like he went after me.

"I can't believe I'm saying this, but you looked handsome with that beard."

He's wearing shorts that display his muscular legs in the video. A soft-looking T-shirt with a *Skid Row* logo. His scruffy beard looking all manly and bearlike. His blue eyes twinkling wickedly.

James was dared to leap off the third floor of a building and into the pool.

"I can't watch." I'm breathless as I watch him head to the railing of a third-floor balcony.

"Jimmy . . ." Charlie sounds concerned. "I don't know if this is a good idea."

James grins at the camera. "Of course it's a good idea. A thousand dollars is always a good idea." He's climbing the balcony rail. But when he glances at Charlie, he loses his balance and slips onto the other side of the rail. His arm flies out. And he grabs onto the rail at an awkward angle. There's an odd snapping sound, and he slides off the ledge, and suddenly all hell breaks loose. Charlie runs to the ledge, yelling.

"JIMMY!"

Charlie peers over the balcony, where James is crashed among the bushes down by the side of the pool.

"Fuck. I just broke my damn wrist," he tells Charlie as he struggles to sit up, a shit ton of branches crunching beneath him.

"Least it's not your damn head!" Charlie sounds on the verge of tears when the video turns off.

I shake my head.

"What? No laughing?"

"Why would I laugh? That's not funny!" I cry.

"It was. Kind of funny. Admit it, Lizzy."

"No, it's not funny."

"The funny thing was that my doctor's bills were way more than a thousand dollars."

He chuckles softly, the sound rough and low, distracting. As is his big body, somehow pulling the space around him like a magnet. Including me.

Shouldn't you be bracing yourself, Lizzy?

He tucks his phone away. "Oh, come on. I'm all right now."

There's a hot ache, growing and growing inside me. There's concern there. Yearning. Need. *Caring.* "Something could have happened to you! Have you ever wondered what Charlie would do without you?"

James smiles down at me, his chest so close that its warmth teases and taunts me.

When he studies me for a moment and notices the concern on my face, his smile fades. His voice drops as he glances at my mouth. "But see . . . that's the thing. Nothing happens to me. Ever. Not anything that I can't recover from."

"James . . ." I shake my head, nervously licking my lips under his intent gaze. "Do you have survivor's guilt?" I ask.

I'm not smiling anymore.

"No. Survivor's anger, maybe. But the last thing I wanted to teach Charlie was to be too afraid to live. Shit happens. You don't survive this life. You live it. You take risks, and you show people who you are and what you stand for, and if they don't like it, fuck 'em. You make every day mean something. If you're just surviving, what the hell good is it?"

James

Lizzy's worried I'm a loose cannon. I'm not. I've had a healthy outlet for my anger. I've moved on. I'm good—and I'll be even better once Charlie feels good about himself and gets into a better school. But right now, all I want is for Elizabeth to relax and let her hair down. In every sense of the phrase.

Difficult, considering her suitcase hasn't shown up.

I've been hounding the baggage claim carousel for half an hour, and nothing's coming out. The rest of our flight companions have already left.

Lizzy's luggage is still a no-show.

"Until tomorrow?" Lizzy asks the attendant behind the airline counter.

"Yes, ma'am, we're sorry; it seems to have remained in Atlanta."

"I really need that suitcase." Lizzy rubs her temples, groaning.

After fifteen minutes rechecking, I give her the hotel address for them to send it when it arrives. "Thanks. We'll keep an eye out for it," I tell the attendant.

Lizzy groans as she lets me usher her away. "I don't know if I'll survive without my face creams. I have nothing to wear, and I have a dinner scheduled with some really big clients."

"We'll figure it out."

I know this shit is important to Lizzy.

But I have an idea.

And I hate wasting time.

I lead her to the hotel chauffeur who stands with a sign that reads **BANKS** and motion at him to lead us to the car.

She's calmer by the time we arrive at the hotel.

"Checking in. Elizabeth Banks."

I glance around the hotel's sumptuous lobby and resist the urge to whistle.

"Ahh, yes, Miss Banks, welcome back. We have you for two rooms—"

I reach out and lean on the counter. "One."

The girl glances up in surprise, then shoots Lizzy a smile. "One?"

Elizabeth remains rooted to the spot, a gorgeous blush up her cheeks. "Two," she says, nudging me.

I shrug at the girl. "Two." I look at Lizzy. "Connecting?"

She concedes. "Fine. Connecting."

"We've upgraded you to one of our junior suites, Miss Banks. A king bed with a parlor and the second king bedroom connecting. Enjoy your stay."

"Thanks." Lizzy nervously tucks her credit card away.

"I'll try my best." I wink at the lady and scoop up my key, leading Elizabeth across the lobby to the elevators.

Connecting rooms.

Fuck yeah.

"JIMMY!"

I turn to spot a lanky red-haired guy dressed in yesterday's suit.

"Jimmy Rowan. From YouTube? Damn, I thought that was you! I almost didn't recognize you without the beard. What's up, bro? I'm starwars601—I comment on your posts all the time. You're fucking sick, bro!"

I look at Lizzy and suck in a breath.

"I'm sorry," I say, lifting my chin in the air as pompously as I can manage. "I have no idea who you're talking about. Have a good night."

I adjust the collar on my suit jacket, offer Lizzy my elbow, and walk away with her on my arm, saying loudly, "What is this YouTube thing people are talking about?"

Lizzy shakes her head and giggles.

DINNER

Lizzy

I hear a knock on the connecting door of my room as I'm standing in a towel, looking at the travel clothes I just set out on the bed.

I suppose I can wear my leggings and tunic to dinner if I wear my hair nice. But ugh. I hate how travel clothes seem to suck up the smell of airplanes. It's just not ideal, and I'm stressing like crazy. Presentation is everything in my line of business. I dread that my buyers will think that I'm not taking their time seriously. I'll just have to explain what happened.

That's when I open the door and see James, standing there in his travel clothes. "You going to shower?"

"In a minute. I was down in the lobby. Got you something." He sets a bag down on the bed. Fishes out a toothbrush and toothpaste.

"Thank you."

"And this." He pulls out two things he seemed to be holding behind his back. One is a shoebox, the other a long garment bag. He sets down the box and unzips the garment bag. And James holds a perfectly gorgeous ivory-colored dress.

"Oh my god! Where did you find this?" My eyes widen as I register the satisfied male look on his face as he then flips open the lid of the shoebox to reveal the most gorgeous strappy nude heels I've ever seen. "James . . ." I'm breathless all of a sudden. Truly touched by the gesture. "James. Let me pay you back."

"No." He sets the hanger down and tugs at my towel.

"Yes."

"No." More sternly now.

"I'm your boss, Rowan," I protest while he's too busy pulling my arms up and sliding the dress over my head, then down my body in a delicious silken cascade.

"I didn't get it for my boss," he whispers in my ear. I shiver as he drops a kiss on the back of it, then zips me up, his fingers lingering on my back for a heart-stopping moment. "I got it for my girl."

I swallow. My heart skipping helplessly in my chest as he steps before me. He always seems to look taller when he's this close. More and more tempting the more I get to know him. "Now let's have a look at you."

It's hard to get the words out. Because I'm continually amazed by this guy. In so many ways I've lost count.

I look down at myself.

I feel heavenly. Feel like a princess. Like someone who's getting spoiled in the very best way.

"Thank you," I breathe, impulsively leaning up on my toes and pressing a kiss to his lips. James grabs me by the back of the neck and tilts my head just so . . . so he can kiss me a little more. Then he pushes me back a fraction and studies me almost as thoroughly as I do when he's wearing our Banks suits.

"Stunning," he says as verdict.

Another little leap in my heart.

I shake off the daze and beam up at him before I grab his shoulders and usher him to the closet where he hung all his things. "Your turn. We can't be late. Make me look good tonight, Rowan."

"Always, heiress."

I brought the perfect suits for James for tonight's dinner. It's the first time we're out in public, with several of our big buyers. The rest of the next week will be just as full of meetings, but this is it.

This can make or break the way the rest of the trip will go.

After tonight, he will belong to the world.

I don't even have to be nervous that they won't accept him. I know they will. I have polished my diamond perfectly.

What am I nervous about? I can't quite describe it, but it's gnawing inside me and making my skin crawl.

I'm pacing in the suite when James steps out with his hair slicked back, the fit of the suit perfect on his athletic body. My breath catches.

My eyes hurt.

In that suit?

James is David Beckham in a suit at the royal wedding.

I'm speechless.

He's beautiful, and though I should feel some pride in playing a part in bringing out this man's beauty, all I can feel is a knot in my stomach. A knot I can't quite seem to loosen, no matter how much I try.

It's starting to hurt to look at him.

Ignoring the sudden weakness in my knees, I step out of the room. He follows me, his tall frame sort of making me feel shorter than I should feel.

What's going on?

I can't think when he's near, and I can't even bear to think what it will feel like when this is over and he's gone.

"I don't know if I can do this monkey shit for a whole evening, let alone weeks on end." He tugs on his tie, already restless and feeling caged in.

I bite back my smile and grab my bag before we step out and ride down the elevator. "Don't say *shit*. Say, 'I don't know if I could get through this ordeal . . .'"

He pulls me close. "I don't know if I could get through this ordeal. I need incentives. Give me some gas."

Before I can even think of what he means, he's already fueling himself. With my mouth.

When we peel away, his eyes are heavy. As heavy as mine feel. "Better."

My voice is barely audible through our breaths. "We need to leave."

"Give me a minute. I just need to cool down." He exhales, his nostrils flaring as his gaze connects with my own.

He eases back for a long moment, gives my mouth a hot look, makes me wet between the legs, and takes my hand as we step out of the elevator.

The restaurant is only two blocks away, so we walk there. I know there's a risk I could see someone I know who might tell my father his daughter is out and about holding hands with some gorgeous man. But at this point? I'm in Los Angeles courting buyers. My father's in China. LB is in Atlanta. The breeze is delicious. The scenery perfect. I'm too far away from all of that to care right now.

"Are you nervous?"

He laughs deeply, sexily. He leans close to my ear. "I just want to get through the night so I can get to the part where I can kiss that smirk of yours to pieces."

I can't just pretend the thought didn't make my heart and every cell in my body skip.

We're on our way to Nobu Malibu—a place frequented by Hollywood's elite and the perfect venue for our first dinner with some of our potential buyers.

The restaurant sits on Malibu beach with the Pacific Ocean stretching out in front of it, the last rays of the setting sun painting millions of diamonds upon its glassy surface. We're meeting with representatives from some of the biggest stores in the US, including Barneys New York, Bergdorf Goodman, Neiman Marcus, and also representatives from luxury online stores such as Net-a-Porter. I plan to have our new line available everywhere to maximize sales and exposure.

As James and I step into the lobby, we're greeted by a tall thin man with perfectly manicured eyebrows and colored hair, who promptly walks us to a round table by the porch, right next to the railing overlooking the ocean.

The breeze catches my hair, and I finally feel myself exhale. The smell of blue ocean and warm sand intoxicates my senses. I catch a glance of us in a wall of windows, and my confidence surges. Damn, he looks fine. "You know how to make an entrance, James."

He smiles and murmurs, "If I was making an entrance, I'd be scaling the side of the wall like Spider-Man. Or maybe skydiving in."

"Not tonight. Do you always see potential stunts in every place you go?"

"Doesn't everyone?"

I laugh and shake my head. "All I see are potential disasters."

And oh, I definitely see potential disaster here. But not for James. James, I think, can do anything. Me? I'm not so sure. I've spent so long grooming him that it'd be ironic if I couldn't pull this off myself.

James pulls out my chair and winks. I walk in front of him, and right before I sit down on the chair he's holding out for me, I feel him plant a discreet but delicious kiss on the side of my exposed neck. "Don't be nervous, beautiful; we got this," he whispers before taking his seat next to mine.

I get goose bumps.

Then, I start to see the buyers float in and fill the remaining seats. I introduce James to all of the buyers.

"Nice to meet you. James Rowan," he says as he greets each of them.

I watch him take charge, completely awed by him.

He's got this to the point that everyone at the table can't tear their delighted gazes away from him.

After some small talk about their flights, the city, and the delicious food we're about to have, we get down to business.

"When I first came up with the idea for the line, I had a very clear vision for what I wanted it to be. I wanted it to be a line made for the young businessman: sleek, modern, elegant, masculine, but still playful and youthful. All of our suits are made to stand strongly as individuals. Even the most streamlined and basic suits have beautiful accents and fabrics that elevate the look and turn the traditional black suit into a statement piece."

The buyers all continue listening intently, sipping on the champagne I ordered for the table before they arrived.

"Which brings me to James." I turn to him and smile, my heart fluttering.

"From the moment I met him, I knew I had found the face of my line. He embodies all the line represents and strives to be. I thank you all for coming tonight, and I look forward to you all getting to know him, because he truly is the heart and soul of this line—in human form."

James winks at me and then says, "I would say I'm flattered, but the lady knows her stuff."

The buyers laugh and raise their glasses. Anthony from Net-a-Porter toasts, "To beautiful men in beautiful suits!"

We all drink, and then the questions start pouring.

First from Anthony. "So, James, what do you think makes the perfect suit? And do these Banks suits fit the bill?"

"Three things come to mind, Anthony," James begins and raises his hand, counting off with his fingers.

"One, the cut. Two, the fabrics. And three, the fit. All of the suits from this line are different and unique in their styles. One thing they have in common, though, is a flattering masculine cut. Second, they are also made with the finest fabrics; they look mattified but with the perfect amount of shine, so when you see a man walk down the street, you will know when he's wearing a Banks. And, of course, fit: you can have a ten-thousand-dollar suit, but if the pants are too long and the jacket is more like a corset, it will look cheap. Banks suits are made to be fitted perfectly to the body, and alterations are encouraged—customers get free fittings whenever they decide to buy one of our suits because we understand how important it is to have a perfectly tailored suit: the goal is to make it look like you were practically BORN wearing a Banks suit."

Anthony raises his brow and turns to me. "Wherever did you find this man, and where can I get more?!"

I laugh.

Melissa from Bergdorf then asks James, "Tell us three of your favorite cities, and match them to a Banks suit."

"Oh, that's a good one . . ." James thinks a moment and then says, "I'll go for the classics: New York, Los Angeles, and, of course, Atlanta.

"New York is fast paced, cutting edge, and ruthless. I would go with one of Banks's darker suits, especially the onyx black with satin side stripes. Paired with a patterned gray tie, it's high end, elegant, lethal, and fierce. Perfect for New York streets.

"On the other hand, Los Angeles is more laid back, beachy, so I would go for one of our white linen suits, with a blue tie. It's perfect for a business meeting, afternoon walk down Rodeo Drive, and then a walk on the beach.

"And last but not least, Atlanta. I would go for a navy suit, with a cool patterned tie and a pocket square. Straight to the point, classy, and masculine."

At this point I'm so blown away I am speechless. He's answering every curveball with a home run.

Melissa is also pleased.

Robert, the buyer for Barneys, who has been rather silent until now, says to me, "My dear, you not only have a face for your line—you got yourself a superstar. I'm in. Send us your catalog."

The rest of the buyers follow suit, agreeing wholeheartedly that James is more than just a pretty face and that his charisma will make the brand a huge hit.

The dinner continues on with more questions and banter. I couldn't be prouder. Seeing James so comfortable and witty, laid back, stunningly handsome, and gentlemanly does shit to me.

This man is so much more than I could have ever imagined.

After dinner, I'm so giddy with delight after witnessing how thrilled our buyers are that I don't want to head to the hotel yet. So we take an Uber to one of the closest LA beaches, and we walk. James with his hands tucked into his slacks pockets. Me with my shoes in my hand and my toes curling into the sand as I take each step.

"Have you ever gone out to a beach without a stunt as a goal? Just for pure . . . I don't know. Enjoyment?" I ask.

"Never."

"Me either." I grin, my stomach fluttering when his white smile flashes out at me in the dark.

There's a breeze. A beautiful crescent moon.

And James Rowan. His jacket slung behind his shoulder. His pants rolled up to his knees. Shoes in the pockets of his jacket.

"You sold them tonight, James. I can't even say I'm proud of you . . . because it was your charisma that slayed them. Not only your beauty, which of course is all my doing," I tease.

"Of course. I'm a bear in my natural form."

"Ha," I laugh exaggeratedly, wishing I didn't have my shoes in my hands so I could have some sort of contact with him. "Maybe now that I've bred you for my world, you can breed me for yours."

James only looks at me, his gaze growing a little more intense.

God. Did I just blurt that out? Did I sound like I longed to be part of it?

I shake my head and laugh at myself, then shoot him a curious glance. "Are you up for a tamer sort of stunt?"

He almost chokes on his saliva. "Say what?"

I stop walking. "You heard me. Are you up for a little game with me?"

He steps closer, his gaze challenging. "I'm game."

"Whoever builds the biggest sandcastle in the least amount of time gives the other whatever they want."

James reaches out to take my shoes. He sets them aside and drops his jacket to free his hands and frame my face. His voice is gruff and rough as he inspects me. "You're on."

He fishes out his phone, turns on the camera, aims it at us, and motions. "On the count of three. One . . . two . . ."

"Three!" I dive down and start digging a huge pile of sand.

James is down on all fours, carving even faster than I am.

I'm getting dirty and laughing as I scoop up piles and piles of sand, digging myself a cute little moat.

I try not to see what he's doing.

But it's hard. I steal a peek, and James already has a huge-ass peak of sand on his side.

"What?"

"Done." He leaps to his feet and dusts off his hands.

"No fair. Yours isn't even a castle. It's like a . . . it's ugly, James Rowan!"

"We said who built the biggest castle. NOT the finest."

He laughs as he settles down next to me, legs stretched out, one of his arms behind me.

"Fine." I glance at the camera. It's still filming. I almost dread asking now. "You get one desire granted."

"Just one?" His brows fly upward.

I nod cheekily.

Wondering what hell or weird dare he'll ask me to do. Go skinny-dipping. Embarrass myself in front of his viewers.

I get nervous as I wait but persist. "Name it. I'll ace it."

He chuckles. While I lift my gaze to his, I realize he's looking down at me intently.

His hand comes up to cup one of my cheeks. Warm. So big half of my face feels engulfed.

"Lizzy Banks . . ." He leans closer to whisper in my ear. "Always craving perfection. You can't help it, can you? You think once you achieve it, you will be loved by one and all, even your father. And it makes you frustrated, shocks you to the core, because you also can't help . . . wanting me . . . even when you know I'm far, far from perfect . . . still. Not quite perfect enough for the likes of you."

I start to shake my head. Because that is not true. That is totally not true. True, I have high standards for myself, and for this project. But I've never really wanted to touch or change any part of him that makes him *him* because he's totally irresistible and . . .

God.

Oh god ohgod ohgod. I'm *falling*. I can't even fight it. I don't even know if I want to fight it. All I know is that I keep wondering about him, this, us. I keep watching him work. Keep discovering more treasures about him to love, admire, respect, want. Tonight he amazed me, excited me. Before I can speak and tell him so, he's easing back to look at me again. "You do things to me."

My heart is pounding. "You do more things to me," I breathe. The beach, usually superpopulated by day, feels desolate. It's like the night is ours. Like the world is ours. Like we're a team, unstoppable. Meant to be.

It's perfect. Tonight. *HIM.*

"So . . . what is it that you'll . . . want me to do?" I hesitantly ask.

"Nothing. Just be here. Right here. And do this." He leans down, and I tilt my head a little upward. He teases my lips apart with his own.

Then we're kissing.

We're feverish as we taste each other, savor one another.

I have to peel away with effort, panting out as I tug on his shirt, "You. In me. Hotel."

He doesn't immediately strip, merely studies my lips with hooded eyes, his eyelids heavy, his pupils so blown up his eyes are nearly black.

My throat feels swollen and thick.

What was I thinking? That I could create a human being, as if it were art . . . and I could remain unmoved, unaffected by it. Unchanged by it.

I thought I wouldn't become affected by it, touched by it, changed by it. By him.

How wrong I was.

Every part of this man has touched my life. Every part of him that I've touched has touched me back, and the parts that I had nothing to do with have outright shone on their own. Near blinded me. There is *so* much to him to admire.

I see him now and can't hide my admiration. I don't know if I'd have been able to stand three months of feeling imperfect—perfection has been ingrained in me. As if anything less is bad. But when I'm with him I want to shed that skin and just be me, the girl who tries to be perfect but never really buys into being all that. The girl who just wants to be happy, succeed in life, have her father's love, joke around, and yes, even fall deeply and madly in love with the guy who will make her feel happy. Complement her perfectly.

My eyes water as I stare at the face of that guy—the one that has awakened all those feelings in me. The one I've been falling for since he was dirty, crass, bearded bar brawler Jimmy. Only to get rid of the static and outward differences to meet the man within—and to be swept off my feet and stumped by what I've found.

I've never met a human being that made me feel as alive—as perfect, even with my flaws . . . as seen . . . as happy . . . as free—as him.

♥ ♥ ♥

We go back to the hotel. I shakily pull out my key card and hand it over, and he swipes it in the elevator and pushes the button to our floor.

The doors seal shut. And James looks at me again. His lips a bit shiny around his mouth—from my kisses.

His eyes heavy lidded as he runs them up and down my body.

Anticipation bubbles in my veins as he takes my fingers in his when the doors ping and leads me out.

He uses my key to let us into my room. As soon as the door shuts, he leans me back against it and growls as he sweeps down to push my lips apart again. I part my mouth, groaning when he gives me a toe-curling, soul-crushing kiss that has me liquid against him.

His tongue is hot and wet on mine, and when he groans, the sound pulses through me. Causing another wave of desire to ricochet through my body. He's so sexy I can barely stand it.

My legs feel gooey as I grab his hand and lead him to the bedroom and pause as soon as we're inside; I'm starting to undress him when he stops me.

"Elizabeth." He shakes his finger at the window. "Out there, you're the boss. In here, I make the rules."

My heart skips a lustful little kick, but I protest out of conviction. "That's not fair."

He slowly lowers the zipper and lets my dress puddle on the floor.

"I'm not playing fair with you." His eyes darken, those blue devil's eyes drinking me in, in my naked state, darkening by the second. Darkening as his voice drops lower and lower, gruffer and gruffer. "Not now. Not a month from now."

A month . . .

I can't help but wonder if the timeline is deliberate. He said a month. As if he means to keep me bound to him until we aren't working together anymore.

I refuse to think about letting go when I haven't really had him in the first place.

"I feel you shutting down on me, and that can't happen. Not with us."

His fingers weave through my hair. I hold my breath as he ducks to my neck, and his lips channel more magic than a wizard's spell. There's probably nothing I wouldn't do to finish out the night with James Rowan fucking me, taking me to new places, as he gives me the ride of my life.

He holds me by the back of my head, pinning me in place as he drags his lips up my chin and toward . . . god, yes.

Another burning kiss turns my knees to mush. I want him inside me, so desperately I might ask him to skip this whole thing. But I'm having too much fun for that—not that sex isn't fun, but this body-to-body grind?

THIS is foreplay, and by god, I want to enjoy it.

His hands fall to my hips, and he looks down at his stretching cock, blatantly visible through the open zipper, teasing me with the heat of his arousal, teasing himself with the heat of mine.

"I'm on the pill," I blurt, perhaps ruining the moment.

"No worries. I'm not going to need to run out for a condom tonight." He pulls a strand from his slacks pocket.

I whistle. Impressed. "Somebody was confident."

"Hopeful." He drops them to the ground and grabs me closer, then lowers his head and kisses me until I see stars, his mouth working me over like the only thing that matters is showering me with complete adoration, and if this is adoration? I can't wait to see him when he's full-on committed to the cause.

God, just the thought makes me clutch all over.

I can practically feel my freedom slipping away. In some ways, we've been dancing long before this night. Dancing around the issue of him and me. Our differences . . . and our insane pull toward each other.

If we sleep together . . . when we sleep together . . . everything will change. I should be running scared.

As much as I'd like to take a few minutes to figure out how I feel about that, I can't.

His attention to detail as he kisses and laps at me is like a sexual awakening, a movement that's all about the experience, hunger, need.

I want him.

I can't resist him. I won't.

I want everything that I see in his eyes.

James

I kiss her, devour her mouth like it's my last taste.

I'm in too deep, but there's no turning back now.

Her body against mine is ruining me for all other women. The way she moves against me, the way her kiss melts my heart.

I can't help myself.

There's no help for a man like me with a woman like this.

There's just Lizzy and me. Us.

And that's scary as fuck.

"Are you sure?" I ask as she leads me to the bedroom.

Since when have I asked a woman if she's sure, and when have I ever cared? I always felt like if things were moving along at a good pace, then a woman would stop me if she changed her mind.

And I sure don't want THIS woman to change her mind, and yet I ask?

"I want you to be sure."

And ask again?

What the fuck, fucker!

She nods, and I won't say another word. I want to enjoy this moment, this sweet and fucking hot-as-hell moment.

The moonlight peeking through the sheer curtains provides a perfect view of her. I drag her closer. Watching her chest move quickly up and down as she throws herself at me and I catch her in the air, boost her by the ass to my mouth. Her lips meet mine, and she guides the kiss, her mouth parting for my tongue as her sexy little body rocks against mine.

"Promise me you won't treat me like I'm fragile," she begs me.

Fuck me, my brain is spinning a thousand miles an hour. I want to make love to her and fuck her at the same time. I want her to scream so loud everyone in this building knows she's mine.

I scoop her up closer and carry her to her bed. "You're not fragile, sweetheart. You're rare, and that makes you pure gold."

I lay her down and then straighten back and strip, aware of her greedy little eyes taking me in.

Caressing every single one of my muscles. I smirk down at her, feeling fucking high as I lean over her, not getting enough of her mouth.

I run my hands up her abdomen, cupping her breasts.

Her hands cup my face, and I have no words. I'm dying here, dying to taste her, dying to feel her trembling beneath me.

Lizzy shivers more when I pull off her top and drag the tip of my tongue across her nipple. Slow, licking in circles. I love how she arches, how she's ready for me, wanting me, waiting for me to thrust inside her, take her. Ravage her.

Savagely fuck her.

I suck her nipple, rolling my tongue against her soft flesh as I roll her thong down to her ankles. Flinging it away, I move between her legs and ease a finger inside her, loving the way her quivering walls close around my finger as she lets me take her a little bit at a time.

I'm dying here, dying because I've never moved at such a slow and easy pace but also dying because if I rush this now, I'll fucking lose it.

And I can't. Lose it.

Not yet. Not now.

Not when I'm right where I've wanted to be since the first day we met.

One of my hands pulls up one of hers, keeping her partly thrashing as I finger her again, finger her and lap at her lovely tits.

I ease back to jerk off my undershirt, then my slacks and boxers; then I crawl back over her, wanting her hands on me.

"James." She blinks up at me as if she's seeing all of me for the first time. And I'm so fucking sunk. I admire the pure look of flushed satisfaction, that marked look of insatiable pleasure washing across her flawless face.

By this time, I'd already be fucking for the finish, getting in, fucking long and hard, and getting out. Going home.

Except now I want it slow.

So I sheathe myself and grab her hips, take her lips, and ease in . . . slow.

Slow, focusing on slowing down the roll of hips, the rocking of bodies. I want to feel this energy we have, feel the way we connect and latch on to that.

She gasps and rocks faster, wanting me to go harder and quicker. But I won't.

"Shh," I quiet her, lifting both her hands now and pinning them beneath mine.

We're palm to palm, body to body, locked in this eye-opening moment, a moment that suggests maybe, just maybe, a woman like Lizzy could fall for a guy like me. Not the perfect man she's making, the one that she'll soon show off to the world, but just me, the YouTube guy, the guy who has something intriguing enough to catch her eye just like she caught mine.

I need her to fall FOR ME.

I need her to know that she's mine.

Her hands slip free, and she grabs at my hips and pushes me down harder, showing me how she likes to fuck.

That turns me on.

That hits home. Cranks me right the fuck up.

She drives me so fucking crazy.

"Like this?" *Feed that rhythm.* "Or this?" *Slow that grind.*

"There," she rasps. "Right fucking there."

I'm hard as hell as I stroke her.

Fuck her.

Claim. Her.

I want to stay right here, right like this, until she comes and I come. I want . . .

. . . it all.

"Tell me what you love, gorgeous. Right there." I splay my fingers against her back and pull her up, closer to me. "Here?"

She nods vigorously.

Go slow, Jimmy. Take it fucking slow.

And I try.

God knows I try.

But this little vixen throws her hips against mine and begs me to fuck her. Begs me to give it to her.

I'm living the ever-loving fucking dream.

"Harder." She moans and licks my lips. "Fuck me crazy."

And I do. I go at her like I've never loved on another, burying myself so deep for so long that I'm just part of her now.

So fucking lost I'm soon doing mathematics in my goddamn head just to keep from coming.

'Cause I want it to last.

Last and last and fucking *last*.

I want her to be willing to go on and on. More of her sweet cunt around me. More of her moans. More of her.

She gives as good as I do, and before I know it, I can't help myself. I can't stop. I won't stop.

1,345 minus 204?

769 plus 69 plus another 69 plus . . .

Fuck me, this girl's got me riled in the best ways.

She comes with a soft cry, and her walls squeeze around me. I clench her body to mine as the milking motions of her pussy make me groan. I drive my dick as deep as I can go and yell as I come with her, shooting off several times, increasing my tempo to prolong the pleasure.

When we finally fall against the sheets, entirely spent, I wonder what the hell just happened.

I tip her nose with a quick kiss. "I've always heard that you have to watch the quiet ones," I tease her.

"Probably," she croons, smiling up at me.

I watch her for a minute, liking that she isn't hiding from me. The soft white sheet is folded under her breasts, and I want to touch her again, just touch and kiss her, give her the kind of pleasure that she'll never forget.

"Oh, and I BET you like the quiet ones, right?"

"Right now? No. I don't want quiet, Lizzy. I want you to scream *Jimmy*, over and over and over again."

"James," she moans.

"That'll fucking do."

JAMES ROWAN

Lizzy

I slept with him.

I slept with James Rowan.

My creation, perfect-man-in-progress. My manbabe, like Jeanine would say.

And *my*, is he a manbabe.

I glance around my rumpled bed, reaching out in want to trace the muscles on his back with my fingertips. I glance at the time and stop myself before making contact. Nope. No time for that.

"James," I say, nudging his thick shoulder.

He groans and grabs my hand, stilling it at his side.

I squeeze his fingers. "Jimmy," I coax in his ear, forcing myself to my feet and opening the curtains.

James groans in bed. "Did you just call me Jimmy?" He lifts his head, turning to blink at me in confusion.

"No," I lie.

He's like a beast awakening from slumber.

My beast, I think before I can stop myself.

I run my eyes along his back.

Wait.

Are those red streaks catlike scratches?

Did I do that?

Me? Elizabeth Banks?

James flops to his back and drags his arm to shield his eyes. "What time is it?" His voice is groggy with sleep. It's . . . sexy.

A strand of dark hair falls across one eye.

His arms ripple as he sits up halfway on the bed, his neck propped on a bunched-up pillow.

I walk over and try not to notice all those inches of sexed-up beef-cake in my bed as I reach out to brush the hair out of his face. Ignoring the skip in my heart, I sternly say, "Time to wake up. We need to go. We have a lunch with an important client."

He smiles at me and slowly reels me into bed, on top of him.

I'm sunk.

God, I'm so done for.

I'm creating this perfect man, this man who has easily stepped right into his role at Banks LTD, and suddenly I don't know what to do with him.

He shows me a new side of himself when I least expect it and somehow manages to make me feel like he's just a man and I'm just a woman, but together we're so much more.

As he caresses my cheek and stares into my eyes, I watch the twinkling lights in his eyes. He's so gorgeous—I'm breathless. Everyone at Banks LTD loves James. They've bought the act. No one would believe that I found this guy in a bar fight.

But the thought makes a knot of fear curl in my stomach. Because what if Dad ever finds out things are not quite what I've made them out to be?

"What are you thinking?" He tilts my face up to his.

"How can I think at all after last night?" I tease.

"Good answer." He kisses my forehead and whispers. "Let's get you fed and ready."

I'm beaming as my luggage arrives, and we leave the room a little later. I'm beaming because I'm happy, because I don't remember ever being this happy, but also because I never thought sex could be like last night with Devil.

He makes me feel protected and precious, yet strong and independent. I wonder how he does it and makes it seem so effortless as I let him hold my hand in his grip.

That's when it hits me. It's easy because when I'm with him? I can be me.

♥ ♥ ♥

At lunch, he exudes the same charm as we meet the buyers for Dray's, a famous department store from Florida with over twenty stores across the continent.

"James Rowan," James immediately greets the group of buyers as we introduce ourselves across the table.

"Wow," one of the women tells me breathlessly as she invites me to the seat next to hers. "We saw the ad on GQ dot com. He's a bona fide god. We're fans already. We're in."

I smile, thrilled that it's up already. I watch her click on an image on the screen of her phone, where a huge ad of James on the *GQ* home page appears.

She turns the screen to him, and I see his eyes widen momentarily before he shields his gaze with a cool smile and leans back in his chair, all poised and collected as if he's not one bit surprised his face is that big, that *live*, on an online site.

"I'll send you the PDF of the catalog," I tell her, back to business.

She motions to James then, her hand sweeping in the air from the top of his perfectly combed hair to the tips of his perfectly polished leather shoes. "We want what he's wearing. Not just what he's wearing— we want it all," she laughs, then winks at him. "Right down to the socks."

He plays along and winks back.

I shoot him a scowl, and he smiles a look at me that says, *You want me to play along or not?*

Afterward, I'm so happy I think I might die.

"We got an order for five thousand pieces!" I leap on him, kiss his jaw. "You're slaying, James."

"She wanted my dick. I just made her think if she ordered a few pieces she might get it."

"Stop it," I laugh, and he raises my chin.

"We got anything tonight?"

"Of course we do. We're booked solid until the last night."

"Well, save that night."

"Why?"

"Thought I'd take you out on that date."

He leads me, and I am confused as to what he's talking about. "You've already got me where you want me. You don't need to do any-thing special."

"Oh, lady, there's a long way to go to having you where I want you."

"What do you mean?"

"Only that when we get to that last night, you're mine for the evening. The *whole* evening."

OUT

I'm standing in front of the mirror, applying lipstick and having a conference call with my father, who never made it to Los Angeles after all.

Which is actually a *very* good thing, considering that though the meetings have been amazing, I don't think he'd be too happy with what's been going on *after* those meetings.

"The press has been positive," I say. "Did you see the piece in the *Times*? They said James Rowan is America's answer to James Bond."

"Hmm," he says. "LB says he never actually met James in person."

I frown. "Well, we just ran out of time. But the proof is in the pudding, Dad. We've gotten great response so far."

"Yes. I'm encouraged," he says.

Encouraged? That's . . . positive. No, he didn't say "good job," or that he was impressed, but this is good! I suppose that's the most I can hope for from my dad.

"Thanks," I say, my whole body prickling with goose bumps.

I end the call and set my phone down. It's the last night of West Coast Fashion Week. Everything has gone amazing. Orders have been steadily pouring in. This is probably the most successful launch Banks has ever had.

But that's not what's got me excited.

What's got me excited? I'm going out on a date with James.

This isn't a big deal, really.

And yet why am I locked in the bathroom?

Staring at myself for the dozenth time?

Checking to see that not a single hair has escaped my updo?

That the dress—a simple, curve-hugging, navy-blue number—still hugs my body attractively like it did three seconds ago?

I reach for the glass of wine that I poured before stepping into the shower and take a long gulp before looking at myself again.

There's a knock, and I jerk at the sound.

"You okay in there?"

It's James. He sounds amused and just a tiny bit confused.

"Yes, I'm coming."

Oh yeah, you've got that right . . . I think to myself.

Inhaling a deep breath, I step outside. And spot James standing there, just two feet away. In black slacks and an electric-blue shirt that brings out the bluest blue in his eyes. His hair freshly showered, standing up attractively atop his head. Perfectly shaven. His thick, kissable lips shaping the most delicious smile as his eyes rake me, top to bottom, several times.

"You're fucking gorgeous."

My heart does a little happy dance.

I think my choice of dress was spot on.

"Thank you. You clean up nice yourself."

I offer him my arm, and he tucks it into the crook of his as he leads me toward the balcony. "Where are we going?" I ask, still trying to catch my breath from my excitement.

"You'll see."

I suddenly have a feeling I might end up getting drunk tonight. Even without alcohol. Because the thing is . . . being with James? I get drunk on him.

He opens the door, and there is a beautiful candlelit dinner for two. For just me and James. There is a light wind blowing off the ocean, the sun is setting, and I've never seen anything more romantic. "I thought you wanted to take me out?"

"No," he says. "We've been out enough this week. Tonight, I want you all to myself."

I couldn't have wanted anything more.

♥ ♥ ♥

We eat in a leisurely way, talking about our successes of the week, our legs tangled under the table.

When we are done, he stands up so fast that the chair rattles behind him. Then he walks us into his room, holds me in only one arm as he shuts the door as quietly as he can, and then stumbles us frantically to the bed, where he drops me and strips me in about three beats of my frantic, eager little heart.

He's got me naked, and he is still in his slacks, looking down at me.

He spreads my legs open and up over his shoulders, bracing me against the wall as he buries his head between my thighs. I gasp. My fingers wildly clutching fistfuls of his hair. I want to pull him closer, but at the same time I can barely take the excruciating pleasure of those deep, wet flicks of his tongue. I thrust my hips up and fist his hair so hard that I'm afraid I'm hurting him. But I can't be hurting him, or if I am, he's not aware of it. Because he's groaning between my thighs, only driving his tongue in for a deeper taste. A better taste. A taste of . . . me.

I push him back on the bed. He falls on it, but not before he clutches my hips and brings me down with him.

"Ride me," he says.

I'm straddling him, leaning down, my hair falling like a curtain down the sides of my face as I drop my head—taking from his hot, wicked, and delicious lips again. He palms my ass, squeezes and massages it as he slithers out his tongue to give me a kiss to remember. A kiss for all kisses. THE kiss of kisses.

He shoves his fingers up the back of my legs and works them along the fissure, caressing my ass cheeks with nothing separating us. When he slides his index finger into the fissure of my cheeks and drags it up and down my clit, I jerk with a gasp and arch back with a soft moan. "Oh god."

I love it. I CAN'T control myself. "You make me lose it," I gasp.

He rolls me to my back and pulls one of my legs, draping it around his shoulders. "You haven't lost it enough."

"What do you mean?"

"You've yet to come all over me," he says, pushing me down and thrusting in without a condom, eyes flashing with desire as he watches me take every thrust and meet him with a thirsty roll of my hips.

"We ran out of condoms." I pout, which is a feat in itself.

"I'll pull out—I'm safe. Do you trust me?"

We stop for a moment, our breaths coming in gusts. I hold his gaze and feel myself nod. "Yes," I gasp.

He pulls my hair back to expose my neck and give it a thousand and one fierce licks.

He groans as if he likes my taste. I clutch his hair and count my lucky stars that I'm on the pill. I can't stop him. Won't stop him. Want him, this, desperately.

My breasts heave up and down from the force of each of those breaths. His body covers mine, all muscle and sinew, so hot that we're both sweating from the combined heat of our bodies so close together. Draped in sweat from the absolute ideal and perfect exercise that we're both doing as we fuck like rabbits.

I go off with a soft cry, and James lifts up and smothers the tip of one of my breasts in his mouth, groaning my name as he pulls out, grabs his dick in his hand, and pulls as he comes all over my abdomen.

I groan and watch his semen fall like rain on my skin, my whole body clutching in fresh new arousal.

"Best I ever had." James shoves his two longest fingers into his mouth and pops them out, a growling *ummm* following. Then he smiles down at me. My smile silently admits to him the feeling is mutual.

GOING HOME

I'm giddy when we get into Atlanta. The first thing I did at LAX was pick up the hot-off-the-presses issue of *GQ*, and there, in a full-color spread, was gorgeous James, wearing a black Banks suit. Just as I'd hoped, the ad popped like crazy. He's going to make Banks LTD a mint.

But having that gorgeous man in the seat next to me isn't the reason I'm giddy.

Holding James's hand in mine, I'm thinking about what he said. Life without risks is just surviving.

I want to live.

So right there, I make a resolution. I'm going to tell my father who James is, and that he and I are together.

My father will think I'm insane. He will be disappointed. He might not speak to me, and this could drive a wedge between us, which will make my assuming the reins at Banks impossible.

But I don't care about that. Not as much as I care about James. And if my father really loved me, he'd support me.

"You look like you're thinking some really deep thoughts," James says, leaning in, his breath tickling my ear.

He's completely oblivious to every woman on the plane looking at him. And they are all looking, probably wondering what movie star he is. It only makes me more certain that this is what I need to do. I say, "Just thinking about some things I need to do when we get back."

"We have more shows, right? More places where you need to show me off?"

I nod. "We do. A few. My father and LB will be at those. But you've impressed everyone so far. I'm sure you'll continue to do so."

"That's the name of the game, Miss Banks," he says.

"You can cut the formal act," I say to him. "It's not like any clients are here."

"But we're still in public," he says. "And I can't say I hate it so much, anymore. It's growing on me."

I suppose it is. I didn't tell him how to dress for the flight, and yet he put on slacks, loafers, and a button-down and looks about ready for drinks with the rest of the Rat Pack. Me? I slipped into jeggings and an oversize sweater, for comfort. For the first time around him, I feel a little underdressed.

"What I was thinking," I tell him, "was a little more about us. You and me."

He raises an eyebrow. "You mean, how things are going to be, now that we've . . ."

I nod, hoping he'll tell me exactly what his intentions are. *I want to spend the rest of my life with you* would fit in so very nicely here.

Instead, he says, "Well. Let's just play it by ear. We shouldn't get too far ahead of ourselves yet."

I nod, bristling as I think of Daniel, my ex. That's just something Daniel would've said. *Let's not get too carried away, let's play it loose, let's take things slow . . .* He was a master at deflection. And then he'd totally screw me over when I needed him most.

I'm not going to let that happen again.

I can't pretend a little part of me doesn't deflate when I answer, "Right. Of course."

Maybe I'll wait a little bit before telling my father that James and I are together.

Yes. That makes more sense.

When the plane lands, we walk up the aisle and step up the ramp. When we reach baggage check, there is a huge crowd of reporters waiting at the end of the escalators. As we descend upon them, I wonder if there really was a famous person aboard the airplane. Then I realize that they're all shouting for James.

I blink, amazed that the publicity campaign that was launched simultaneously while our traveling began—in *GQ*, on several city billboards, and on bus and metro ads—has already had such a massive impact. James looks around as if this is surreal. Which it is! Banks LTD has never had such a crazily successful advertising campaign. He looks at me and gives me a wink. "This is wild," he murmurs.

"You're famous," I say to him, mind blown, too, by James's effortless charisma—noticeable in his YouTube channel and even more so now after getting the kind of exposure we're giving him. "But if you think this is wild, wait until New Yo—"

I can't finish because he's suddenly swept away from me, and I'm pushed aside. More and more bodies crowd between us, all people eager for a piece of him. It's exciting how enthusiastic people are. He's looking back for me, but eventually he just gives in and starts to answer a question a reporter is asking as a microphone is thrust under his nose.

I know I need to get to him. He's my property, after all. I need to make sure he's giving the Banks-approved answer.

But maybe he can do this all on his own. He's already proven he can handle himself. Maybe he doesn't need me.

"Are you with that hottie?" one of the reporters, a redheaded woman, asks me. "James Rowan?"

I nod. At least I'm not invisible. "Yes, he's the face of the new—"

"He's a dream, is what he is. Sexy, smooth, complete sophistication. He could sell me anything. Whatever it is, I'm buying."

I smile at her, a little knot of worry growing in my stomach. I'm wondering if this is a bad thing. Maybe he's too good. Maybe he's so beautiful he'll outclass and outshine the very thing we're trying to sell?

Or maybe he'll outshine and outclass me?

No, that's ridiculous. He's Jimmy Rowan. He's real. He's not like all those other stuffed shirts walking around in designer suits.

I break through the crowd and hear the redheaded reporter say, "James, the entire female population of Atlanta wants to know, Are you single?"

I wait with bated breath for the answer and go completely cold when he hitches a shoulder.

"And looking," he says smoothly, giving her that million dollar smile.

We rehearsed that answer. He's supposed to be a bachelor. So he's not supposed to give any allusion to having a serious girlfriend.

So why does it bother me so much to hear him say it?

The flight might have been excruciatingly long, but suddenly, I wish I'd never left the plane. Because maybe if we hadn't, I could've kept whatever we had in LA.

It's stupid, because I knew life would go on. We couldn't stay in that little bubble together. And I was the one who changed him.

But right then, I wish that I hadn't.

I wish to god that he were still Jimmy.

James

A week after Atlanta, I finally get a breath of air from the whirlwind of press and appearances I've been making, so I go down to Tim's to see Luke.

"So when were you going to tell us that you were a supermodel?" Luke says, frowning as he slides a glass in front of me. "When's the swimsuit competition?"

"Funny." I look around. I figured Luke would find it out eventually. He's a smart guy. "Keep that down. I'm trying to keep it under wraps as much as possible."

He starts to pour my tequila and then stops. "Or would you prefer a martini? Shaken, not stirred?"

I shoot him eye daggers. "Pour the fucking drink."

He does, then opens up the latest copy of the *Atlanta Journal-Constitution* to the second page, where there is a massive full-page ad of me. Throws it down on the bar. I can't look at it. "Is this what you and Miss Hoity-Toity have been working on together?"

"Yeah." I lift the glass to my mouth and toss it back. Not as subtle as the shit I've been getting used to, it burns my throat. "Another."

"And what does Charlie say about it?"

"Charlie's cool about it."

"But what about the YouTube channel? Everyone was wondering when you're going to post a new video."

I shake my head. "Can't. Not until my contract is over." I shrug. "And maybe not ever, after that. You know, I'm all Charlie has. I have to think about his future."

He studies me. "I'm sorry. Who the fuck are you? You look a little like a guy I knew named Jimmy. But you can't be."

I hitch my shoulder and spin on the bar. There are people I know there, people who used to root for me, watching me. Now they're all looking at me like I'm a stranger. I'm wearing slacks and a white shirt, which is all I've been wearing these days. But I'm still the same guy. Do they even recognize me?

"Hey, Luke?" I say, not looking back at him. "Set up a round for everyone in the bar. On me."

"Mr. Big Bucks, huh?"

As I'm spinning back, I catch sight of Denny. Oh, shit.

Just what I need.

"What's wrong, little princess? Did they run out of dresses for you to wear for your photo shoots?" he says, sauntering over to me. Behind him, three of his brothers are there.

I glare at Luke. So, does everyone know?

Of course they do. How could I keep it a secret? I knew it was a mistake to come back here.

I throw a couple of hundreds on the bar and say, "I'll see you later, Luke."

Then I go outside.

I'm halfway down the block when Denny calls after me, "Charlie told my brother that you're going to be sending him to private school. So that's how you settle your fights these days? Running away? Pussy."

It takes everything I have not to whirl at him, fists blazing. But I have more meetings tomorrow and can't get into this shit. I promised Lizzy. I start to walk faster, as I hear their footsteps pounding on the concrete behind me. Before I know it, one of them smacks me on the side of the head.

I spin on them, fists raised.

Then I lower them. I am not Jimmy Rowan, no-good, classless asshole anymore. I'm beyond that. And I have a contract that says it. "Look, guys. I'm done. Stay away from Charlie. Stay away from me. And let's all just live our lives, okay?"

They stare at me for a second of complete silence. Then the three guys all look at Denny.

I turn to continue down the street.

"Fuck you, Prince James." The first punch hits me in the side of the head, catching me unaware. The ground rises up to meet me, and I'm out before the second impact hits home.

GOLDEN BOY

Lizzy

I go home after another stellar day at the office, checking my phone.

I have one message from James. Busy as hell. Hope you're having a better day than I am.

I smile and sigh. Funny how a text can get me horny. But that's all I'm getting from him these days, sadly enough.

I'm the new hero in my office. Everyone absolutely loves James. He creates a buzz everywhere he goes. They've been pouring so much love on him that this is the first time he's even texted me since LA. I've seen him, briefly, for appearances, but he's always surrounded by people. And at night, does he stop by? No. He's completely MIA.

I understand. He's busy. He's working from morning to late at night, every day, earning that million dollars.

I know this because my father has me working on compiling all the press for his appearances. I wonder if Dad simply wants me to have some experience with all the aspects of Banks LTD before I turn CEO, or if he secretly knows I crush on James and wants to torture me—but whatever the reason, there is *a lot* of good press. So while I've been seeing the dirty details on everything he's doing, and I've scheduled most of it along with LB, I haven't truly felt a part of it. It's like I created him, and now he's left the nest, never to return home.

And I feel like the stupidest mother bird on earth.

As the driver pulls up in front of my building, I see a man leaning against a bright-red Porsche 911 Turbo, checking his phone. He's hot. If it weren't for the bruise over his eye, I'd have thought it was James. I pause, half out of the car, when he looks at me, that unmistakable lopsided smile on his face.

It *is* James.

My stomach starts to flutter.

"James?" I ask, looking at the car. *His* car? "You . . . cashed the check?"

He nods. "Well, I delivered, didn't I?"

"Well, only half, so—"

"You only gave me half the money. Like it?"

"Yeah, but I thought you were going to send Charlie to a private sc—"

"I'll do that too," he says, wiping some imaginary dust off the hood of the car. "It's a lot of money."

"Not that much," I tell him. "I can put you in touch with a financial advisor, who'll—"

"Lizzy, what did you say when you gave me this?" He holds up his phone. "I needed James's phone. Well, I needed James's car too. Right?"

I gnaw on my lip. "I guess. But you still have to be careful, because . . ."

"Relax." He pushes away from the car and clicks a button on his key chain to secure the door locks. "Anyway. I need your help."

"Come up, come up," I tell him, every part of my body buzzing. I don't think we'll be able to make it to my bedroom. I want him so bad. Now.

In the elevator, he kisses me, tangling his hands in my hair. "Mmm," he murmurs. "God. Fuck, I missed this."

I taste the blood. When he pulls back, I study his face. His nose is bleeding, and he has that black eye. I don't know; I'm kind of glad about it. It shows there's still some of the old Jimmy left. "I thought you said you weren't going to fight anymore?"

"This is what happens when I *don't* fight. When I try to follow the contract," he growls. "Your father called me this morning. He wants to meet me and take me out to some place for dinner. With the people from . . . I can't remember. Saks?"

I swallow. "My father is taking you to meet with the people from Saks?"

He nods.

Oh god.

"Did he forget to ask me?"

"He said you were busy with another project."

I frown. James *is* my project. "I'm not too busy. I should call him and see if he wants me to go instead."

Up in my apartment, I dial my father as I watch James go behind the bar. He sets out a tumbler and pours himself a splash of Macallan. When he answers, I say, "Hi, Dad. Listen, James just told me you have a meeting with Saks. I'm sure you're busy. Don't you want me to—"

"No, Lizzy. I think it's better if I handle our model from now on."

"What?"

"There have been some rumors of inappropriate behavior on your part with our model."

I freeze, and my eyes flash to James. "What?"

"Yes, Lizzy. I have it on very good authority that you were seen after hours with him. And you were hardly coming into the office, acting suspiciously, so people were talking. So I think you need to step back from this. Got it?"

I press my lips together. That good authority? LB. It had to be.

"Fine, but—"

"But nothing. Leave James to me. Thank you."

And he ends the call.

I stare at the screen for a good ten seconds before I grab my phone in my fist and almost launch it across the room. The next thing I know, James is holding a tumbler of scotch in front of me. "Looks like you can use this."

I swallow miserably as he tries to put his arms around me, but right now? That's the last thing I need. "My father . . ."

"I know," he says. He reaches over and touches my face, but I flinch.

I shake my head. "No, you don't understand the pressure I'm under."

"I don't?"

Well, I guess he is under a lot of pressure too. But it's not the same. He can go back to his old life. Me? This is my one and only life, and I'm stuck with a father who I can never please.

"My father thinks I'm such a fuckup. He thinks you and I are together."

He gives me a confused look. "Well, aren't we?"

"I don't know!" I cover my face with my hands. "I don't see how we can be, right now. Maybe ever. It's dangerous, James. I told you, he doesn't like mixing business with pleasure, that's for sure. And if he finds out where I found you . . . he won't just think I'm a fuckup. I'll completely embarrass him. My father is so . . . strict. He's strict in all aspects. He wants perfection in me and demands perfection in whoever I date. If he knows that I faked perfection in you . . . that it wasn't, well, really who you were . . . that you're not what he thinks you are . . . he'll never let me touch any part of Banks LTD again."

"I got it," he says, backing away. "Well, I shouldn't be here, then. It'd probably look bad if I was seen coming and going from your apartment."

I reach for him. "But wait. Don't go. Let me clean you—"

"I've got it," he says, his eyes cold, distant. "Don't worry, heiress. I won't let you down."

And he sets the tumbler down, opens the door, and closes it behind him.

Leaving me alone.

I pace the room, a bundle of nerves. What did I think would happen if I contracted with James to be my model? How did I actually think I would be able to pull this off and emerge unscathed, without losing massive bits of my heart and my mind in the process?

I look at the glass of Macallan that he poured for me, then throw the whole thing in the bar sink and pour myself a tall glass of Patrón. I *really* need it.

James

It's time to put on the magic for Saks. Harold Banks, Lizzy's father, is a real, honest-to-god blowhard. He reminds me of an unsmiling version of the mascot in Monopoly, sitting in the back of his limo in his tux, drinking his scotch. He pours me one and says, "My boy, you've become quite popular, haven't you?"

The cabin is dark, so he doesn't see my black eye right away. I take the drink, swirl it like Lizzy taught me, and say, "I suppose."

"You're making me a mint. Let's toast to that."

We do. I chew my first sip, as instructed. "I do what I can."

He's still frowning. "But I have a question for you that I hope you can help me with."

"Of course," I say.

He straightens in his seat. "Who the fuck are you?"

My smile fades. I clear my throat. "I'm sorry?"

He grinds his teeth as he looks me over from head to toe. "My daughter would like us all to believe that you materialized out of nowhere or came down from heaven to be the face of Banks Limited. But I know that's not the case. Your reputation as the face of my upscale clothing line is built on the belief that you're a successful businessman in your own right. And yet my men can't find a single entity that's headed by a James Rowan, anywhere."

I let out the breath I didn't know I was holding. "Well, I—"

"What's your net worth?"

"I—"

"Stop. Don't answer that. We already have you in our ads, so there's nothing I can do at this point. Just know that if you're playing some game with me, and if the world finds out who you really are, I'm not going to stand idly by. And I'll be damned sure to put my lawyers on you to get whatever money we promised you back. You understand?"

"Yes, sir."

"Keep your private life private, boy. And you'd better not fucking show up at a meeting with a black eye again. Got it?"

So he did see it. I nod, wondering what the hell else he might have noticed about me. No wonder Lizzy is scared to death of him. By the time I've spent fifteen minutes in the limo with him on the way to the restaurant, I feel like I've been through a war.

The chauffeur comes around and opens the door for us. "And one more thing," Harold grinds out.

I hold back, somehow knowing this isn't an afterthought. From the way he's looking at me, what he's about to say is the main point. "Yes, sir?"

"If I find out you even touched my daughter," he says in a low, threatening hiss. "I'll nail your fucking ass to the wall so hard you'll be taking the rest of your meals through a straw. You're not, and will never be, good enough for her."

I exhale.

Knew that was coming.

And I wouldn't care, if I didn't know that this man means more to Lizzy than anyone in the whole world.

I frown at him. "You're right. I'm not. I don't care what you do to me. Just—if things don't go the way you want them to, blame me.

Don't take it out on your daughter. All she's ever wanted to do is make you look good."

He blinks, surprised. He might have just expected me to nod along, as I get the feeling most people do around him. He strong-arms everyone into silence, I'll bet. But he's not going to do that to me.

He nods. "Fair enough. It doesn't give me pleasure to come down on Lizzy. I assure you that won't be the case with you."

Bring it, old man, I think, stepping out of the car.

The meeting with the people at Saks goes well. Mr. Banks turns on his charm and is actually smiling and jovial with these clients. But every time he looks at me when no one else is paying attention, I get a threatening, icy stare. I do my best to put it off, but it's like navigating a minefield. I find myself wishing again and again that I had Lizzy by my side. That I could touch her, hold her, go back to her apartment with her and celebrate another win.

But I fucking can't. Not now.

At the end of the evening, I finish my Macallan and my cigar at the bar with Mr. Banks and the rest of the clients. When we say goodbye to the clients, Mr. Banks claps me on the back and says, "Good show, boy. Keep it up. Let's go home."

I shake my head. "I think I'll just stay here a little longer."

"All right," he says. "Remember, we're golfing tomorrow with some buyers from Neiman Marcus."

Golfing. Shit. Golfing?

I should be in a panic. But I've been on high alert all evening, and I don't think things can get much worse. I can't have Lizzy, so I'm fucked any way you slice it. "Looking forward to it."

He leaves.

I summon the bartender.

"Another Macallan?"

I shake my head. "Give me a tequila," I mutter to him. "The cheapest shit you got."

"Sir?"

I'm not a sir. I'm a fucking fraud, and her father knows it.

"Just pour the fucking drink," I mutter.

I need to get shit faced, as soon as possible.

Lizzy

It's been a week since I last saw James.

Well, in person.

He's everywhere now. On every city bus billboard that I see. On TV, in all of the special appearances we scheduled for him, and even in some new ones that I didn't even know about. In newspapers. When I walk down the street, if a man has his hair or his build, I think it's him. But it's never him.

And he never texts me anymore either.

After I found out my father knew about us and he left my apartment, I wished I hadn't said what I had.

But I had to. We had to put the brakes on. All of our futures hang in the balance.

James is the picture of class. He is sophisticated, smart, sexy . . . everything a woman wants. I saw a news story where women were just throwing themselves at him. One woman actually fainted in his path, she was so enthralled.

Even if he isn't real, he sure looks it. My creation has outclassed me.

I'm lying in bed, staring at the ceiling, not wanting to get out and face the day.

This is for the best. Banks LTD has never done better, and that's all that matters, isn't it? When I gave my father the latest update on how well all of the marketing featuring James was coming together, he actually stopped me and said, "Good job, Lizzy."

I'd been waiting all my life to hear those words.

But for some reason, when I heard them, they bounced right off me, like I was wearing a suit of armor.

I barely cared.

How stupid am I? To have gone and gotten myself so wrapped up in a man that I can barely get out of bed? He's just street rat Jimmy Rowan, a nobody. He'd be nothing if it weren't for me. So I guess the joke is on them.

Ha ha. I can't stop laughing. Really.

I roll over in bed and see that the clock says it's noon. I should be in the office, but I can't bring myself to think about work right now. I stumble out of bed and go to the kitchen, where I grab a bag of potato chips, the closest thing I have to junk food in the house. Then I go back to bed, feeding myself handful after handful.

The phone rings. I look to see that it's Jeanine as I reach for another handful and realize the bag is empty. Darn it.

I answer. "Hello?"

"What is going on with you?" she asks me. "You haven't returned any of my calls."

"Sorry," I mumble, tumbling back out of bed to see what else I can scrounge up in my kitchen. "Been busy."

"I can tell. James is a sensation! I can't believe all the amazing press he's getting. Your father must be so happy with you! And you must be thrilled too. He almost passes for a real gentleman."

"He is. He's fooled everyone." Even me.

Finding nothing in the pantry, I open my fridge. Just yogurt. Gross. What I wouldn't do for a gallon of cookie dough ice cream.

"I saw a news report of him on the greens at Ansley with your dad," she continued. "He'd obviously never played golf before. But he was so goddamn adorable nobody cared."

I sighed. I'd heard that he was going to play golf. At first I was nervous, because maybe I should've given him golfing lessons. Turned out he didn't need me. He pulled it off in fine style. He even ended up with a pretty respectable score. He can do just about anything. Without me.

"Anyway," she says breezily. "I was wondering if you'd get me a ticket for the New York launch at Fashion Week? I'm going to be in town that week, and I thought I'd stop in and see the sensation strut his stuff in person."

I nod absently. Even if my father tries to chain me to my desk, I'm going to New York. I don't care what I have to do, but I will be walking James into the ballroom we've rented for the East Coast launch if it kills me. "Oh. Sure."

"I can't believe you didn't get with him." She sighs. "You had him at your disposal, willing to do anything you said."

I don't know why I say what I say next. Maybe it's because I feel hurt, left behind. Maybe because I know it doesn't matter, since it's over. Maybe because she *always* gets the man, and I want her to know that once upon a time, I was wanted by this amazing, sexy man that everyone desires. "Oh, I did," I say lightly.

"You did?" I can almost hear her jaw drop to the ground. "Really? When? Spill!"

"In LA. It wasn't a big deal. Just a fling, like you said. He's . . . really good."

She lets out a little squeal. "Oh my god! Is his body amazing? I would totally lick him from head to toe, like a lollipop. Did you?"

"Well, we had breakfast in bed. And there was syrup involved," I say.

She squeals. "Nice and sticky! So was he yummy?"

I swallow. I'd expected to feel better when I told her.

But now I just feel worse. My stomach roils, which I expect has less to do with the potato chips in my stomach than this topic of conversation. "Um. Yes. He was just like you thought. Amazing." I sound toneless, dead, my words hollow.

"And?"

I try to summon the details she obviously wants, but I can't. It's too painful even to think of, and it's making me feel more and more like burying my head in the floor, ostrich-style, for the rest of my life. "I'm sorry. Someone's at the door. I have to go. I'll tell you more later."

"Boo," she says, disappointed. "But I'm proud of you! It must've felt good just to break free, just once, for some good old meaningless fucking."

I end the call and throw my phone down.

I guess I'm the moron. Because that meaningless fucking felt far from meaningless to me. In fact, it felt like everything. I'd never experienced anything like being with James. And who knows if I ever will again?

At that thought, I feel nausea bubbling in my throat. I go to the bathroom and take a shower. By the time I've cleaned up, I feel better.

And I've decided I need to do something.

I'm my father's daughter. I don't just sit around and mope in times of crisis. I always feel better when I'm taking action.

I get into my Audi and drive down to James's house, not sure what I'm going to find when I get there. I knew he had a late night last night, promoting the line at some high-end nightclub, so maybe he's home. I pull up to the curb and see his fire engine–red Porsche parked in the driveway. It looks so out of place in this modest neighborhood.

I climb out of my car and knock on the door.

A second later, the door swings open. It's Charlie. "Hi," he says, a little confused to see me here. "Jimmy isn't home."

"Oh." I'm disappointed. "Do you know where he is?"

He shrugs. "Big limo came and picked him up a half hour ago."

I rack my brain, trying to think of his schedule. "Why aren't you in school? Are you home alone?"

"I have pink eye. I'm contagious. And no, Jimmy got me a *nanny*." He rolls his eyes.

"A nanny?" I ask. I'm picturing someone young, blonde, and possibly Swedish.

He nods. "Yeah. We're also in the middle of packing up to move to some fancy apartment somewhere."

"Really? You're moving?"

"To be closer to the private school he got me into."

"Which school?"

"Westminster."

I blink. "I went there! It's an amazing school." I swallow. "You're moving to Midtown?"

He shrugs. "And you saw the car." He scrapes his eyes over it and wrinkles his nose.

"You don't sound happy."

"The new school's okay, I guess," he says, sniffling. "The problem is my brother."

"Why?"

"He's never home. And he's being a little bit of an asshole."

"He is?"

"He's changed. He's too busy. Too important. He don't have time for me anymore."

My heart breaks as I look at the little boy. No, they didn't have much before. But Charlie was happy, because he had Jimmy. Maybe James really *is* a monster now. Am I responsible for this?

"Well. Will you tell him I stopped by?" I reach into my purse and pull out the envelope James gave me almost three months ago. I hand it to him. "Your brother gave this to me to keep safe for him, and I'm giving it back. He said it was his most precious possession."

He opens it and looks at it for a long time. Sniffles again. "I don't know if that's true anymore," he mumbles.

I start to tell him that of course it is, but he isn't listening. He gruffs out a goodbye and closes the door on me.

And I didn't think it was possible to feel any worse than I already did.

James

I'm about to blow a gasket.

The movers are coming in a week to move us into our new high-rise condo in Midtown. The New York launch is in three days, and I have another big dinner tonight, and a list of things I need to accomplish before I get on the plane tomorrow. And Charlie's acting like a little asshole.

"I told you that you needed to start packing your shit up before I got home!" I shout, storming into his room. All his LEGOs and action figures are all over the place. He hasn't done shit. I grab an empty box and start tossing stuff in. "What the fuck do you think you're doing?"

Elsa, the nanny I hired, is Hispanic and doesn't speak English well yet. She's giving me a blank look. I say to her, "Did you not understand? He had to pack?"

She's staring at me, confused.

"Where the fuck is he?"

She shrugs.

Forget it. I don't have time for this. The house is a fucking shit hole, made even worse by the state of chaos it's in. I can't say I ever formed an attachment to this place, since we moved here after my family died, and we've been renting it. Charlie's going to love this condo in Midtown. It's hot.

Almost as hot as the apartment belonging to another Midtown resident I know.

But I can't fucking think about her now. Even if she's going to be right across the street from me. Her father's orders.

Yeah, it's been weighing on me. I think about her almost every minute of the day. But like she said, this is for the best. She never tried to get in touch with me after our argument, when she told me we needed to cool it.

I yank open a closet, only to find it full of his clothes. Really, he's done less than shit. All he had to do was throw everything into the boxes. Easy. I start to grab the hangers and toss them one after another into the box, muttering, "I'm doing this for you, Charlie. So you can have a better life. And this is the fucking thanks I get?"

When I reach down to the bottom of the closet for his shoes, I see something move in the darkness. I squint at it.

"What are you . . . are you fucking hiding in the closet? Really? Get out."

I start to yank on him, but he pulls himself up into a ball. "No! Go away!"

"Charlie!" I growl.

Then I scrub my hands over my face. I'm not going to catch many flies growling at him like this. I count to ten, force myself to quiet down. I sit on the edge of the bed. "Look, tiger. I'm sorry. But I'm at the end of my rope here, and I really could use the help. I'm trying here. For us."

"No! You're not doing any of this for me! It's for you and your giant ego. Get the fuck out! You're being an asshole!"

I clench my fists. "Come out, Charlie. I don't have time for this."

He doesn't.

Losing my patience, I lunge into the closet, grab him by the back of the neck, and yank him out. I'm holding him there, and he's looking up at me, shaking, terrified, when it hits me, right between the eyes.

I *am* being an asshole. I've never put my hands on him before, and now . . . who the fuck do I think I am?

And I thought I was trapped before. Now, maintaining this image . . . I feel like I've been stuffed in a fucking straitjacket. At least when I was Jimmy, I knew who the fuck I was. And Charlie liked me.

I let him go. Smooth his hair. "I'm sorry, Charlie. I didn't mean to . . ."

He starts to sob against me. I pull him to me and hug him, hard. Then I lift his head. "Look at me," I tell him. "One more week. I've got one more week in this contract, and I promise, things will change. Okay? When I get back from New York and we move into our new place, I'll take a weekend off. We'll go somewhere, and we'll do whatever you want."

He sniffs and wipes his nose with the back of his hand. "Whatever?" I nod.

"Can we make more videos? Like we used to?"

I clench my teeth. I promised myself I wouldn't go back to that. That's not who I am anymore. But Charlie's looking at me, his big blue eyes full of tears. "Yeah. If you really want me to. That's what we'll do."

He wraps his arms around me and hugs me tighter.

"So, here's the deal," I say to him. "You're going to love your new room in the condo. It's, like, ten times the size of this. And there's a bathtub in the place you can snorkel in. No kidding."

He smiles.

"So get your ass packed, or else we can't go."

He nods. "I will. But I'm gonna miss this place."

"Yeah. Me too. I've got to go out to a meeting in a half hour, but I promise I'll be home tonight to tuck you into bed at ten. Okay?"

He hugs me again. "Yeah. Thanks, Jimmy."

Feeling a little more relaxed, I shower, change into a new suit, and head out in my Porsche to downtown Atlanta, where I'm meeting with Quill. I'm not sure who they are, or why I'm meeting with them, but it's been a fucking whirlwind, so when I got a call from a woman named Kim, director of marketing at Quill International, who wanted to book me in for dinner and I saw my calendar was free, I went with it. I figured it was just another meeting with more buyers.

Kim, a knockout redhead in a business suit who's a poor substitute for Lizzy, shakes my hand and escorts me to a table in the corner with no fewer than eight old men in suits. I shake hands all around, help Kim into her chair beside me, and get ready to launch into my spiel, which I know by heart from repetition, about why Banks suits are the best.

The oldest of the men, who is in the very center of the table, says, "It's fantastic to meet you. Obviously we've heard much about you. And we wanted to see you for ourselves."

I order a Macallan 25 neat from the waiter and spread myself out. "Well, here I am."

Kim leans over and whispers in my ear, "You don't disappoint. We're so impressed."

I start to speak about Banks, when the older man holds out a hand and says, "I'm John Quill, the owner and CEO of Quill Couture. Do you know of us?"

I stroke my chin. I don't, but I've been a very convincing liar. "Of course."

"So let's get down to brass tacks," he says, leaning forward. "We have it on good authority that Banks only locked you in until the end of New York Fashion Week. Is that true?"

I feel my confidence flounder but get it back. I look over at Kim, who's waiting for an answer. They all are. "Yes."

Smiles all around. I've said something that pleases them. One man says, "Big mistake on their part," and the rest of the men laugh.

My drink comes. I forget to swirl or chew. I just swallow.

Then I feel Kim's hand on my knee.

"Perfect," John Quill says. "This is very fortuitous for all of us."

I look over at Kim, who is running her hand up to my thigh, kneading the muscle. I can't pretend it doesn't feel good or turn me on. But it's fucking not what I need right now. I lace my fingers in front of me and try to concentrate. "How so?"

"Because, Mr. Rowan," he says, "we'd like to offer you a three-year contract to be the face of Quill Designer Suiting for, say, ten million a year?"

I try to chew my next sip of scotch, but I end up biting my tongue. I can't control my expression or pretend to be the face of total sophistication. I find myself stammering, unable to push words out. My collar suddenly feels too tight. I yank on it. *Keep it together, Rowan.* "Ten *million?*"

"Yes. A year. With the option to extend as necessary," John Quill says, just as Kim begins to brush her hand over my cock.

My rapidly stiffening cock.

"That's . . . an attractive offer," I say, shifting in my seat. Thirty million dollars. I can't . . . I never thought fucking Jimmy Rowan would be worth that much in a hundred lifetimes. "I'll need some time to mull it over, though, of course."

"Of course," Quill says, as Kim starts to zero in on my cock, stroking it harder. It's throbbing now. "If you give us the name of your lawyer, I'll draw up the papers and send them off to take a look and make sure all the terms are agreeable."

I nod, thinking, I don't know any fucking lawyers, anywhere. Wait. Jeanine. Lizzy's best friend. Lizzy trusts her. She can help me out. "Of course."

The rest of the evening goes by in a blur. I try to speed things up, but they keep ordering more drinks, and by ten I know I'll never make Charlie's bedtime. Goddammit. I promised.

I am a fucking asshole. But I'm about to become a rich fucking asshole.

A rich fucking asshole who might just be good enough for Harold Banks's daughter.

Kim leaves her hand on my cock, even when I try to shift away. During dinner, when she needs to use both hands, she briefly removes the one on my lap only to promptly set it back down on my cock. At the end of the meal, I'm drunk and hard as hell. I can't get up because my cock is tenting my slacks.

The rest of the men shake my hand as they leave. I hang back, saying I'm going to have another drink. I order my tenth—eleventh?—Macallan 25 neat, vaguely aware that Quill wants me so bad they've dropped thousands of dollars tonight, just on scotch alone.

But Quill wasn't the only one in the restaurant who had its eye on me. Unfortunately.

"Listen," I say to Kim, when she hangs back and orders another drink. "I'm sorry. But if I'm seriously going to consider your employer's offer, I can't have any romantic entanglements."

She smiles at me. "I don't want romance, either, James," she says, running her tongue along her red lips. "I just want you to fuck me tonight. No strings. You name the place."

CHANCE MEETINGS

Lizzy

I hurry into the Banks headquarters, trying to keep my head down and stay focused on the millions of things I need to do. I fly up to New York tonight, and I still haven't put together the proposal that my dad requested of my suggestions for what James should wear at the big launch. I also have a list of about twenty things I need to do to get myself ready to be there.

I still haven't talked to James. When I stopped by his house, I thought for sure he'd at least text after Charlie gave him the message. Now I'm pretty sure he's just avoiding me.

As I'm walking in through the revolving door, I get a call from my dad. "Hi. I'm on my way up," I tell him, breathless.

"I'm not up there, Lizzy."

"Oh." I check my watch. It's after ten. "Are you in New York already?"

"I'm at Piedmont."

My heart clenches. "The hospital? What—"

"It's not a big deal. I went in for a normal checkup, and they found my blood pressure was elevated. They're trying to get it all back under control. I admit I've missed a few doses."

"Dad, do you want me to come and—"

"No. Listen. I don't want anyone to know I'm here."

"Not even LB?"

"He knows already." Of course. "You know how LB is. He's on top of everything and wants to be sure his boss is tip-top. Under that hard-ass shell, that boy cares for me."

"Nobody can ever possibly care for you the way I do, Dad," I whisper. "Especially not LB." I groan.

I want to tell him that LB has been *betting* on my failure. That he is my dad's right-hand man but an expert left-hand man, too, intent on keeping me from claiming a spot as CEO. But I can't. I can't say all that to my dad, who is no fool and obviously values the guy. I don't want to risk him thinking I'm being overdramatic.

He sighs. "I don't want to give anyone the impression that I'm not well. Got it? So no visits, no flowers, nothing. I'll be out as soon as I can."

"Dad! You should rest. Don't rush yourself," I scold. "And I have to come visit you."

"No. Lizzy. You don't. What I want you to do is man the New York launch. Give my presentation. Can you? The notes are on my desk."

My heart starts to flutter. He asked me to. Not LB. "Yes! Of course!" I blurt.

"Good. I'm depending on you."

"I won't let you down. And Dad?"

"I know, I know. Take it easy. Goodbye, Lizzy, and good luck."

I end the call, worrying about my father but excited about this opportunity. Putting me visible like this means he trusts me. It means that I'm finally getting my due. There will be over two thousand of the biggest and most influential names in couture in that room. Allowing me to speak as the ambassador to Banks LTD and introduce James as the new face of our line is a huge honor. LA was the starting gate, but this . . . *this* is the checkered flag. The official launch party people will be talking about for weeks, or if all goes well, that's so big it'll be recalled for years after.

I'm smiling as I walk past the café in the lobby, toward the elevators. As I do, I see Jeanine, sitting at a table, talking with a man in a suit.

I briefly wonder if she came to look for me but then can't remember that we had anything set up for a lunch date, or a business meeting either.

She's facing me, and the man is facing away, so I wave at her, but her eyes are so intent on the man she doesn't notice. I come up closer, still waving, and she suddenly blinks toward me. "Lizzy," she says, instantly smiling. "Hi."

"Hi. Sorry. I don't mean to interrupt your meeting, but you'll never guess what my dad—"

I stop when the man turns around.

It's James.

The floor suddenly wavers under me.

"Oh. Hi," I say, my knees weakening. I take a step back. "I'm sorry."

Why are my horny best friend . . . and my horny ex-fuck . . . together?

I can think of a million reasons . . . all of them bad.

"On second thought," I say to Jeanine, "forget it. I'll tell you later. Maybe."

I turn on my heel and start to rush toward the elevators, my face burning and my head spinning as I try to process why the two of them are together. No, it's not like I saw them with their tongues down each other's throats, but still. I know Jeanine. And I know James. And I can't help thinking that if you put two beautiful people like them together, it can't end well. For me, at least.

Wow, now I'm totally sounding crazy, aren't I?

Blame it on James Rowan that I can't even *be* reasonable Elizabeth anymore. Only crazy Lizzy, only Lizzy who doesn't feel so carefree and young anymore.

I've made it halfway around the fountain in the lobby when I hear footsteps quickening behind me. "Hey."

James.

I turn around. He's beautiful, breathtaking, and I know if I look at him I'll be lost. So I look everywhere else. The floor. The ceiling. The wall over his shoulder. "I'm fine. I'm not asking for an apology. I mean . . . whatever it is you two are discussing, it's okay."

He's confused. "I just wanted to say hello. I haven't seen you."

Oh. I gnaw on my lip. Fidget. I am so not the sophisticated woman I was when I first met him. I feel like a bull in a china shop. "Oh. Well. Hello. I suppose I have to go. My father . . ."

He nods, plunges his hands into his pockets. "I miss you, heiress."

I feel whatever wall I've been slapping together crumbling under the weight of his blue stare. "I miss you, too, James."

"You going to New York?"

"Of course," I tell him. "That's what I was so excited about. My father can't make it to New York, so he's having me introduce you at our launch party to kick off Fashion Week."

A smile breaks out on his face, and those baby blues are suddenly so lit up that it almost hurts to see it. "Seriously? That's fantastic, Lizzy. See? I knew your father would see your worth. He's a smart man."

I feel it in the way he looks at me. No jealousy. No ulterior motives. Unlike the other suited men in this lobby right now, James is genuinely happy for me. As if my success is his success.

And I know it, like I know my own name.

It doesn't matter how many days or miles or men I put between us. I will never, ever get over James Rowan, as long as I live.

So I stand there, basking in his presence a little longer, wanting to say that to him but knowing that it'll only ruin everything. What would come of it if I told him that I loved him and didn't give a shit about being CEO of Banks? He'd have to walk away from me, or else he'd be breaking the contract. And I doubt I'm special enough to him for him to do that. He clearly needs and likes this life and the money too much. It's his ticket for Charlie.

But his gaze is so penetrating that I'm tempted to take the chance, even if. . .

No. The spell is broken when Jeanine comes over, sending me a look that maybe means she'll talk to me later? I have no idea what's going on. She points at her wrist, signaling to look at the time, when it suddenly hits me.

"Are you having a . . . business meeting?" I ask with a raise of the eyebrows.

He nods. "Needed a lawyer. Called her over for an informal query 'cause she's the only one I knew."

"Oh!" I sigh, relieved. "That's great. I mean she's the best. I whole-heartedly recommend her."

"I just wanted to let you know, though," he says. "I'm working on something. For after our contract is up. I hope you'll stick around for it. Okay? I haven't forgotten."

I nod at him. "Of course, James."

"See ya, Liz—" He stops. Thumps the side of his head. "Pleasure to see you again, Miss Banks."

And then he jogs off.

Leaving me smiling, swooning, and wondering just what the heck he's working on but knowing Jeanine won't be able to tell me because of client confidentiality, which makes me sort of frustrated. And . . . he hasn't forgotten what, exactly? Stick around for what? I'd have stuck around for anything he was offering, right then.

Anything.

James

She's all I've been thinking about, ever since that meeting with Quill Couture. After untangling myself from Kim after dinner, who was about as persistent as a spider spinning a web around me, I went home and sat at my kitchen table the whole night, thinking.

Sober by morning, I gave Jeanine a call and agreed to meet her for lunch in between some of my other meetings with the Banks team. If I'm worth thirty million, I'm not no one. I'll never think I'm worthy of Lizzy, but maybe if I line my pockets with this money, if I'm really rich as opposed to just pretending to be, her father will think I'm worthy of her.

That's the plan, anyway.

I go back to Jeanine, who is reading over the contract. "It looks fine," she says. "The terms are very agreeable. Of course, there are some things I'll have to question. But not too much. You're going to be a very wealthy man soon."

I nod. "And it won't be in violation of the current contract?"

She shakes her head. "Nope. Though I feel bad. You're obviously valued by Banks LTD. I am sure if you went to them with these terms, they'd match it or perhaps offer you more. They'd hate to lose you to their competition."

I press my lips together. "No. It's been good. Really. But with Lizzy, things are . . ."

A sad smile spreads over her face. "I get it. She told me. So you want to put some distance between you two?"

"Well, yes. As good as they've been to me, I don't want to be employed by her family. For the plans I have, it would be better if I was doing my own thing, outside of the Banks umbrella."

"Ah. I understand. I'm in law, after all. And entanglements like that can be very sticky," she says, with a cheeky smile. "Though I hear you like things sticky?"

The mischievous look in her eyes is unmistakable. Lizzy . . . told her about LA? When she knew that it could mean I was violating the contract?

Why the fuck would she do that?

Why? Because they tell each other everything. They're best friends. I think about the time Lizzy rambled on to me on the phone, describing in great detail what she wanted to do to me.

"What are you talking about?" I say, frowning. "The contract?"

She shakes her head, laughing. "Don't worry! Lizzy doesn't know I'm talking to you about this. Your contract with Banks is safe. I wouldn't ever harm her, or you. But I mention this because you two need to be careful. If someone else found out . . . it could destroy Lizzy, *and* you, and even this contract." She sighs as I absorb that. "I think you should talk to her about this decision. Because I know that you two have more than business on the line."

"She'll discourage me, and I don't want her to." I shove my hands into my slacks pockets.

Jeanine leans back in her chair. "James . . . Jimmy . . . let me tell you something. Lizzy has been my friend for a long, long time. We're very close. And yet I can assure you that the way she is with you, the way she looks at you, acts a little bit jealous around you . . ." She shakes her head, her expression amazed. "I've never seen my friend act like this around any guy. Ever."

I don't know why, but my chest suddenly feels constrained. Like my jacket just shrank.

"You care about her too. You don't need to pretend you don't. And if I were you, I'd weigh that into my decision. Because this contract"— she waves it in the air—"is going to take you far, far away from her. And I'm not sure that's what you want. And I can definitely tell you for certain that's not what she'll want."

I eye her quietly as I pick up the contract. "Thanks for that." I pluck the contract from her hands, fold it, and tuck it into my back pocket. "I will decline."

I walk out of there and dial the number on the card Kim gave me, asking where I can meet her. I figure it's polite to decline in person, considering I'm turning down $30 million. And Lizzy's taught me to be a better man. While Jimmy might have texted and said, *No thanks—hasta la vista!* James knows better. *I* know better.

♥ ♥ ♥

I meet Kim at a nearby hotel. I asked to meet her somewhere *else*, but she said it was this or nothing at all. So whatever. This will be the last time I have to see her anyway. Now she's sitting across a fancy European-like settee from me, crossing her legs slowly from one to the other. She offered wine, but I asked for coffee instead. She's finishing her glass, listening to my decision.

"You're saying . . . you decline?"

"Respectfully. Yeah." I nod my head and shove the contract down at the table and push it closer to her side.

She glances at the contract and laughs, raising her eyes to meet mine with a gleam of anger there and something else.

"You can't. You can't decline, James."

"I just did."

"Oh, James," she laughs, pushing the contract back with two manicured fingernails in my direction. "You want out of there. Don't deny it. You and Lizzy's relationship is complicated, and she'll never give you what I can . . ."

She starts to stand, and so do I.

"I . . ." I was about to say "ain't interested" but swiftly correct myself. "I'm not interested."

She laughs and comes around the coffee table. "Oh, come now. You don't have to pretend with me, Jimmy. You can say *ain't*." She continues winding slowly around the table. "You said it all the time the other night, and I find it to be quite sexy. Along with those other little secrets, especially that big LA secret. And about where Lizzy found you. Big boy."

I freeze as she stops before me and leans forward, batting her eyelashes seductively at me.

"You think you're not good enough for her. Oh yes, I deduced as much when you let it out as a reason for rejecting me. It's her you want, but you don't think you're deserving. Even after LA, when you were so close you were pretty sure 'I ended where she started and vice versa.' See? I remember quite clearly."

I'm frozen, my mind spinning as I register what she's saying.

I let that secret out too?

To Lizzy's competition?

What the fuck was I THINKING?!

Drinking?!

Doing?!

"What are you talking about?" I say as she curves her arms around my neck. I wrinkle my brow, racking my fuzzy brain for the shit I said that night as I tried to politely but firmly pry myself out of her grip. "I'm sorry. I'm not following."

She straightens as I step back. Flips her hair again as she comes forward once more. "Well, of course you're not following. You didn't really realize what you were saying. But I could read between the lines, noticed your hopeless devotion to Lizzy, which is cute but not happening. Because if you think you two stand a chance, Jimmy . . . I know a way that things may fall apart."

I cross my arms, stunned by what I'm hearing. "Go on. I'm listening."

"If it somehow got out just who you are? The sewer you slithered from?" She smiles. "That Lizzy has been lying . . . to the world. To her father. A man like that, taken for a fool? How do you think that would go? I bet if the truth of you got out, you'd destroy Lizzy. You'd destroy Banks Limited, and you'd probably destroy any chance of this new contract, too, since there's a clause in here that says that as the face of their line, you'll need to keep a squeaky-clean image. So my ass is on the line, too, champ. This secret can stay just between us . . . where it is. It's more . . . *intimate* this way. Don't you think? Nobody else needs to know, Jimmy."

I stiffen, fury boiling in my veins. "What do you want?" I bite out.

"Simple. You. In New York. I'm going to be there, and I want you to be with me after that launch. Your contract will be over. And I want you to give me what you gave Lizzy."

"Why? You just said it yourself. I slithered from a sewer."

She shrugs. "What can I say? I have a very dirty mind." She leans over and straightens the lapel on my suit. "And I like my men dirty."

It doesn't matter what I wear. To women like Kim, I'll always be dirty. "And if I don't?"

She pulls out her phone and holds out a picture of me, before Lizzy found me. Then shows me an after one. Where every detail of my features is marked for comparison and obvious similarities. "This is just the beginning. I can get plenty more that shows without a doubt that you were once Jimmy Rowan, the YouTube daredevil. And darling? I'm not beneath hiring a person to get me pictures of you and Lizzy outright . . . *you know* . . ."

I reach for my coffee, but it's gone cold. "I don't get it. You're beautiful. You don't need to do this, Kim. Why would you . . ."

Her nose wrinkles. She rolls her eyes. "I know I don't *need* to. But you don't get it, do you?" She crosses her arms. "Lizzy Banks is a total bitch."

I pull on my collar, anger roiling in my guts. "I'm sorry. What? She's done nothing to you!"

She snorts. "Not personally, but her existence bothers me. Her perfection bothers me. All my life, I've had to work for what I get, and Lizzy has been given everything on a silver platter. She wants something, and she just gets it. She's always lived in her little ivory palace with her daddy giving her the world. Well. This time, Quill and I will be the ones laughing in the end. And I'll be the one that gets what the whole world is gushing about."

I scrub a hand over my face. "Jesus, if you're so jealous of Banks and their success, why involve me? Why not just spill the beans and get it over with?"

She gives me a mischievous smile. "Because this way, I get something that I want too."

She bites her lower lip and eyes me hungrily.

Goddammit.

This shit with Quill is not even about the thirty million anymore—this is about *Lizzy* now, and me choosing between ruining her career or sucking it up to help her save face.

I'm not even doing it for the money anymore. I don't want to hurt her. I'd rather hurt myself first.

But I still don't have to relish it.

"I'm fucking sorry I ever met you."

She leans in and gives me a kiss on the cheek. "Baby, you won't be sorry in New York. I promise you."

She packs up her briefcase and starts to leave.

"I'll give you a call, James. And like I said, if you don't want me to tell all of New York what a worthless piece of shit you really are, you'd better answer."

I step back into my place and stare at my phone—fucking James's phone—for three seconds before I call Jeanine and tell her I'm signing.

"What do you mean? What happened to change your mind?" She sounds shocked. And disappointed.

"Nothing," I brusquely reply. "I'm just done with Banks Limited, and Lizzy and I are never going to happen. I better get real here." I mean, have this bitch sabotage what Lizzy has worked so hard for? And knowing *I'm* the fucking idiot who spilled the beans while drunk and having her hand on my cock, coaxing me to take her while I kept insisting I couldn't because she and I . . . because I had feelings for Lizzy?

I hang up and glare at the phone as if I could make the thing explode.

Fuck. Me.

I've never hated myself—or what I've become—so much.

NEW YORK COUTURE

Lizzy

I'm here. New York City, the world's fashion center, for the start of Fashion Week. I peek into the main hallway, where people are already gathering—the lobby is buzzing with the industry's most fashion forward. I check my phone. Ten minutes until we make our grand entrance. Then, he'll do a little schmoozing for about an hour before I get up to the podium and formally introduce him.

Where is he?

I search down the back hall, but he's not here. I texted him and told him to meet me fifteen minutes before, wearing the Banks Intrigue tuxedo—our most expensive and elite piece.

I clasp my hands in front of me, but that doesn't help. Then I reach into my bag and pull out my index cards for the speech I'm going to deliver. It's very simple:

Welcome, everyone, to Fashion Week, and Banks Limited's launch event for our most exciting line yet. I'm Elizabeth Banks, and when my father started the line over thirty years ago, he wanted Banks to be synonymous with style, elegance, and sophistication. The face of our newest line, James Rowan, embodies all that. A successful businessman himself, James is a man's man, but he also exudes class and appreciates upscale luxury. He is the true twenty-first-century man, one who is at home on the links, at the theater, or at an elegant dinner affair. He enjoys the finer things in life, and that's why he wears Banks, the finest men's couture in all the world. We are so happy to introduce James Rowan!

I know it by heart, but my, that doesn't stop my heart from seemingly wanting to escape out of my chest wall and go running out the door. I fan my face. It's so hot.

I open the door and am looking outside, thinking I might faint, when I feel a presence behind me.

I whirl.

James.

Oh god. Why does he take my breath away, every time? I've never seen him look more elegant, more built for this role.

I reach over and straighten his already-straight tie. "You're amazing," I breathe, tears pricking the corners of my eyes.

He sees them, brings a hand to my cheek, gently blots them away with the pad of his thumb. "You're beautiful."

I smile at him. His gaze is as penetrating and moving as always, but there's something sad in the way he looks at me. Maybe because our contract is near its completion. We can talk about extending it, of course. My father will want me to, because sales have been so good. But I guess there's all this uncertainty there. We don't know what will happen next.

All I know is I want "next" to include him.

However it can.

I open my mouth to say that to him as LB squeezes through the doors. He looks at James, brushes his sleeve. "You two ready?"

I nod.

LB smiles. "Well, it's certainly been a whirlwind. I have to say I had my doubts. But James, you came through in high style. I've never been so happy to be proven wrong."

I'm a little shocked to realize LB sounds genuine.

Cool as a cucumber, James nods and winks at him. "You can make that check for two hundred thou out to James Rowan," he says, lifting his chin.

LB's eyes grow as wide as platters.

James ignores him, extending his crooked arm to me. "Shall we?"

I smile. "We shall."

Then he opens the door for me, and we make our way to the ballroom.

The room is packed—everyone who is anyone in the city is here. All the movers and shakers. The most influential reporters, bloggers, you name it. I grip his arm tighter as he leads me into the ballroom of the five-star hotel we rented out for the launch. I suppose I'm more nervous than he is. I glance up to my left and see his chiseled profile, and my stomach clutches. He has a face that—until now—only existed in my dreams. Hard jaw, sculpted to perfection. Firm, plush, kissable lips. Sharp, pristine blue eyes that feel like lasers zeroing in on me. He catches my gaze, and the devil's smile suddenly playing on his lips is worth a million bucks.

That's exactly how much it cost me. What *this* guy cost me. I would've paid so much more.

It's like he's the only man in the room. Like he belongs here. Confidence oozes out of his every pore. Masculinity envelops him as perfectly as his custom black suit. He walks like he owns the place. My heart beats harder and harder for him.

I can't believe I got him to agree.

Women are vying for his attention. His moves are smooth. Sophisticated. Elegant.

"An autograph?" a young woman asks shyly.

He takes the notepad and pen she extends and scribbles his name, his voice low and rough. "There you go." Beneath all that polish is his raw masculine energy. The determination that brought him here.

"James . . ." I halt him before we go any farther. "Whatever happens . . ."

He looks at me. A thousand words lingering in his look. "I know."

But does he? I've fallen in love with my own creation. I polished a diamond, and now it's flawless. Perfect. But it's not mine to keep.

He is not mine to keep.

"I'm feeling a little woozy," I tell him as we descend the staircase. "I think I'll just go to my table for a moment."

He nods and takes me to the table, pulls out my chair, and helps me into it like he's been doing it all his life. His breath is warm on my cheek as he leans over. "You going to be okay?"

I'm not sure. I don't think I will ever recover if things go badly tonight. That's what it feels like. Like this night won't just make or break Banks. It'll make or break my entire life. Like if I walk out of here without him, I'll be losing the best thing that ever happened to me.

And I'm scared to death.

"A lot of people want to speak with you. You should make the rounds," I tell him. "And then, at eight, I'll make the official announcement. Sound good?"

He nods, stroking my bare shoulder with his finger, and then he's off.

I watch him go, thinking of that old saying *If you love something, set it free.*

I love him. I love James. I love Jimmy. Both of them. I love every little part of him, no matter who he is. Rich, poor. It doesn't matter.

And after this contract ends tonight, he is free.

Whether he comes back to me is up to him. But if he doesn't, I know one thing for certain: I will never meet another man who makes me feel the way he does.

I'm watching him make his way around the room, drinking water as if it's going out of style, when Jeanine sits next to me. She's wearing a gold gown and has her shiny hair piled atop her head like a blonde goddess. "He's something," she breathes.

"I know." Clearly I'm not the only one who thinks so. I'd be hard pressed to find another woman who isn't taken by him.

"And you created him. How does it feel?"

I shake my head. "I didn't create anything. He was already amazing on his own."

She looks at me, eyebrow raised. "Aw, girl, don't tell me you fell for him."

I look over at her, realizing my palms are sweaty. I wipe them on the front of my gown. "No."

You can't fall for a star when it's in the heavens and you're on the ground, can you?

"Well, that's good to hear. I know how soft that little heart of yours is. I'd hate to see it damaged. Because he's moving on, hon."

I look at her. "What?"

"That was why we were meeting. He signed a huge contract the other day with Quill Couture. He's going to be their face, starting next season."

I frown. "Wait, how did . . . you're not serious? I thought we had him . . ."

"No, you had him for this season only. I didn't think we needed to put in a clause that we got the right of first refusal on subsequent seasons. Who knew that he'd become so sought after?" She seems worried and apologetic, but that is nothing compared to how I suddenly feel.

My body goes numb as the words sink in. *He's moving on. James is moving on. Without me.*

So that was what he was working on? Screwing me over and leaving me panting in his wake? I watch him across the room, smiling, shaking hands, being adored by everyone, and all the while something hot and dangerous is building inside me. "How can he do that? How can he

251

move on without even asking us? I'm sure my father would've matched the offer!"

She sighs. "I know. I told him that. But he seemed adamant; I think Kim . . ."

I stare around the room and find Kim.

I stare, horrified, as it dawns on me that she's beautiful, perfect, and simply . . . not me. Not the girl who always wanted to change him. Someone who sees only the new him. Someone who will pay him anything he wants and more.

Someone who . . . is actually, maybe, truly perfect—unlike me.

I swallow, and Jeanine follows my gaze. "I'm sorry, sweetheart, I was sure he'd pick you. I told him to talk to you, to reconsider, but he simply came back and went with them. I was so disappointed. He might look like a Prince Charming, but he's really just a toad. A really, really hot, lickable toad, but a toad nonetheless." She tosses her bag on her plate. "You want me to get you some champagne?"

Champagne?

Jeanine squeezes my shoulder to catch my gaze, but I can't even breathe, much less drink. The room is spinning. My vision is bending. So I gave him everything, transformed his life, and how does he repay me? He fucks me and then ditches me?

Sounds perfect.

Just another wildly successful addition to my massive collection of loser men.

I can just see my father saying *I told you so.* But this is even worse. He wasn't an Ivy League grad or a successful businessman; he was a nobody. I took him out of the garbage and made him who he was. And in return, he used me and tossed me in the garbage.

Maybe I'm the nobody, and he knows it.

Was I a joke to him? Was he planning to ditch me all this time? Was he just laughing at me, waiting to get back at me for thinking I was better than him?

I feel the tears coming. I can't cry here, in this room, with James. "I have to go. I need some air," I mumble, climbing to my feet.

But I don't think air can help me now.

As I go past the bar station that's making fruity, exotic blue drinks, I see my answer.

When the bartender's back is turned, I grab a nearly full bottle of Patrón and push out of the ballroom doors.

James

By the time I get back to the table, it's a quarter of eight. Almost showtime.

But Lizzy is nowhere in sight.

As I scan the ballroom for her, fielding a few people asking for my autograph, I see her approaching. The Black Widow herself, Kim.

"Not fucking tonight," I murmur to her, not looking at her. "I told you. Any time but tonight. You're not fucking this launch up for her."

She shrugs. "We'll have our time soon. I wasn't coming to talk to you about that, James. I thought you might want to know where Lizzy was. You looked a little concerned."

I frown. "Where is she?"

"Well. About fifteen minutes ago, she went out that door. With a bottle of tequila."

A bottle of tequila? Shit. I've had about enough of Kim's fucking with me. Speaking of Kim fucking with people, when I was making my rounds, I looked over and saw Jeanine and Lizzy talking, and Lizzy was looking at Kim. "What did you say to her?" I grind out. Remembering the look of horror in Lizzy's eyes when she spotted Kim here.

She bats her eyelashes innocently. "Nothing! We've never crossed words!"

I grab her shoulders. "What the fuck—" I stop when I see heads swinging toward me. I let her go. She's smiling up at me, as if she knows she's gotten the best of me. "If you said anything to her, so help me, I'll—"

I stop again. What can I do? She's got me by the balls.

Pushing my chair in, I stride out the doors, glancing up and down the hallways, looking for her. I hurry into the other empty ballrooms, to the outer lobby, down past the check-in desk and the concierge, to the bar, the hotel restaurant . . . No Lizzy.

Fuck. Where is she?

Fisting my hair in my hands, I turn around, wondering where else she could go. Outside?

Kim has followed me. She reaches for my hand. I yank it away.

And I'm done. I'm fucking done with this. With these fake people, who pretend to like you but only care about one-upping each other. If that's what's called sophistication and elegance, fuck it. They can keep it all.

She puts her arms around me. "Come on, *Jimmy*," she teases with a lilting voice. "I know just how to make you feel better."

She buries her face in my neck, and before I can think to push her away, I look up as Lizzy walks in from outside, still clutching the bottle of tequila, now half-empty.

She freezes.

And the look she gives me is like the end of the fucking world.

Something I know I will never recover from, so long as I live.

Lizzy

When I went outside with my bottle of Patrón, I thought I couldn't feel worse.

Then I got corralled by a doorman, who told me I'd better return the bottle to its proper location if I didn't want him to call the cops. By then, I'd drunk half of it. At first, it'd burned, but as I stood outside, taking a swig in front of the man, it went down like water. Like a total spoiled bitch, I said to him, "Don't you know who I am? I'm Elizabeth Banks. That's my party you're hosting in there!"

"All right, Miss Banks," he said condescendingly, holding my elbow. "Why don't we get you inside, and you can return the bottle?"

I shook him off. "Why don't you stay out here and fuck off?"

And I took another swig. That was when I started feeling a little chilly. Chilly and warm, actually, at the exact same time.

I went inside, and it turns out I *could* feel worse.

Because now I'm looking at Kim, my competition, making out with my . . . whatever he is. My nothing? My nothing that feels like *everything?*

The second he sees me, James tears out of her embrace and stalks toward me. I drop the bottle on the ground with a terrific crash, glass shards spraying everywhere. He opens his mouth to say something, and I run off toward the back of the hotel. Anywhere. I just need to get away.

Somewhere he can't follow.

The restroom.

I don't make it that far, though. He catches up to me before I can slip inside. He grabs me by the shoulders and pulls me into his arms. For three seconds, he's holding me, repeating my name over and over again, like it means something to him.

It hurts too much.

He's hurt me. SO much.

"Did you fuck her too?" I ask, blubbering now, struggling to free myself from his hold as I try to stop crying.

"No. NO."

"Well, *why not?*" I sound hysterical. Still sobbing as I push myself free. "What was stopping you? What's stopping you from fucking every woman in the place? They all want you, Mr. Sophistication. Mr. PURRRRFECT!"

He grabs my shoulders again, giving me a squeeze to catch my attention, his fierce blue gaze pinning me down in frustration. "No, Lizzy, something *is* stopping me. Don't you get it? It's—"

"Oh my god, it's James Rowan!" a middle-aged woman screams across the lobby, barreling toward him. "Everyone! It's that hot guy on the side of the building in Times Square!"

"Go," I mutter, pushing at his chest. "Greet your adoring public. Show them what a PURFFFFFECT man you are, James!" I scaldingly grit out.

Suddenly, a slew of women are heading this way. He turns, bracing himself, allowing me just enough time to slip out of his arms and into the restroom.

Maybe he tries to follow, but I don't care. I slip into a stall and need almost an entire roll of toilet paper to stem the tide of my tears.

I'm too drunk; I can barely stand up straight. The walls of the stall are bending and squeezing in my vision.

Maybe a minute or an hour later, I hear a rap on the door, and someone—I think it's LB—says, "Lizzy? You're on in two!"

His voice sounds like he's underwater. Or speaking through wadded-up cotton.

Two minutes. For what?

Right. I have to give my speech.

I don't even know how I walk across the room. I push open the door to the stall and blink to focus on my face in the mirror. Everything's bleary, like I'm looking at myself through a kaleidoscope, but I know I don't look my best. My hair's a mess, and my face is red.

But what the fuck. I'm game.

Let's get this show on the road.

Anger starts replacing my hurt. I blow my nose hard into a paper towel, toss it away, and stalk out of the bathroom. When I get to the ballroom, I trip over my own feet as I make my way to the table. I grab my purse, fumbling with the clasp as LB looks at me. "Are you okay, Lizzy?"

I salute him. "Never better, Little Bitch."

Whoops. I probably shouldn't have said that.

Ah, fuck it. He'll get over it. My daddy pays him enough.

I climb up to the podium. Or stumble is more like it. I don't care. Suddenly I could laugh at this all, because *I don't care.*

My gown suddenly has too much fabric swishing at my calves, and it's too fucking in my way. I yank it out from between my legs and pile it all on my arm. Grabbing onto the podium for dear life, I signal for the band to cut the music, and stare at the dumbstruck faces in the audience.

"Okay, people!" I scream into the audience. "Let's get this party started!"

That really quiets them down, almost too effectively. You could just about hear a pin drop. But really, all I can hear is my blood rushing through my ears. It sounds weirdly squishy.

I blink and look down at my cue cards. The writing's too small. And did I write this shit in Chinese?

I toss them to the side.

I look up, just to make sure I have everyone's attention. Yep, they're all still there. God, they're so quiet and still. Is this an audience or a photograph of an audience?

"All right," I say, trying to think of what I was going to say. "So. Why are you all here today?" I point at random people in the audience, stalling for time. They all look like deer caught in headlights. "That's a good question."

I can't remember shit.

I look over at LB, hoping he'll give me a hint, but little bitch that he is, he's just staring at me, mute. Thank you, fucker.

Part of it comes to me. "I remember now. I'm Lissy Banks." My name comes out all wrong, and I know that and vow to be more careful with the next thing I say. But for some reason, the next thing I say sounds like "Coshureweeksbankslaunch."

Someone coughs. I think I'm losing them.

But I feel good. Like I can take on the world. I can turn things around.

"Sorry. Let me start over." I grab the microphone and decide I might be better off walking the crowd. Because maybe if I move, even with this stupid too-much-fabric gown of mine, I can keep up with the room, since it's spinning around me. A flash of inspiration hits me as I stumble out into the audience. "When my father started the company over thirfty years ago, he wanted Bangs to be symomomous with style, elegance, and sopisticashion. The face of our newest line, James Rowan . . ."

I'm supposed to say "embodies all that," and that is when James is supposed to come out, with the spotlight on him, and do his little twirl on the runway. He does, exuding confidence and control, but I can't get those final three words out. His eyes sweep over me, full of concern.

Some concern. He's such a fake. Like all of them.

I wanted to make the perfect man. But I made another dime-a-dozen phony.

I stare at him. My voice falters.

And something inside me just cracks.

"The face of our newest line, James Rowan, is . . . *a fucking fraud.*"

His eyes fall on me, hard. I look away to avoid his gaze, but every other eye in the audience is on me.

"It's true. Everyone thinks he's such a sop—sop—" I can't get the word out. "*Elegant* person, the epitome of style and grace. Bull *fucking* shit! He didn't fucking know what a butter knife was before I met him. Three months ago, he was practically living on the street, in a bar, doing dares on YouTube for peanuts. He's nobody, and you all think he's the greatest thing since sliced bread. You're all so stupid, falling over him like he's the Second Coming. You put a sewer rat in a suit—he's still a sewer rat."

I glance around the room, at all the faces, white with shock, and I just don't care anymore.

"Introducing the new face of Banks LTD, James Fucking Rowan, liar and asshole extraordinaire."

Then I drop the mic to the ground and run away, as far and as fast as my high heels will carry me, leaving the ballroom in absolute silence.

James

It isn't how I thought I'd spend my first night in New York City.

After Lizzy ran out on me, leaving me alone on stage with two thousand faces staring at me, I slowly exited the stage and went after her.

But she was gone.

Jeanine came out a few minutes later. "Well. Look at that," she said. "You're nobody again. I guess she fucked you both—"

I held up a hand to her and silenced her with a look. "Don't. Don't even talk to me or Lizzy again."

And then I stormed outside, loosening my tie, ignoring the stares from people on the streets. I wanted to see Lizzy, but I knew she was done with me. Maybe I could've explained things to her, but I was tired. Tired of all the shit.

I navigated aimlessly for hours, until I found myself in the middle of Times Square. And there I am, right on the side of one of the buildings— a giant, ten-story-high billboard of me, leaning against a wall, in the same Banks Intrigue tuxedo I have on now. Though I'm surrounded by a million other ads, I'm the focal point.

Holy shit.

I pull out my phone, think about snapping a picture for Charlie, then stop myself.

Charlie doesn't want a picture of me. He wants me.

I open my web browser and switch my flight to tomorrow morning. There is a packed week of meetings scheduled, but from the way everyone was looking at me, I get the feeling I'm done here.

Since I won't complete all those meetings, I won't get my second half of the money.

My contract with Quill is a no-go.

I also owe LB $200,000, and after all the purchases I made when I first cashed the check, I don't think I'll have enough in my account to cover it.

But none of that matters.

Not the car, or the apartment, or the nanny, or even the fancy private school. Not a single thing.

She's what matters.

And I fucked her over, big-time.

How hard would it have been to just put her first? To say *fuck you* to the money, to my fake image. She knew who I was and didn't care about any of it, and yet I had it in my head that I couldn't be worthy of her unless I became this asshole. I trashed my people, Charlie, and everyone I cared about for this bullshit.

I deserve this.

"Hey!" someone calls to me. "Aren't you James Rowan?"

I shrug. James. Jimmy. I have no fucking clue who I am these days.

When I don't answer, they leave me alone.

I turn my back on my billboard and dial Charlie. When he answers, sounding sleepy, I realize it's past his bedtime. "Hey, it's me," I say.

"Jimmy? What time is it?"

"Doesn't matter. I wanted to tell you I'll be home tomorrow morning. Okay?"

"You will?" I can sense the excitement in his voice. "What about—"

"Forget all that. I'm coming home to you because you're the most important thing to me, now and always." As I walk, someone bumps me, but I don't care. I'm feeling stronger already. "Okay?"

"Yeah, Jimmy. Hey, Jimmy?"

"Yeah?"

"I didn't tell you 'cause I was mad at you. But Lizzy came over. Last week."

She did? No wonder she thought I was blowing her off. "That's okay, tiger."

"And Jimmy? I haven't finished packing."

"Forget the packing. What if we go out this weekend and shoot some videos?"

"Yeah?"

"Yeah. Check the email and see if there are any good dares you think I should do. Okay?"

I can just imagine him doing a fist pump. "All right!"

"Sleep tight. I'll see ya tomorrow."

"See ya, Jimmy."

Who am I? James? Jimmy?

When I hang up, I already know the answer.

DAY OF RECKONING

Lizzy

Monday morning, I'm waiting for the elevator, thinking I might puke.

Again.

I spent the entire night after the launch in my hotel room, hunched over the toilet, retching long strings of tequila-tasting spit and bile into the bowl. In the morning, when I woke up, my diaphragm hurt, and I couldn't get out of bed even to check my phone. On Sunday, when I finally started feeling better, I checked my phone and saw a text from my dad.

COME HOME ON THE NEXT FLIGHT.

Just like that, all caps.

And I immediately started feeling worse.

It had gradually begun to dawn on me what a complete mess I'd made of Banks LTD, James's career, my relationship with my father, and my own dignity . . . in that tiny five-minute period on stage.

But honestly, it didn't faze me at all. I didn't care when everyone in the lobby was looking at me and whispering as I tugged my suitcase toward the exit. I didn't care when I looked up at the television in the airport and saw that my little appearance and James's downfall had made national news. CNN, go me! And I don't care now that I'm probably going to be fired.

Really, what difference does it make? I'll end up in my prettily decorated apartment, helping Ugandan nonprofits, and feeling just as empty about my life as I do now.

I take the elevator up to the top floor. This time, I'm an eleven o'clock, not even close to being first, because that's where I rank now, in my father's all-important scheme of things.

When I step out into the reception area, my father's secretary says, "Oh! Hi! Elizabeth!"

I can tell the whole office is abuzz with what I did. She seems surprised I have the gall to show my face here again.

"Your father's meetings are running late. Have a seat. Can I get you some coffee?"

I shake my head and sit in the waiting area, tapping my fingers on my knee. My father was released from the hospital the day after he went in, so nobody found out he had been in there, which is what he wanted. Unlike me, he was able to pull off his deception.

As I sit there, I practice over and over again in my head what I'm going to say to him. *I'm sorry* doesn't seem like enough for how royally I screwed up. But I feel like I could be apologizing until the end of the world, and it'll never repair the damage I've done. So maybe I shouldn't even try.

Finally, his secretary looks up at me. "You can go on in."

I nod and whisper thanks to her, walk to the heavy double doors, and push them open.

My father is sitting behind his massive wood desk, hands tented in front of him. "Lizzy."

I walk in and realize that LB is sitting there too.

Of course.

I sit on the very edge of the seat next to him.

My father's frown is scarier and deeper than usual. "What have you got to say for yourself, young lady?"

All the apologies I was going to say just fly right out the window.

I did all of this because I felt like I needed to bend over backward for my dad. Because I wanted him to see me as worthwhile.

But why the fuck should I have to?

I throw up my hands. "I couldn't get anyone else. And I just wanted to prove to you that I could handle this. That I could make a man that everyone would fall in love with. So that you would finally see that I can make sound business decisions and I'm not just a pretty face."

"Sound business decisions? You call this sound?"

My breath catches in my throat.

"I was thinking on my feet. I needed a man. And I found one."

He slams his hands on the table. "Have you been fucking him?"

It hits me out of nowhere. I swallow.

"I'm in love with him," I whisper.

He rolls his eyes to the ceiling. "You think he loves you? You're out of your mind. That thing that you found—I hesitate to call him a man—will use you for your money."

His words themselves don't hurt me. "It doesn't matter," I murmur. "He doesn't love me. We're over."

He studies me for a long, long time. "Lizzy. You have everything. That man can offer you absolutely nothing. Why would you want to—"

"Because I do, Dad!" I scream at him. "That should be enough! I'm your daughter, but I'm not *you*! What I feel and want and like . . . why is that never enough for you? Why do I always have to want what you want, even if it'll make me miserable? Why?"

I start to sob into my hands.

My father looks at LB. "Leave us."

"But—"

"We'll discuss that later."

I hear him stand, and a moment later, the door clicks closed.

When I look up, he's studying me. "Tell me what you want, Lizzy."

"I want you to see that I'm trying. That maybe my thoughts aren't the same as yours, but they're still valid. Maybe I'm not the best in this business, but I love it more than anyone. And everything I've done has been for you, and for the company. I didn't want to pull James from a sewer. I did it because every other guy on the list turned me down, and I wanted to make you proud of me. That's all."

I'm sobbing so hard I can't see straight.

There's a long pause. Suddenly, my father booms, "No. I mean . . . what do you want when it comes to this man? This James."

I blink. "It doesn't matter. He's been practically ignoring me since we got back from LA. Whenever I see him, he—"

"For god's sake, Lizzy. He's doing that because I threatened him."

I freeze. "What?"

"I told him that if he came near you again, I'd nail his ass to the wall. He said he didn't care what happened to him. He just wanted to make sure that if anything went wrong, you wouldn't be held responsible for it."

My mouth hangs open. "He . . . did?"

He stands, pushes away from the desk, and comes around to sit on the edge of it.

He hands me a piece of paper.

I look up at it, blinking through my tears. It's a check. For $500,000. Made out to James Rowan.

"What is this . . . ?" I begin. Money to get him away from me?

"That's how much you promised him, yes? To fulfill the contract?"

I nod. "But—"

"Do you think he would be interested in signing on with us for the next, say, three years?"

I blink. "What?"

"LB just brought in the latest figures from the weekend. Turns out that sales of Banks Limited are surging. No such thing as bad publicity, I guess. People don't want James Bond; they want the possibility of turning an ordinary man into something extraordinary. He's quadrupled our sales projections for the year already."

I gape.

"Part of this business is knowing when to take risks. You took a huge risk, which I never would have done. And it paid off."

I blink at the check and then look up at him. I can't speak.

"And yes, you have your own mind, and I'm glad that you're not afraid to use it. I can't say the same for anyone else in this company," he says, glancing at me in silence. "I'm proud of you, Lizzy. You did this."

He lifts me into his arms and pulls me in for a stiff, awkward hug. But it's a hug.

My father is hugging me. For the first time since . . . when? I can't even remember.

"But—"

"I can't say I approve of James. But at least he had the balls to show up. And that? I respect that. A hell of a lot."

I pull away from him, shaking, my eyes wide. "Dad?" Is he saying what I think he's saying?

He nods and motions me to the door. "Now, get the hell out of here. I've got work to do."

I walk outside, my head swimming. No, it isn't a giant glowing Harold Banks seal of approval, but I don't think that exists.

And James just got the closest thing I've ever seen.

James

I clap my hands in front of the camera as Charlie starts to film. "All right. What I've been dared to do today by viewer sickkid09 is to stand on the bed of this truck here as the driver plows me straight into this wall of light tubes at thirty miles per hour." I affix the goggles over my eyes and the helmet on top of my head. "That'll get me what, Charlie? Five hundred?"

Charlie nods.

"Five hundred. Easy money. Let's go."

We're in the middle of a deserted field south of Atlanta, and the sun's starting to go down. The old fluorescent light tubes were free from the dump, but the wall frame took forever and a fucking day to assemble. I only have one take for this, and it isn't the light tubes I have to worry about, though I'll probably get some cuts from that. It's falling off the bed of the truck that could really do me in.

I ruffle Charlie's hair and take him to a safe distance where he can stand and point the camera. "Got it? Don't move from this spot, no matter what. Okay?"

He nods. "Get it, Jimmy."

I wipe my hands on my jeans, fix my gloves on my hands, and fasten them at my wrists.

Luke gives me a wink from the cab of the junker truck we got from the dump. I climb up to the bed and get myself situated behind the cab, standing with my legs shoulder-width apart for a solid base. "You getting this, Charlie?"

He nods.

I bang on the top of the truck, signaling to Luke to put the pedal to the metal.

And he does. We're far away so he can build up speed, and I'll be hitting the glass tubes at around thirty miles an hour. As the truck speeds up, I catch sight of a gray sports car streaming down the road toward us, kicking up a cloud of dust.

It looks like Lizzy's Audi.

But it ain't Lizzy's, of course. The last time I saw her, a week ago in New York, she called me a liar, an asshole, and a fraud.

All things I've owned up to.

What I haven't done is capitalized on my fifteen minutes. I got calls from every news outlet in the country, including *GMA* and *Today*, wanting me on to discuss what had inspired me to go through with it. I turned them all down.

What inspired me? Not the money. Not the clothes. Not the chance to be someone I wasn't.

Lizzy inspired me. She inspired me right out of Tim's Bar, because I had a feeling about her.

She's inspiring me now to be something other than a liar, an asshole, and a fraud.

Inspiring me to just be me.

Even if she hates who I am, that's the best I can do right now.

I hear the car's brakes squeal to a stop as the truck reaches full speed. I place my gloved hands on the surface of the truck's roof and brace for impact, when out of the corner of my eye, a dark-haired wet dream steps out of the car.

I lose it.

Impact.

Glass shatters in my face. A million little knives sting my skin, and the truck jolts to a stop, but my body is still moving. My boots lose contact with the truck bed, and I'm propelled over the cab of the truck, flying forward weightless into the dirt, headfirst.

"Jimmy!" voices yell in chorus.

Charlie. Lizzy.

LIZZY?

Everything goes black.

A minute or an hour later, I blink and hear Luke saying to me, "Hey. Jimmy. You all right, man?"

I lie there in the mud, dazed, on my side. "Gimme a minute."

Luke again. "Hey. Count to ten. One. Two. Wiggle your fingers." I do. "One. Two. Wiggle your toes. That was sick, man." Then, farther away. "He's okay. Just got the wind knocked out of him."

"Thank god." A familiar female voice now.

Lizzy?

I open my eyes and grab on to Luke's arm, pulling myself up. Lizzy. She's here. Like I've died and gone to heaven. "What are you doing here?" I croak out, shaking glass particles out of my hair and lumbering toward her, rubbing my neck.

"You're bleeding." She sounds concerned.

I wipe my face. I have blood and glass shards embedded in my cheeks. "Then you should be happy, huh?"

Charlie says, "Jimmy. I'm still filming."

Right. I almost forgot. I have him face the camera toward me, and I say, "Well, sickkid09, you're five hundred dollars poorer. To all my viewers out there, thanks for watching, and see ya next time."

He cuts the camera. I punch him in the shoulder and tell him to go hang out in Luke's pickup for a minute.

"Why, so you can talk to your girlfriend?"

I flick him in the head. "Get outta here."

He runs off.

I look at Lizzy. She's about as out of place as a girl can be, in a gray suit, her pumps sinking into the mud. But damned if she isn't a sight for sore eyes. "Well, heiress, this is a little out of your zip code."

"Where's your Porsche?" she asks.

I wave that away. "Piece of shit kept getting stuck in the mud. Got myself a used F-150. *And* I can still afford to put Charlie in Westminster. Drive's a bitch, but whatever."

"Hmm. I see you got right back into your daredevil stuff," she says, her words clipped.

I shrug and rip off my helmet. "Yeah. Well. You can take the street rat out of the sewer, but you can't take the sewer out of the street rat. Right?"

She winces. "About that . . . I was dru—"

"You were right, Lizzy. This is who I am. My only mistake was in pretending I was someone else."

She shakes her head.

I nod.

She stops shaking her head and just stares at me, biting down on her lower lip as if to hold back from saying something. She reaches into her purse and pulls out an envelope, which she hands to me. "Here."

I open it. It's a check for $500,000, made out to me.

I hand it back to her. "I don't want this."

"What? Of course you do. It's a lot of money."

"No, Lizzy, I don't. I got all I need."

She hands it back to me, her voice a little uneven. "It's yours. You fulfilled your end of the contract. In fact, Banks has never been so successful. My father wanted me to ask you if you'd be interested in a three-year contract."

I shoot a disbelieving look at her. "You're serious, heiress?"

She nods.

"And what do you want?" That's all I wanna know.

She looks confused. "What do you mean?" Before I can say more, she says, "I was wrong, what I said about you. I shouldn't have said those things. I'm a liar and a fraud too." Her voice cracks.

I tear off my gloves, take the check, and tuck it in her expensive purse. "Tell your dad thanks, but no thanks. I'm good. That world? It ain't me."

It takes everything I got to turn away from her. When I look back, she's still standing there, frozen.

Finally, she says, "Okay. If that's what you want."

And she turns to leave, stumbling a little, her heels sticking in the mud.

I watch her wobbling a few steps away, a thousand things I want her to know flooding my head.

"It ain't you, either, you know," I call.

She turns.

I take a breath, stroke my week-old stubble. "All I seen when I was in your neck of the woods were people who'd cheat. Disrespect. Blackmail. Treat others like lesser beings because of how they made a living. I should've told those people to go to hell, but I found myself thinking I needed to join them in order to get what I wanted. But you ain't like that.

"So as far as I'm concerned, the whole of 'em can go to hell." I rub my neck and fix my stare on hers. "Except you."

A small smile appears on her lips. She looks like she wants to say something. She looks vulnerable, *unsure*. Frustrated and hurt. All at the same time. "Take care of yourself, James."

"It's Jimmy. And don't let those assholes eat you alive, okay? You're better than all of them."

She starts to walk to her car, and every step she takes makes me wonder what the fuck I'm doing. She drives away in that car, I'm never going to see her again. Our worlds are too separate.

By the time she gets into her car and pulls away, I'm already regretting this.

I'm mad as shit at myself. At life. At myself again. At everything.

I stuff my gloves into my pockets and shove my helmet under my arm as I walk back to the truck, where Charlie and Luke are waiting.

Just my luck. I'm in love with a fucking princess who I'm never going to be worthy of.

And I hate myself for not being up to snuff.

The boys are sitting in the cab, giving me identical looks like I just shot Bambi between the eyes.

"What?" I mutter, angrily throwing my shit in the back. I motion for Charlie to scooch to the center and climb into the cab of the truck.

Luke shrugs. "I don't know why you let her go."

Charlie nods. "You love her, don't you?"

I look at them both. Grab my ball cap and fix it down low over my eyes so they won't see it when I lie. "Just drive."

Charlie grabs the cap from my head. "Answer the question."

"Yeah," Luke adds. "Listen to the boy. Answer the question."

I sink down in the seat. "Yeah. So what? She's a princess. And I'm—"

"A prince," Luke finishes. "Believe me. She thinks so. We all do."

"Not the kind that can give her a single thing she wants in this world."

Charlie laughs. "She already has everything, Jimmy. Maybe she just wants you."

I put my hat on Charlie and smash it down on his head as Luke says, "For the last time. Listen to the boy. He obviously got the brains in the family."

Yeah. Maybe I don't belong in her world.

But . . . I think she'd fit like a fucking glove into mine.

Would she do that?

Would she give it all up for me?

"You're telling me to . . . ," I mumble, the wheels in my head turning as I look down the winding road stretching through the woods toward the highway. Her Audi's already disappeared from sight. "What are you saying I should do? Go after her?"

They both nod like bobbleheads.

Charlie holds up the camera. "I dare ya."

Damn that kid. He knows there ain't nothing I won't do on a dare.

"All right," I tell him. "But if you're gonna film it for my channel, I'm gonna do it right."

CHANNEL

Lizzy

"Thanks, LB," I say from my home office when an email pops up in my inbox. "I'll take a look at them and let you know."

"All right, Lizzy. Take care."

"LB. Wait!" I say before disconnecting the call.

At some point, I'm going to have to eat crow and admit that I was wrong about him. We've been getting along great lately, and I don't want to hold back on what I have to say. "LB. I'm sorry for what I said at the launch. I was mean and rude, and you've been a great help to me after this—"

"I didn't only do it for you, Lizzy. I did it for your dad, and for Banks Limited. Though I may have also done it for you," he adds with a smile in his voice. "You're a Banks, after all. In all probability, you are going to be my boss someday."

"You may end up being *my* boss," I say.

"Yeah. Well. I wouldn't mind it the other way," he says.

I smile when I hang up. I guess I should be happy. My father charged me with finding next season's new face of our line. Someone who can be rugged and sophisticated, like our last model, who shall remain nameless. LB is helping. I see now why my father trusts him. He knows his stuff, and he's loyal to Banks's success.

It's okay that my dad decided he's postponing making a decision on Banks's future CEO for the time being. Maybe I'll be CEO one day because of my outside-the-box thinking, or maybe LB will, because of his longevity with the company, but either way, Banks LTD will be in the hands of someone who is totally devoted to it.

And that's all I want.

That's a long way off, though. My dad embarked on a new exercise program after his health scare, and he's been feeling better than ever.

And Banks LTD is doing just as well. The buzz died down about James after a couple of weeks, but the ads with James are hands down the best-performing ads we've ever done. Our line is killing it. My father was upset about not being able to snag James for additional seasons, but he's glad he wasn't snapped up by the competition.

And of course, I haven't seen James.

It's been two weeks since I left him in that field south of Atlanta. Since he turned down the rest of the money. Since I drove away, wishing to god he'd come after me and call me back. I would've settled for anything. A call. A text. Just a little something, to know he was okay. I thought about texting him, but we're of two different worlds, and I didn't think I could bear it if he never responded.

Sometimes, I'll drive around his area of town. I'll go past Tim's Bar and think of going in. I imagine him sitting in there, in his "office" in the corner, with all of his fans. I even went past his house once, but I didn't see an F-150 in the driveway.

The only thing I have now is YouTube. Aside from the stunt I witnessed firsthand in the field, he hasn't uploaded anything new. His Facebook page says he's planning something really big, but he's been mum on what.

I think about doing stunts of my own.

Of breaking free of this ivory palace where I live.

Of not just surviving, but *living*.

Turns out that I wasn't the only one doing the teaching during our time together.

So I'm going to live. Jeanine and I always joked about backpacking through the wilds of the Australian Outback. We said we'd never survive two days out there without breaking down and crying over a broken fingernail.

I booked a trip. Next summer, I'm going. Even if Jeanine ends up with some last-minute lawsuit that keeps her from coming, I'll go alone.

Without anyone to hold my hand or pay my bills or buy my groceries or tell me who I can or can't associate with.

I'm living.

I wish I could tell James that. I think he'd be proud of me.

I open up the files for all of the potential models that LB has sent me. They're handsome and rugged, yes. But not one of them is James. Not even close.

I'm starting to type in my recommendations so that we can narrow it down to three men to bring in for interviews when my phone rings. It's Michael.

"Hey," I say, happy to hear from him. I haven't spoken to him since just after Fashion Week, when he told me that he was devastated that he'd never have a chance to dress James again. "How are you?"

"Honey," he coos. "Do you hear the sirens?"

Sirens? I pull the phone away from my ear. Yes, there are definite sirens in the distance, coming closer. "What's going on?"

I start to rush to my balcony when Michael says, "Woman. Turn on channel four news, quick."

Heart in my throat, I switch directions, find the remote, and flip on my TV. What, is the building on fire? My eyes bulge when I realize there's a reporter standing in front of my building, the Paramount. "Wha . . . ," I breathe out as the reporter begins to speak.

"If you're just joining us, we're at the site of one of the tallest condominium complexes in Midtown, where it appears a man is trying to scale the side of the building in a tuxedo, with absolutely no climbing equipment."

No.

NO.

Numb, I walk toward my balcony and throw open the french doors.

I step outside, still holding the phone to my ear. Michael is talking a mile a minute, but I can't make out a word he's saying. I slowly edge to the railing and peek over.

James.

"Hey, heiress," he calls out, as if he's just out for a morning stroll.

He's about three floors away from me, hanging on to the bottom of one of the balconies below me. And I'm on the twentieth floor.

"James! What are you doing?" I shout.

"Jimmy. Told ya. This is how I make an entrance."

"Oh my god," I mumble, watching him easily scale the balcony so that now he's standing on the rail of the balcony two floors below me. It's actually like perfect steps, if you're feeling a lot adventurous, or a little suicidal. But still . . . the view from here gives me vertigo. "You could've just used the elevator."

"Now where—" He pauses and stretches up, grabbing the railing of the balcony directly underneath mine. "Would be—" He pulls himself up, so now he's dangling, using all his upper-body strength to pull himself up. "The fun in that?"

I hold my breath as he easily lifts himself onto the balcony, pausing for a second, hunched over, hands on his knees.

He holds up a finger, catching his breath. "Good workout. Almost there."

I'm just staring at him, half-scared to death he's going to fall, half-embarrassed. Because now there's a fire truck below, and residents are all stepping out on their balconies. Two police cars are out there too. A police officer with a bullhorn is shouting something I can't make out. Somewhere, I bet Charlie is filming this.

And I can't . . . even . . . believe it.

He starts to climb again, reaching for the railing of my balcony. When he pulls himself up a little, I realize he's wearing a Banks Intrigue.

"Are you crazy, Jimmy Rowan?" I say to him as he leans his torso on the rail and grins at me.

"Yep. And I'm also probably going to jail." The second he gets up, I grab him so he won't fall, though I know he's got it. I pull him over the railing, and he collapses on the floor of my balcony. "Bail me out?"

"Of course. But why did you . . . ?"

He shrugs, gathering his breath. "Because I was dared."

"You were . . . dared?"

He stands up and takes my hand, bringing me to the edge of the balcony. He waves at the people below and the helicopter that's now circling nearby to let them know he's okay. "Yep. Dared to show and tell you how batshit-crazy in love with you I am."

I am sure this is a dream. I must be dreaming. My voice comes out a breath. "You are?"

"I sure am. So now I've got a dare for you, heiress."

"You do?"

He smiles, his gaze on me hotter than a thousand suns. "Actually, more of a very lucrative offer."

I'm still dazed. "I'm listening."

"Yeah. It's going to involve drinking large amounts of crappy tequila. Eating shit with whatever fork is clean. No shaving," he says, rubbing the scruff on his chin. He pulls on his tie and sends it flying over the side of the balcony. "And fuck the bow ties."

He reaches over and unbuttons the top button on my blouse, and I swear, for the first time in weeks, for the first time since LA . . . I can breathe.

It's all him.

It's what being with him does to me.

"And another thing—you'll be expected to talk about fucking as much as humanly possible. As long as it's with me." He fixes me with a hard stare. "You in?"

My whole body is a field of goose bumps. It's a scary thing I'm up this high, because I feel like I can fly.

I nod, drinking in those blue, blue eyes of his, that dimple, and the way he looks at me. "How can I refuse an offer like that?"

He pulls me flush against him as the people watching us start to whoop and cheer, and as if it doesn't matter—as if all that matters is us—he puts a finger under my chin and lifts it for a kiss.

"Some stunt," I murmur, breathless as he whisks his lips across mine first.

"No stunt, Lizzy," he says, nibbling my lower lip, then licking off the sting. "Just living. And I want you to do it with me. Ready?"

It might have taken me twenty-five years of following other people's stars, of doing what was expected and wanted of me as society girl Elizabeth Banks. But nothing has ever felt as right as when I gaze into his eyes, seeing every bit of my future there. Maybe I set out to make him, but my dirty, sexy, hot-as-hell daredevil made me, and now? I wouldn't change a thing.

Yeah.

I'm ready.

EPILOGUE

Two months later . . .
James

I'm the million dollar man. That's what my fans on YouTube call me since Lizzy appeared on my channel. My 3,000,300 fans.

Oh yeah, she ended up helping me expand my channel more than I ever imagined.

She said, "I think people like things that are real, so we should be real with them." So we had Charlie film us both as she and I chatted about everything that happened to lead up to that debacle at the Banks menswear launch that made me even *more* famous.

My channel exploded. It went viral. Everybody knows my girl hired me for a million dollars.

Everybody knows becoming James was the biggest stunt of my life.

Not that it's just a stunt . . . because I *am* James.

Hell, I'm not pretending to be the perfect man.

I am her perfect man.

And I'm bewitched.

I see her heart and own her soul.

She lets me have whatever I want. Gives me everything I'll ever need.

As I inch closer, she curves her arm around my neck and gives me an impish grin, one that says she's got this under control.

I don't doubt that for a minute.

"Now what, heiress?" I shrug off my jacket. Unhook my belt. Drop my damn zipper.

"Watch." She slides my navy slacks to my knees as she goes down to the concrete. "Wait." She touches my cock, eyes the tip, and kisses the crest.

NOW. I'm dying.

NOW. I can't wait to fuck her.

But wait I will.

This is her night. She's the boss. She's taking the lead.

Her mouth inches closer, and that wicked tongue slips across her lips. I grab hold of her ponytail and guide her over my cock. She's a tempter, a woman who no longer protects her inhibitions or adores her privacy.

Where's the fun in that?

Her mouth is any man's ruin, but her mouth is mine, and I'm hers to ruin.

She dips her head but lifts her eyes. Her tongue strums. Her fingers get busy.

Good lord, this woman is hot as summer, sweet as honeydew.

She grabs my cock with a determined grip. She strokes and pumps. Her fingers touch. Her lips swell with the sweetest kiss.

The flush of skin.

The look of lust.

Her gorgeous face. That sexy little body.

Oh. Dear. God.

"Come here, Lizzy." I pull her up and straight into my arms. Lifting her, I lock her legs around my hips as I find the table behind us.

"Don't you dare be careful with me."

I grin at a memory.

She doesn't want careful. That's good. Perfect. Because I can do reckless.

We can be reckless together.

She hikes up her skirt, and I curse a little because Lizzy has me. She has me wrapped around her itty-bitty finger and knows it. When we're apart, there's this empty pit in my stomach, in my heart and soul, and it's then when I realize that I'll do whatever she asks of me.

She doesn't want careful?

Fuck careful.

I want Lizzy bare. I want to feel her quivering walls closing around me, trembling as we finish, pulling me tighter as I come.

I want to ride her without protection because I want HER.

Every. Last. Bit.

After everything we've been through and everything we can still go through together, I want her for the rest of my days and nights, hours and weeks.

She's mine. All mine.

I'm hers. All hers.

And I don't care if we're in her brand-new office in her dad's Banks LTD building, and the whole world or some guy with binoculars watches. Now and for the rest of our lives, we'll remain inseparable and completely insatiable—just. Like. This.

"Make me yours, James."

"Honey, you're already mine."

She beams, and I stroke. I'm taking what I want because it's already mine. She's already mine.

And I couldn't be bought. She couldn't be sold.

That's love for ya. And we've got plenty of that.

ACKNOWLEDGMENTS

Although writing is a personal thing and sometimes quite a lonely profession, publishing is a whole other beast, and I couldn't do it without the help and support of my amazing team. I'm grateful to you all.

To my family, I love you!

Special thanks to Lauren and Holly at Amazon Publishing and Montlake, for believing in me and taking me under their magic wings.

Thank you, Amy, and everyone at Jane Rotrosen Agency!

Thank you to all my writing friends; I appreciate each and every one of you so much.

Thank you, Nina, Jenn, Chanpreet, Hilary, Shannon, and everyone at Social Butterfly PR—you are amazing!

Thank you to Melissa,

Gel,

my fabulous audio publisher,

my fabulous foreign publishers.

To all of my bloggers for sharing and supporting my work—I value you more than words can say!

And readers—I'm truly blessed to have such an enthusiastic, cool crowd of people to share my books with. Thank you for the support. xo

Katy

PLAYLIST

"On the Loose"—Niall Horan
"Home"—Daughtry
"Love So Soft"—Kelly Clarkson
"She (for Liz)"—Parachute
"Coming Back for You"—Maroon 5
"Red Lights"—Tiesto
"Better Man"—Paolo Nutini
"Flicker"—Niall Horan
"Halo"—Beyoncé
"Heartbeat Song"—Kelly Clarkson
"Terrified"—Katharine McPhee

ABOUT THE AUTHOR

Katy Evans loves family, books, life, and love. She's married with two children and a dog, and she spends her time baking healthy snacks, taking long walks, and taking care of her family. To learn more about her books in progress, check out www.katyevans.net and sign up for her newsletter. You can also find her on Twitter @authorkatyevans and on Facebook: AuthorKatyEvans.